ALSO BY AMY YORKE

The Wilderise Tales
The Good and the Green
The Bright and the Blue
The Ancient and the Amber
The Silent and the Silver

The BRIGHT *and the* BLUE

Book Two of the Wilderise Tales

Amy Yorke

GLASSLOOK
PRESS

For anyone who lives for sun-drenched days
and campfire nights

WILDERISE
HEROT'S HOLLOW
Weldan House
FOSSHOLM
Gull Bay
SUDPORT
SALLIN SEA
LANDSEND
LOEGRIA
ARCAS DYRNE
Castle

Pronunciation Guide & Glossary

CHARACTERS

Alison Lennox: AL-ih-son LEN-nox
Keir Ainsley: KEER AINS-lee
Rinka: RINK-a
Drystan Droswen: DRISS-tan DRAHS-wen
Gwenla: GWEN-la
Lady Sibba: LAY-dee SIB-ba
Weyland Gilroy: WAY-lend GIL-roy
Aras: AIR-as
Lydiach: LID-ee-ahch
Mezec: MEZ-ek
Nolwynn: nole-WEN
King Derkomai: KING DER-ko-mye
Prince Idris: PRINCE ID-riss
Princess Ceridwen (Ceri): PRINCE-ess KAIR-id-wen (KAIR-ee)

Wilderise: WILL-duh-rise
Loegria: LOW-gree-uh
Arcas Dyrne: AR-cuss DERN
Landsend: LANDS-end
Sudport: SOOD-port
Herot's Hollow: HAIR-uts HOL-low
Sallin Sea: SAL-lin SEE
Weldan House: WELL-dun HOUSE

OTHER

Korrigan: KOR-ih-gen
Spriggan: SPRIG-gen

Fulling: FUL-ling. The full-height races of the world: humans, elves, orcs, dwarves, mermaids, sirens.
Halfling: HALF-ling. Not a separate race; rather, the offspring of a Fulling and Quarterling or Eighthling.
Quarterling: QUART-er-ling. Races that come up to knee-height on humans: korrigans, hobgoblins, goblins, selkies.
Eighthling: EIGHTH-ling. The smallest races: fairies, pixies.

Chapter One

TALKING TO STRANGERS

Rinka

Sure, there was more blood coming from Rinka's nose than was ideal, but at least she had made it. She was on board the rail-wheeler and on her way to join her friend Alison in Wilderise.

The day had started well enough. Rinka had packed everything she owned into the largest trunk she'd been able to find and had lugged it to the station an hour before her rail-wheeler was due. She had spent the time since pacing the platform, checking her maps and watching the passengers coming and going, wondering how they could be so nonchalant about the whole thing.

Rinka had never left the city of Arcas Dyrne before. Her family left the orcish strongholds for the city generations before she was born and never looked back, her mother insisting that the orcs who remained were "uncivilized" and "barbaric." And while most city dwellers took at least the occasional holiday to the coast, Rinka's mother found those people to be "lazy" and "unscrupulous."

Truth be told, Rinka's mother was a judgmental old hag.

Rinka had freed herself from her mother's house two years earlier when she moved in with a human number-cruncher named Alison Lennox. Their flat had been small but comfortable, and it had been a short walk to Rinka's job at a butcher shop. A job she hated, but along with Alison's salary, it brought in enough to pay the rent.

Until one day, it didn't. With their landlord's latest rent increase, they were priced out of Arcas Dyrne for good. And thus Rinka had a choice: move back in with her mother, or join Alison in a land she'd never set foot in, a wild and dangerous land she'd only seen at the picture show.

She chose the latter.

Morning light flashed from the open windows of the rail-wheeler as it rounded the final curve into Arcas Dyrne's North Station, the great black engine billowing smoke and pulling a dozen red cars behind it. A crowd had formed on the platform, primarily human and dwarven families heading out for one of those "unscrupulous" early holidays. Rinka lifted her trunk with ease despite its size, planting it and herself just a step from the platform's edge.

The rail-wheeler slowed. Rinka could not resist the urge to take one final look at her maps and the letter from Alison with instructions on each step of her voyage, even though she'd had them memorized for weeks. She reached into her leather satchel, but when she removed the papers, a sudden gust of warm wind from the rail-wheeler swept through the platform, sending them into the air.

"No!" cried Rinka, snatching with her strong grey arms. She came away with only one of the documents: the map of her home country, Loegria. The one she needed the least.

Rinka pushed through the crowd as they inched closer to the platform's edge in anticipation, elbowing a dwarf in his ear ("Watch it!") and nearly tripping over a tiny Halfling child as she followed the papers, which swirled and flapped in the breeze as if they were birds in flight. She caught the corner of Alison's letter just as she reached the part of the platform where the first-class passengers waited, shouting an apology that frightened a lady elf in a fine silken dress back into her partner, who huffed in Rinka's general direction.

The rail-wheeler had pulled to a stop, and the platform grew even more crowded as the overnight passengers from Landsend pushed through the outgoing travelers on their way from the station. A human man in a hurry batted the final paper—the most important one, the map of Rinka's destination, Wilderise—out of his face and down to the concrete of the platform floor, where Rinka lost sight of it as it tangled in the legs of the passengers.

She grabbed at something on the ground, coming away with a folded and yellowed object that greatly resembled the worn map Alison had sent her, but it was only a human newspaper. The crowd thinned as the passengers began to board. Finally, Rinka spotted the map caught on the armrest of the last bench before the end of the platform. She sighed with relief as she tucked it back into her satchel, content to have everything back in its rightful place.

Her joy was short-lived.

Turning hastily to make her way back to the third-class section, she crashed face-first into a cart of luggage pushed by a human valet.

For a moment, everything went black. And then stars danced in her eyes as she blinked to refocus them. She smelt something metallic and felt a warm drop of liquid slide from her nose to the top of her lip before she felt the pain.

"I'm sorry, miss, but you should watch where you're going," yelled the valet. He had not stopped to see the damage; Rinka doubted the elf he accompanied would have allowed it if he'd wanted to.

Her nose hurt, badly. She wiped at her face and came away with a surprising amount of blood on her hand. She reached into her satchel for her handkerchief, staining her maps with her own blood.

"Pixie's britches," said Rinka to no one in particular.

There wasn't anyone to speak to.

The platform was nearly empty now, the waiting passengers having finished boarding during her struggle. Ignoring the blood streaming down her face and the throbbing of her nose, she sprinted back to her abandoned trunk, the rush of air pulling tendrils of her auburn hair loose from its bun.

"All aboard!" shouted the conductor.

"Wait! Wait for me!" yelled Rinka as the rail-wheeler's wheels squealed into motion.

Rinka tossed the trunk up the stairs of a third-class car just as it began to move away. But when she reached out her hand to grab the railing and pull herself on board, she came back with empty air.

The rail-wheeler was picking up speed quickly. Rinka's reflexes were normally excellent, but the pain had sent tears into her eyes, obscuring her vision and making it hard for her to find the stairs to the next carriage as it rushed past.

"Look, Mummy," said the Halfling child Rinka had nearly trampled earlier from the approaching stairwell, tugging on his mother's sleeve and pointing to Rinka. The Halfling's mother, a human woman, shook her head at the child and muttered something about the impoliteness of staring, offering no help whatsoever.

As Rinka turned to the final stairway, her teary eyes caught the motion of a figure sprinting across the platform. She couldn't quite make him out, but he appeared to be as tall and broad as an orc. He certainly moved like an orc, covering the gap between the platform and the moving rail-wheeler in one great leap.

"Please!" yelled Rinka. She had just one last chance to get on the rail-wheeler before it carried everything she owned away to Landsend, leaving her behind.

The stairwell would be in front of her in seconds. This was it. She had to time the jump just right—

"Grab on," said the stranger. Rinka blinked away the tears—he was standing in the stairwell, reaching out to her.

She didn't think, she just thrust her hand into his. The stranger pulled with incredible strength as Rinka fired the muscles in her legs as hard as she could.

It was enough. Almost too much, actually. Rinka very nearly knocked the poor man over.

"I'm sorry," she said as she pulled herself up slowly, being careful not to lean too far back into the open air behind her as the rail-wheeler cleared the platform. From the top step, the stranger extended an arm again, and Rinka gratefully accepted. "Thank you for helping me," she continued, but her voice was muffled by the blood in her nasal passages.

"My Gods, are you alright?" asked the stranger.

Rinka saw herself reflected in his dark eyes—crimson streaks running down her face and onto her pretty green dress, eyes filled with tears, and, worst of all, her hair was a total mess. It was so pathetic she couldn't help but laugh.

"My father always said it's not a party if no one's nose is bleeding." Rinka's father had a number of sayings that were in no small part responsible for her parents' divorce, at least according to Rinka's mother. But Rinka always found them charming, and in this case, surprisingly appropriate.

The corner of the stranger's mouth twisted a bit in bemusement or perhaps bewilderment. "Looks like it's a party, then." It was clear that her first guess had been incorrect—he wasn't an orc—but there was something strangely familiar about him.

She studied his face as he fumbled in his pockets for something, trying to guess at his background to give her a clue as to where she might have seen him before. Humans could be as large as orcs, sometimes even larger, and they were frequent patrons of her (now former) employer. But there was something about his face that wasn't quite human. While his eyes had the almond shape of traders from the Far East, the rest of his features were sharper and thinner, more like the elves from the high mountains of Loegria.

His ears, which would have given her more of a hint, were unfortunately hidden behind his dark hair. She couldn't quite place him, although she did have a guess.

"Have you ever been in a picture show?" she asked him as he held out the object he'd been seeking: a handkerchief.

He furrowed his brow and looked from her—no doubt wondering just how much injury Rinka had sustained to ask such a question—and then to his clothes, which were tattered and stained. "No, I can't say that I have. I've never even seen one."

"Never?" asked Rinka. She pulled the handkerchief to her face and was surprised by its pleasant floral scent. The fabric felt fine in her hands: silk maybe, or a very fine cotton. She nearly asked the stranger where he'd gotten it, but as she looked from his ragged clothes to the handkerchief, she realized it must have been stolen.

Rinka wasn't one to judge. She'd seen enough of life in the city to understand the difficult choices that had to be made at times, and the stranger had been kind enough to help her when no one else would.

The bleeding had slowed to barely a trickle, but Rinka was grateful to be able to clean herself up. As she wiped the blood from her face, the soothing touch of the fine fabric seemed to wipe what was left of the pain away.

Rinka followed him into the carriage. There were no seats left together, but as the two of them approached the first row, a Halfling gentleman in overalls stood abruptly to offer his seat, his face registering alarm at the disheveled man and the orc in bloodied clothes.

"Poor fellow," said Rinka. "My trunk is in another carriage. I'll have to get changed quickly before I scare away the rest of the passengers."

"Never mind the passengers," said the stranger as he gestured for Rinka to take the seat by the window. "Are you sure you're alright? May I ask what happened?" His voice was warm and deep with a bit of a rasp, as if he'd spent too long by the fire or had smoked one too many pipes.

"Just a mishap with a luggage cart. I'm Rinka, by the way." Rinka held out her hand to shake.

"Drystan," he said.

"Just Drystan?" Rinka asked. Humans tended to have surnames, and elves were almost all nobility of some kind, Lords and Ladies of ancient lands Rinka knew nothing about. Drystan sounded like an orc's name, or maybe a dwarf, but he resembled neither of those.

"Drystan Droswyn," he said. "But you can call me Drystan."

That was curious, too. Humans preferred to be addressed by their surnames unless you were closely acquainted.

Still, Rinka could hardly see the point in arguing with a stranger about their own name.

"Nice to meet you, Drystan," she said.

Rinka leaned back into her seat and sighed in relief. She had made it on board the rail-wheeler, her maps and instructions safely in her satchel, her trunk safely on board (if a few carriages further away than she would have liked), her nose no longer hurting, and all was well.

"It's a beautiful day to travel, isn't it?" she asked Drystan as she looked out the window at the great buildings of Arcas

Dyrne shrinking in the distance. The landscape beyond the city quickly transitioned into fields of green and yellow and brown, some growing high with the last of the winter crops and others freshly planted and ready for the warmer weather to come. Rinka had seen it all before, but only in the grey tones of the picture show. It did not prepare her for how bright and blue the sky could be beyond the city's smog, for the way it reflected on the water, the perfect mirror images of cotton candy clouds in the stillness of a lake. For the gentle ripples that danced on the surface as the rail-wheeler rushed past.

Rinka turned back to Drystan when he didn't respond. He was looking at her incredulously.

"Oh, my clothes," said Rinka, guessing at his confusion. "Excuse me for a moment—I'm going to go see to my trunk and change into something a little less alarming."

Rinka made her way to the carriage where she'd thrown her trunk, ignoring the stares and frightened comments of the passengers. She retrieved a clean dress, a pretty yellow number she'd made herself after admiring a similar one in a shop window.

After she had changed in the water closet, she retrieved her sewing kit from her trunk. Mending Drystan's clothes would give her something to pass the time, and it would repay him for his kindness.

"That's better," she said when she returned. His eyes lingered on her, but there was no hint of mockery in them. "Now, off with your trousers."

"Excuse me?" Drystan's face registered genuine surprise.

"Your trousers," repeated Rinka. She shook the sewing kit in its biscuit tin, the notions and needles rattling.

Rinka studied the torn trousers as he considered her offer, assessing where to start. But there was something odd about them. There were rips and small holes, but not in the places you would expect. Rinka had mended enough of Alison's trousers to know that the fabric usually wore along the cuffs and the seams, and sometimes at the knee. The imperfections in Drystan's trousers were in the good, strong parts of the fabric that rarely caused Alison trouble. It was almost as if they'd been placed there on purpose.

Almost like a costume.

There was something about him that didn't make sense. The clothes and the bag at his feet were too exaggerated in their humble appearance to have belonged to someone truly down on their luck. And Rinka had known few of even the lowest stature in society who did not take some pride in their appearance. Especially rare were those who would take the trouble to shave their faces but not wash their hair. "You're sure you're not from the picture shows? What about the theatre—"

"Tickets!" Rinka's line of inquiry was cut off by the ticket taker's arrival in the carriage. Luckily, Alison had prepared her for this possibility. Rinka reached into her satchel and withdrew her ticket, frowning at the bloodstain.

Beside her, Drystan tensed. He didn't reach into his pockets or make a move at all.

He didn't have a ticket, she realized.

Rinka knew she should be suspicious of him. He had jumped onto the rail-wheeler without a ticket, and the handkerchief he'd offered her was likely stolen. She knew exactly what her mother would say: *"He's an unsavory sort, and King Derkomai's finest will see that he gets what's coming to him."*

But Rinka didn't want to see the only person who had helped her thrown off the rail-wheeler. And if that made her naïve, so be it.

"I know," she whispered to him. "We'll just say that you lost your ticket when you were helping me onboard."

"That's very kind of you," he said. He smiled at her. "But I'll handle this."

Rinka didn't have time to imagine what he meant before the ticket-taker had arrived.

"Tickets, please."

Rinka handed over her ticket. "Sorry about the blood," she began, but the ticket-taker had already marked it and returned it to her.

She held her breath as she watched Drystan slip something to the ticket-taker she could not see.

"Of course, sir," said the ticket-taker, winking at Drystan. "Have a good day."

"What was that? What did you—"

Drystan pressed his index finger to his lips. A bribe, perhaps? But if he could afford to bribe the ticket-taker, why not just pay for a ticket?

"Who are you?" Rinka whispered, only it came out so loudly half the carriage turned to look. "Are you a criminal?"

At this, Drystan laughed. "Do you always ask suspicious men if they're criminals?"

"Only if they're behaving like criminals."

He turned to her, his shoulder blocking her view of the aisle. "Is that really your best theory? An actor or a criminal?"

Rinka stared at Drystan for a long moment, failing to understand his meaning.

Then it hit her.

"You really are someone else, aren't you?"

He shrugged a single shoulder as if to say he could neither confirm nor deny it, but there was a playful intensity in his eyes that gave him away.

She was right—there was something else to him.

Chapter Two

AN UNEXPECTED ARRIVAL

Alison

The dwarf squeezed Alison's hand with so much force, Alison thought she would break it. Alison reached her other hand into her trouser pocket, producing a handkerchief to wipe the sweat from her brow.

"Almost there," said Keir. He was at the foot of the bed, peeking his head out from under a white sheet. "Just one more push."

"I can't," said the dwarf. Her full cheeks were as red as her hair, and she shook her head back and forth on the pillow. "No more."

"Come on, girl," said the midwife. She was a dwarf as well, and her face dripped with sweat, too, as she held the soon-to-be mother's other hand. "Show them what you're made of."

The laboring woman took a deep breath and strained hard, delivering another unbelievable squeeze to Alison's hand as she let out a primal yell.

"That's it," said Keir. "Dorna?"

The midwife wrenched herself free of the new mother's grasp and took the baby into her arms just as it began to scream.

"A boy!" she yelled back as she carried the baby to a waiting nurse at a washbasin across the room.

"A boy," cried the mother.

"We're nearly ready for the next one," said Keir to the midwife. "Minra, you're doing wonderfully. You're almost there. Alison, are you alright?"

Keir came up to check on them. His dark hair was matted to his head with sweat, and there was blood splattered on his collar, but his eyes were filled with purpose. Despite the exhaustion, Alison was glad to be here with him, to see him like this, to bring new life into the world alongside him. Her heart swelled with love for him she hadn't yet expressed. "I'm fine," she replied.

"Oh, he's so perfect!" cried Minra. The nurse held the tiny dwarven babe up, clean and swaddled in a tartan blanket. "Let me hold him."

"Soon, dear," said the midwife, returning to the mother's side and once again taking her hand.

The next series of pushes took longer than the first. Keir asked the nurse for something called "forceps," which Alison regarded with sympathetic discomfort as she saw him pull the metal object beneath the sheet.

"This is it," said Keir. The midwife joined him beneath the sheet.

Minra groaned, bearing down hard.

"Come on," said Keir. He emerged from under the sheet with the second infant.

This time, there was no cry.

"What's happening?" asked the mother, her voice strained.

Alison wasn't sure. Keir told the midwife to take over as he rushed the baby over to a table.

"Nothing to worry about, dear," said the midwife. "This is why we called the doctor. Sometimes one twin takes a bit longer than the other."

The midwife brought over the firstborn, placing him in his mother's arms and blocking her view of Keir.

Alison's eyes were on him. His back was turned, but she could see him reaching for a bulb of some kind and some vial of medicine from the nurse.

"Come on, little one," she whispered. She held her breath.

Then, finally, a cry. It was a good, hearty cry, and Alison felt tears spring to her eyes too.

"A girl," said Keir. The baby's thick head of hair was still matted with blood, but he held her up to show her mother nonetheless.

He winked at Alison on his way back over. Alison thought of the man she had met just a few weeks ago when she first arrived at Herot's Hollow, of how he had been trapped in the trauma and pain of his past, and of how far he had come since then.

She was unbelievably proud of him.

He would give her all the credit, of course, as he always did when asked. But although they had gone through their experience in a world built from old magic together, it was Keir's bravery and willingness to accept his failures that pulled them from it. And it was his tireless work since then to heal not just his own heart, but the hearts and minds of the town he'd been estranged from, that enabled him to take back his place as the village doctor. To get back to work saving lives as he'd done for the baby dwarf girl today.

"They're so beautiful," said the mother as she received the second baby in her arms. "Thank you, Dorna, doctor, and especially you, my dear Alison," she said. "I swear when you held my hand, it was like the pain was halved. I should be sorry to see you go."

Keir gave Alison a puzzled look. The new mother was not the first person to say this.

"Call on me again if you need anything," said Keir to the midwife. He led Alison from the room and into the living room of the hillside home, the only room of the house with a window.

"Well?" asked a dwarf man. He and several others sat around a table near the fireplace, a pile of cards and coin in the middle.

"A boy and a girl, both healthy. Minra is fine as well."

"A boy and a girl!" shouted the dwarf, on his feet to shake Keir's hand. "Oh, Durtaz is going to be thrilled when he comes up. Can we poke our heads in?"

"Yes, but only for a moment. They need their rest."

"Will do, doctor. Will do," said the dwarves, the friends of the father standing in for him while he labored deep in the mine.

Keir opened the door of the dwarven abode into the cool night air. The breeze felt wonderful on Alison's skin.

He led her by the hand down the mountain trail towards Herot's Hollow, pausing as they rounded a bend out of earshot of the dwarven settlement.

He took her in his arms, kissing her forehead lightly and brushing the dark strands of her hair away from her face.

"You were amazing," he said. "How do you feel?"

"Euphoric," she said. She knew the exhaustion would reach her soon, but her mind was still in the bedroom, hearing the sweet relief of the baby girl's cry. "I've never felt anything like it. I know it isn't always like that, but I see why you do it. Just one moment like that would sustain me for years. It's a gift, Keir."

Keir stroked Alison's shoulder as he led her on. "I wanted to talk to you about that," he said. "Gifts. What Minra said in there about you taking away her pain. Rory Wilson said that last week as well when I set his arm. Is that something people have said to you before?"

His face had an innocent, inquisitive look that Alison now recognized as hiding a deeper concern. She thought about the substance of his question before considering what he was implying. "I've been told I have a comforting presence, yes."

"But taking away pain specifically?" There was a bit of tension in his arm that Alison felt was more than necessary to keep their balance on the steep road.

"What are you implying?"

"Nothing. Never mind. I'm just wondering how I got on without you. If you grow tired of your poetry, you should consider medicine. You'd make a fine doctor yourself, you know."

Alison was dissatisfied by his answer, complimentary though it was, but in truth, she too was too tired to argue. As they made it around the final switchback, Herot's Hollow became visible down in the valley below. The tiny hamlet lined the sides of the river with quaint stone buildings thatched with straw. In the still hours before dawn, the streetlamps were the only source of light, their flickers catching on cobblestones slick with the last of spring's showers.

Alison and Keir walked hand in hand in silence through the empty streets. When they reached their turn, they continued past Alison's cottage to Keir's larger home at the end of the lane. Although Alison preferred her own bed to his, she did not protest. His well was easier to draw from, and they both needed washing up before going to sleep.

By the time Alison reached Keir's bed, she was so spent that she nearly crushed Willow, their neighbor's tabby who had come to split her time evenly among the houses in the neighborhood. The cat grumbled something about humans and their clumsiness, but Alison didn't hear it.

She was out the moment her head hit the pillow.

Alison woke the next morning to a familiar banging sound.

"Use the flap, Dinah," she muttered, rubbing the sleep from her eyes and squinting as a bright ray of sunlight slipped through a gap in the curtains. Dinah had belonged to the distant relative Alison inherited her cottage from, and she wasn't sure whether it was the cat's city upbringing or just something contrary in her nature that made her resist anything Alison did to make her life easier.

One of the first things Alison had done to improve both her own cottage and Keir's home was to install cat flaps in the doors. Willow had appreciated the effort immediately, but Dinah refused, even after Willow had explained that while it wasn't dignified, it was better than having to beg to be let in and out.

The rapping on the door continued. Keir stirred next to Alison. "I've got it," he said. "Go back to sleep."

Alison nodded, never lifting her head from the pillow. She felt as though she had only been out again for a few moments when Keir came back, leaning over her and gently shaking her awake.

"I'm sorry to wake you, my darling," he said, tucking her hair behind her ear. "It wasn't Dinah. It was Aras."

"Aras?" asked Alison. Another of their neighbors, Aras was a fairy shepherd who was generally too busy tending his flock and farm for them to encounter him often. Not to mention that he had been dragged into the magical vine ordeal as well, ending up trapped in the magical manifestation of Keir's worst memory until they had found a way out. Though Alison and Keir had apologized, they felt a certain degree of guilt and tension where he was concerned and resolved to stay out of his way as much as possible.

"He brought news from town. The king is coming."

Alison bolted upright in bed. "Coming here? King Derkomai? When?"

Keir moved out of the way as Alison leapt from the bed, dressing in a hurry. "King Derkomai and his entire court as I understand it. They arrive within a fortnight to Weldan House. My father's invitation."

Alison paused from pulling up her stockings to see Keir's reaction. His relationship with his father the Duke of Merelor, the lord of the lands surrounding Herot's Hollow and its neighboring town Fossholm, was strained to say the least.

Keir's face was regretful but not bereft. Alison finished dressing and took his hand, guiding him to sit with her on the bed. "I'm okay," he said. "I'm not the one who needs you right now."

"Are you sure?" asked Alison. "Do you want to stay here? I'll stay with you as long as you need me to."

"No," he said. "I'll come with you into town."

Alison and Keir retraced their steps from the night before, this time in a rush to get down the lane and up the High Street to the blacksmith's forge just at the base of the mountain.

A small crowd had gathered there in the open-air portion of the workshop. The fires had gone cold beyond them.

A dwarf with grey hair and a warm, round face greeted Alison first: her neighbor, Gwenla. "Oh, I'm so glad you're here. We heard Minra's labor kept you out late last night. What terrible timing. We should all be celebrating the twins, and instead we're dealing with this nonsense." Gwenla led Alison to the person at the center of it all, the reason they had gathered there: Weyland Gilroy, the town's blacksmith, a former prisoner and slave of King Derkomai's, and one of Alison's dearest friends.

Weyland, a red-headed giant of a man, could never appear small exactly, but he did seem shrunken as he hunched over a workbench. Beside him was Lady Sibba, his elvish love, her long and lovely brown arms wrapped around him.

"Alison is here," she said to him gently. He looked up at Alison, carefully avoiding the stares of the other onlookers.

"I really don't know what all the fuss is about," he said. "I'm fine."

Lady Sibba gave Alison a knowing look, both of them hearing the lie in his quavering voice. She took Alison by the hand and sat her down on the bench to the other side of Weyland. "You don't have to put on a brave face for us—"

"He's not even coming here. I won't even see him if I don't go. I doubt he even remembers that I'm here at all."

Alison had spent the past several weeks working with Weyland on an illustrated poetry book that was nearing completion. In that time, she had gotten bits and pieces of the story of Weyland's captivity. He never liked to speak of it at length, but she had cobbled together enough of the disturbing narrative that she imagined she knew more of it than anyone except Lady Sibba.

Years before, when Weyland was a young man, he had been apprenticed to a blacksmith in the city of Sudport, the large southern port city Alison traveled through on her way to Herot's Hollow and where Rinka would be arriving any day now. He was unnaturally talented at smithing of all kinds, from ordinary iron to dwarven steel to elvish silver and gold. His work quickly gained him a following, and when he returned home to Herot's Hollow to set up shop, it attracted the notice of the Duke of Merelor himself, Lord Ainsley.

The duke brought several of Weyland's creations with him to King Derkomai's court at his castle not far from Arcas Dyrne. The king was so impressed by the craftsmanship, he sent for Weyland to be brought to his court and into his employ.

Weyland relished the chance to prove himself and to experience life among the nobility. He was given access to the king's forge, and his clientele occupied the highest stations in society. He was invited to the castle for dinners, sitting at a table of high honor with some of the most renowned craftsmen and artists in all of Loegria and Wilderise. He outfitted courtiers and the royals themselves, armoring the king, the prince, and even the young princess, although it was largely a ceremonial task as King Derkomai's family had kept peace among the lands for generations.

The next part of the story was the piece Alison knew the least about. It involved an altercation with a particularly unpleasant baron who was displeased with having to wait on his order. Weyland claimed that all he did was shout at the man, and Alison believed him, but she could also see how the baron may have been frightened just due to the sheer size of him. The baron returned not long after with a group of the king's guards, most of whom were friends of Weyland's, men and women he'd personally outfitted. They took Weyland into custody, but rather than taking him to prison, they forced Weyland to build bars around his own forge. The king had decided that rather than stand trial for attempted murder (a charge Weyland vehemently denied), he would be allowed to continue his work as a blacksmith, but without pay. This kind of punishment wasn't uncommon in the king's court, although many from the outside had a different word for the king's mercy: slavery.

For several years, Weyland continued his work in chains. His former friends avoided him, not wanting to be seen with one who had lost the king's favor. And the king, who was prone to rapidly changing whims and flights of fancy, had forgotten about him entirely. It was only when a new smith was found, a dwarf woman from the Far East who crafted exquisitely sharp swords with curved blades, that Weyland earned his freedom.

He would never forget Mo Ye, the smith who saved him by lying to the king and telling him he'd be better off without Weyland. Nor would he forget the spoiled princess who told her father that executions were boring, and they should just let the big sad man go. And he especially would never forget Lady Sibba, the scholarly elf of Herot's Hollow who wrote him all through his captivity and kept his spirit alive.

Alison looked from Lady Sibba to Weyland and to the crowd of townspeople who only knew the barest version of his tale, who had all come over to support him the moment they got the news just the same.

"Do we know how long the court is going to be here? Don't they usually have the Midsummer Festival at the castle?" Alison asked. Maybe they could make it through a week or two of a visit without attracting the king's notice. Most of the court could be accommodated in Weldan

House and Fossholm. Herot's Hollow was several miles away, at least a couple of hours on foot. As long as no one mentioned Weyland's name, it was likely there wouldn't be a problem.

Keir, hearing the question, broke from his conversation with Gwenla and joined Alison. "All summer, I'm afraid. They're doing the whole season here. The festival, the regatta, the balls. It's part of the king's plan to increase the investment in Wilderise."

He handed Alison a clipping from *The Sudport Daily News:*

A Most Wondrous Occasion: The King travels to Wilderise for a summer of delight in the picturesque Hill Country

His Royal Highness King Derkomai, ruler of our great nation of Loegria and Wilderise and Defender of the Peace, has designed to endeavor in a most wondrous expedition to our own beloved land this very summer. Arriving at the invitation of Lord Kenneth Ainsley, the Duke of Merelor, the king intends to hold his court from Weldan House, moving the usual summer festivities to a new home, perhaps for good. He will be accompanied by the royal family, the majority of the nobility, and a crew of dwarven industrialists bringing plans to modernize Wilderise into a productive land worthy of investment from the greatest minds and companies in our nation. The king's entourage is expected to arrive in Sudport within the next fortnight in time for the first event of the summer season, the Midsummer Festival, to be held on the lawns of Weldan House.

"You don't have to be here," said Lady Sibba to Weyland as Alison read. "You could come with me to the Rock to see my people. It's beautiful and tropical there. It would be like a holiday. I'm sure Alison won't mind a bit of a delay in finishing the book."

"Not at all," said Alison. "Lady Sibba is right. If you leave now, you'll be gone before any of the royal entourage arrives."

Weyland seemed to consider this as Strelka, his orc apprentice, arrived carrying a tray of mismatched teacups. Alison recognized some of Gwenla's own tan mugs among the eclectic mix, and Strelka had even managed to find tiny cups the size of thimbles for the fairies.

"Thank you," said Alison, taking one of Gwenla's mugs. The tea was good and hot, just the thing for the damp chill that hung in the morning air.

Weyland downed his cup in one big gulp, deciding. "I'm not going," he said. "Not to the Rock—not for this reason, at least," he said to Lady Sibba, who lifted his large hand with some effort and gave it a kiss to show him she wasn't insulted. "He let me go once. If he finds me again, so be it. I can't live the rest of my life in fear. I'll be here, at least until we finish the book. Then you'll find me at the Rock."

Lady Sibba smiled. "Alison can come too. And Keir, of course. You'll be glad we have a doctor on hand, on account of the giant ants, of course."

"Giant ants?" asked Alison, but before she could hear more, Gwenla had come over, having heard the good news.

"Well done," said Gwenla. She sat down her teacup to shake Weyland's hand. "We'll need you, and we'll need all the help we can get if we're going to stop this dam."

"I'm sorry. The dam?" asked Alison. "But we stopped the dam weeks ago. The vine took off and ran the dwarven industrialist out of town."

The vine that Keir had caused, although only Gwenla, Aras, Keir, and Alison knew the entire truth of it. The others thought the surge in the vine, which was born of the old magic, had been the town protecting itself from the threat of a dam being constructed that would put it underwater and off the map for good.

"See here—" Gwenla pointed to the relevant passage. "'And a crew of dwarven industrialists bringing plans to modernize Wilderise into a productive land worthy of investment from the greatest minds and companies in our nations.' More of them are coming, and I'm sure they won't have changed their minds because of a little old vine. No, it's going to take more than that."

"What did you have in mind?" asked Keir.

Gwenla picked up her teacup and took a sip, pausing for dramatic effect. Her grey eyes flashed with mischief.

"Sabotage."

Chapter Three

THREE QUESTIONS

Rinka

"You're a spy," she said, gasping and covering her mouth with her grey hand. "One of King Derkomai's spies."

Rinka had managed to get Drystan to take his trousers off—he changed into his other pair so she could mend them—but she thus far had not managed to get him to admit who he was.

He laughed, a warm laugh that nearly doubled him over. "I'm sorry; I wasn't expecting that."

"So you're saying you're not a spy, then?"

"No, I'm not a spy."

Rinka narrowed her eyes at him. "Exactly what a spy would say."

She lifted her eyes from her needlework back to his face, hoping to find a clue in his expression. His eyes were bright, playful, and entirely too pleased with themselves. There was a dimple in his left cheek from his smile: pleasant, but inconclusive. His lips were soft and had just a touch of red to them—but really, that was a useless observation that gave her no hint as to his character.

"Well, that is a conundrum, isn't it?" he asked her. "What if you guess what I am, but I can't tell you, and so I deny it?"

"Then I guess there's no point in my asking at all, then," said Rinka with a huff, leaning back into her seat in faux resignation.

"Oh, but I was so enjoying it. Why don't we make a deal?" Drystan leaned in conspiratorially. There was a pleasant smell to him, a bit like the floral scent of the handkerchief. Perhaps a hint at his true vocation.

"Do you work in a flower shop?" Rinka couldn't resist asking.

"Hold on," said Drystan, holding up a hand. "I haven't even told you the deal yet."

Rinka had to admit she was enjoying this as well. The man seemed to pose no threat to her, suspicious behavior aside, and she could not resist a good puzzle. "Fine," she said with as much feigned apathy as she could muster. "Let's hear it."

"You can ask me three yes or no questions, and I'll answer truthfully. After that, you can keep asking, but I make no promises about the integrity of my replies."

"Do I have to ask the questions now? All at once?"

He considered it. "No," he said. "You may ask me the questions whenever you like. Just let me know before you ask that you're using one of your questions."

Rinka didn't understand the reason for the gambit, but she did truly want to know who he was, and she couldn't see the harm in enjoying his company during her long journey. "How long do I have? Are you going to Landsend or one of the stops along the way?"

"Landsend, but then on to Wilderise."

Rinka could hardly believe her luck—it turned out he was going not only to Wilderise, but he was heading into the Hill Country too. A companion for her entire journey, and plenty of time to figure out who he was.

Unless…was that really the journey he had planned to take? Or did he change his plans once he heard hers?

"I have family there," he said by way of explanation. Rinka could read no hint of a lie in it, but then she hadn't picked up on any lies so far at all.

Rinka knew what her mother would say about Rinka making plans and deals with strange men. "*Foolish, reckless, irresponsible. Dimwitted fool!*" (Yes, "fool" would be in there twice. For emphasis.)

But meeting someone who not only wasn't afraid of her but actually seemed to enjoy her company had been such a pleasant surprise, she didn't care.

"You know what they say about journeys," said Rinka. "'Every journey begins with—'"

"A single step," said Drystan.

"What? No," said Rinka. "'Every journey begins with three whiskies.'"

Drystan laughed. "Another one of your father's sayings?"

"Well, yes," said Rinka. "Maybe it's an orc thing."

The rail-wheeler's dining cart did not have any whiskies, but it did have a cheap bottle of Loegrian white, which they shared with a small tin of crackers, a bunch of grapes, and a pleasantly sharp cheese. She spent the afternoon asking him a number of questions: where he had grown up (outside of Arcas Dyrne), how many siblings he had (one, a sister), what his favorite dessert was (a pie made with limes and a creamy frosting that sounded heavenly), what his greatest fear was (heights, the first answer Rinka doubted). By the time the rail-wheeler pulled into Landsend late that night, she had mended his trousers and learned much of Drystan, most of which she liked and hoped was true. But she still hadn't worked out what to ask him as her first question that would receive a guaranteed true response.

"Still not ready to take a guess? Even to narrow things down a bit?" he asked her as he followed her to retrieve her trunk.

"I've been thinking of it all day, but I don't want to waste it. Let me sleep on it. Do you have somewhere to stay tonight?"

He raised his eyebrows and glanced at her with a look that made her blush.

"Oh!" said Rinka, as she realized the implication. "I meant—"

"I do. Have somewhere to stay," he stammered, recovering. "But I'll see you on the ferry in the morning?" He picked up her trunk and helped her carry it from the rail-wheeler to a high-wheel carrier taxi just outside the station.

"First thing," she said. "You better be there. I fully intend to use each of my questions." She greeted the driver and gave him the name of her inn (she was grateful to Alison once again for her detailed instructions), and then she turned to bid Drystan farewell. She looked at her hands awkwardly, somehow not quite able to meet his eye despite the day spent learning about him. "Well, good night," she said.

She climbed into the little carriage at the back behind the pedal-cycle before he could respond, her heart racing. Drystan backed out of the way as the high-wheel carrier driver began to pull out into the road.

"I'm going to figure it out!" she called after him, unable to resist seeing his face one more time that night.

"I hope you do," he yelled back. He smiled and waved slowly, and the gesture was so familiar that for a moment Rinka could see him, the real him, standing somewhere grand. But as the taxi turned the corner down the steep slope of Landsend's high street, he vanished from view, and as quickly as it had come, the image was gone.

Drystan had been honest about at least one thing: there was only one ferry a day from the bustling seaside town of Landsend to Sudport, the southernmost tip of Wilderise, and he was on it. The journey across the narrow Sallin Sea would take all of the day, and the carriage Alison's beau had hired would take most of the next day to reach its final destination of Herot's Hollow, the tiny town tucked in the mountains that Rinka would be making her home.

She could not wait, but not just because she'd be seeing Alison again at her destination. A certain mysterious someone had made the journey to get there far more enticing than she'd originally expected.

Rinka carried her great green trunk across the gangway, stopping to help an elderly Halfling gentleman with his cart full of luggage before it crushed him under its weight. Having recently experienced the perils of poor luggage cart handling, she was eager to spare him the experience.

"Oh, thank you, my dear," he said to her. "I would have been squashed."

"It's no trouble at all, sir," she replied. He gave her a smile with several missing teeth. It was one of the brightest smiles Rinka had ever seen.

From the deck of the ship, Rinka reasoned she could understand why. No one could be unhappy in such a place with such a view.

The sky was clear and blue, completely free of clouds. The morning sun cast long shadows on the bleached plaster of the buildings of Landsend, which were arranged in neat rows like the layers of an elaborate, though somewhat wonky, wedding cake. The small town was alive at the early hour: pedal-cyclists travelling up and down the hills and narrow lanes, families dragging great big umbrellas to a sunny strip of beach where turquoise waves lapped onto the shore.

The air was filled with anticipation, not just for the day that had just begun, but for the season itself, the start of the endless summer days and balmy nights that seemed to both last a lifetime and be over in an instant.

Rinka spotted Drystan on the upper deck, leaning over the railing and gazing out at the sea beyond. He had changed into another shirt to go with his mended trousers, a tan tunic that laced at the collar. It stretched tightly across his broad chest, almost comically too small for him.

Not that Rinka was complaining.

She joined him at the railing just as the ferry got underway, the gentle lurch of the ship into motion causing her to stumble a step back.

He reached out for her, helping her steady herself once more. Gods, his skin was soft.

"Sorry," she said, trying not to overreact to how nice it felt when he held her with his strong arms. "Believe it or not, I'm not usually this clumsy."

"Really? That's a pity. I was rather enjoying coming to your rescue." Drystan brushed his freshly washed hair behind his ear, which came to a slight point and gave little indication to his heritage. She did like the way he looked with his hair tucked back, but honestly, she was getting nowhere with thoughts like that.

"I've figured out my first question," she said.

"I can't wait to hear it."

She could see that was true, and so she drew it out a bit, teasing. "You promise you'll tell the truth?"

"I promise." He tapped his fingers on the railing, waiting.

"Alright, if you promise. Here it goes." His anxious smile was darling. She almost regretted actually asking the question—she could have sat in this moment of anticipation for a while. "Are you someone well known?"

Drystan hesitated, looking around for a moment as if deciding how to answer. "Yes, and no."

Rinka was displeased with the quality of his response, to say the least. "'Yes, and no?' Is that it? That's hardly an answer. Do you care to elaborate further?"

Drystan chuckled at her indignation. "I didn't say I would elaborate, but I'll admit the answer is unsatisfying." He waited a moment, perhaps seeing if he would get a rise out of her. She did not take the bait, and so he continued. "Yes, I was once. No, I wouldn't say I am now. Or perhaps I am well known now but seldom discussed. Does that satisfy you?"

"Not even a little," said Rinka.

What could that possibly mean? Someone once well-known but now rarely thought of. A child star, perhaps? He had said he wasn't in picture shows, although he hadn't answered that question under the conditions of their deal, so perhaps it was a lie. But there were also child stars on the stage, although Rinka could rarely afford tickets to the theatre. If he had been a star of the stage rather than the screen, she would never guess who he was.

But even that theory didn't really work. How would a little-known child star manage to get away with boarding a rail-wheeler without a ticket?

Rather than plying him with further questions for him to dodge expertly and weave around, Rinka resolved to try a different tactic during their time at sea: revealing information about herself in hopes that he would slip up and reveal something about himself in response.

She told him many things as they walked the decks of the ferry together: of growing up in Arcas Dyrne, of the family she loved but also couldn't wait to leave, of Alison and the flat they had shared together, of Alison's inheritance and her unexpected attachment to the place and the people, and of the things she would miss in the city.

"Oh, and the plumbing," she said as the light began to turn to gold. They were sitting together on a bench on the lower deck, now more than halfway to their destination. "Aren't humans so clever? They say the dwarves are the great inventors, the great industrialists, but it was a human that invented the toilet, and what an invention it was! Oh, but of course you know, since you're human yourself."

Drystan's dark eyes flashed with recognition. Rinka had made a number of similar bids for information throughout the day, but this one did not have an easy escape.

"I'm not human," he said simply.

"I knew it!" It was only confirmation of something she was already quite certain of, but it felt like a small victory nonetheless.

Rinka looked out onto the open water, searching for her next question, but she was surprised to see there was something out there. "That's funny," she said. "It looks like another ship is approaching."

"What?" said Drystan, on his feet. "Where?"

Rinka pointed. Although she did not yet know what Drystan was, she doubted his eyes were as sensitive to motion as hers. "It's just there, just near the horizon," she said. "But it seems to be coming quickly. Or maybe not, I don't have much experience with sea travel."

"It's coming quickly alright," he replied, squinting off into the distance. His face had lost any trace of joy from the day they had just shared. His body tensed, giving Rinka the distinct impression of a snake preparing to strike.

"What is it? What's wrong?" she asked. Her voice was small. Frightened.

"Pirates," he said.

And from seemingly nowhere at all, he drew a sword.

Chapter Four

A SEAT AT THE TABLE

Alison

Hearing the commotion caused by Gwenla's suggestion of sabotage as the answer to the town's impending doom, the others gathered around her to learn of her ideas.

"Here's what we know," said Gwenla. "The largest group of nobility that has ever visited Wilderise is coming. Most of them have never been to this country, let alone this region."

Alison noted the use of "country," which was in and of itself a controversial stance. King Derkomai's ancestors conquered Wilderise several hundred years earlier and ruled as monarchs over both Loegria and Wilderise. But Wilderise had retained its own identity, and Alison had found that many of its people had more flexible views of the monarchy than those in Loegria's capital were able to express.

And the more Alison learned of the king beyond the reach of his propaganda and restrictions on speech, the more she sympathized with their position.

"It will be up to us to show them what we're made of," Gwenla continued. "I plan to be down in Fossholm when they first arrive to meet whomever I can and to learn of the schedule of events. Then we can form a strategy."

"What kind of strategy?" asked Lady Sibba. The relationship between the old dwarf and the elvish scholar was strained, but they had a kind of mutual respect and understanding. At least they did most of the time. "How are we meant to halt the modernization of Wilderise by getting to know a group of nobles? And truthfully, why would we even want to?"

"I can speak to that," said Alison. "I come from the most modern city in Loegria, a city defined by its industry. And I'll be the first to admit there are truly some advantages to modern living. 'Lectrics, plumbing, transit from place to place. But there are also costs, measured in lives and land. If they construct a dam near Fossholm, our town will be flooded. Herot's Hollow will no longer exist."

"But won't we be compensated?" asked Lady Sibba.

"Do you trust Derkomai to pay you fairly for the schoolhouse?" Weyland asked her in response. "And what about those who rent from our Lord? Do you think he's likely to find them other living arrangements?"

Lady Sibba opened her mouth to argue, but sensing Weyland's mood, she closed it again.

"I'm with Weyland," said Keir. "I don't want to see this town underwater, regardless of what coin changes hands.

But Gwenla, what would you have us do? Let's say we find out what they're planning. How can any of us possibly stop it?"

"You might have a seat at the table," said Gwenla. "If you could talk to your father—"

Alison shot Gwenla a warning look, and she changed her tack before Keir could respond. "Or if we could find a way to convince the right people that this land should be preserved, maybe it could make a difference. Or—and this I'll admit is a stretch, but I think we should consider all options available to us—we could consider asking the spriggan and the other creatures of the forest and the land to help."

"To help or to hurt? You saw the spriggan when we raised the standing stones. He could be dangerous," said Lady Sibba.

"Not to hurt," said Gwenla. "Obviously not. But if he were to scare them a little, well, would it be such a bad thing to do?"

Their debate continued, but Keir pulled Alison to the side to speak with her privately.

"You know what she's going to ask you," he said. "You don't have to do it. I could try to talk to my father. Not to convince him, that's definitely not an option, but if I showed him some interest in getting involved in court life, in learning to manage the estate…"

"You don't need to do that. I don't want you to spend a moment longer with that man than necessary." Alison had learned much of Keir's father from his stories and their one brief interaction the first time he brought a dwarven industrialist into town, and her opinion of him was lower than even Keir's. In fact, Alison's chief concern with any activity involving the new arrivals to Fossholm was getting through a meeting with her (possible) future father-in-law without punching him in the face.

"It's not something I can avoid forever, Alison."

There was a part of Alison that was proud of Keir for suggesting this course at all. He could barely speak of his father when they first met. "I know that," she said. "And it's good of you to try to find a way to help the town, even at a terrible cost. For me, it will be no cost at all to visit the spriggan. And there's another group I can call upon that will have strong opinions on anything that will impact the local waters."

Alison returned to a tense scene between her friends, who all were the type to be very strongly convicted of their opinions, but who also cared for each other deeply and did not want to cause harm. "Gwenla, I'm happy to speak to the spriggan again on behalf of the town. But there's another friend I made when traveling here a few months ago who may be able to offer even more to our current mission. Have you met the korrigans that gather near the falls of Fossholm?"

"You mean the drowners? I heard they brought one before the king himself. I didn't think they'd made it out of there alive."

Recalling the inflammatory rhetoric Nolwynn had used regarding the king, Alison wasn't entirely sure how she *had* made it out of there. "It was that very korrigan that I met, although she would take great offense to being called a 'drowner.' Her name is Nolwynn, and she is both lovely and fierce, and her people are responsible for no drownings as far as I know. I can imagine no greater ally, considering her people will be directly impacted by whatever happens to our waters."

"That's truly terrific news! Lady Sibba here has also had a wonderful notion of using the poetry book you and Weyland are making to educate the nobles about the region and drum up support among the more reasonable in the bunch." Gwenla nodded to Lady Sibba, who seemed pleased to be given some credit.

"We won't be ready by the time they arrive, but certainly before the end of the summer," said Alison.

"Then it's settled," said Keir. "Alison, I wanted to catch Aras before he leaves." Keir gestured to Aras, who had taken a seat on a table near the front of the forge. Aras caught his signal and fluttered over, his tiny white wings flapping so quickly that Alison could only see a blur behind him as he moved.

"Would you mind walking with us a moment, Aras?" asked Keir. "Or flying, I suppose."

"Of course," said Aras.

Alison said her goodbyes to Weyland, gaining his reassurance that he would be alright before joining Keir and Aras as they left the forge and turned back into town.

Once they were out of earshot, Keir turned to the small man floating between him and Alison. Aras looked exactly like a human, other than his Eighthling stature and green hair streaked with white.

"Aras," said Keir. "Over the past few weeks since our ordeal, have you noticed any changes? Anything out of the ordinary? Things you haven't been able to explain?"

Alison looked at Keir, puzzled by his inquiry.

Aras seemed puzzled as well. "What do you mean? It's been a perfectly ordinary spring for me. The winter crops produced well this year, and the summer crops have just gone in. The lambs were good this year as well."

"Extraordinarily good?" asked Keir.

"No, not extraordinarily. Just slightly better-than-average. A few more twins than usual."

"Twins," Keir muttered.

"Why do you ask?"

"No particular reason. There's just been a good bit of luck about lately. Just wondering if it was affecting you as well."

Aras was not so easily fooled. "Ah, I see. You're wondering if my experience in the old magic's dream world had some kind of lasting impact on me. Well, if it has, it has escaped my notice. Has it had an impact on you?" Aras looked from Keir to Alison, piecing something together before Alison managed to do so herself.

"Just a better-than-average year for the crops for us as well. Perhaps the ash from the vine has been the difference. I thought it was worth asking, and maybe keeping an eye out in case anything were to change."

"I appreciate your concern," said Aras. "Since you asked, I'll tell you what I didn't have a chance to during our ordeal. Most of the fairies gave up the old magic along with the old ways long ago when we joined the other peoples. But there are some of my people who resisted the change, who prefer to keep to themselves in the wilder parts of the world. You can find such a group not far from here if you know where to look."

Alison couldn't understand their meaning, but she did see a potential use in making contact with the fairies: their magic could prove useful in whatever plan they concocted to halt the dam's construction. "And where should we look for them?"

"They're easiest to find in the moonlight, particularly under a full moon. They enjoy the cowslips in the pastures, although their time is pretty much done for the season. Around this time, you'll often find them near foxgloves, though only those growing wild. And be careful if they offer you food or drink—foxgloves are delicious to our kind, but they're deadly poisonous to you. I'm sorry I can't be more specific. They are wanderers and won't be spotted in the same place twice."

"Are they dangerous?" asked Keir.

"No, not intentionally. But they don't understand the differences in our kinds, so be on your guard. And beware if they lead you into the woods at night. There are other, fouler things than fairies there."

"Thank you, Aras." Alison shook his little hand, and Aras flitted back to the forge to rejoin his family.

Only once they had turned down the lane towards their cottages did Alison confront Keir.

"What was that about?" she asked. "And don't try to tell me it's nothing or good luck. I saw the look that passed between you."

"I'm sorry, I didn't mean to conceal anything from you. I thought you would have guessed my meaning."

"I haven't noticed anything unusual about you. Any lingering effects from the vine." Although Alison had only met Keir long after he'd accidentally summoned it and wouldn't have known the difference, truth be told.

"It's not me," he said. "It's you."

"Me? That's absurd." Things hadn't been exactly ordinary for Alison, but that was due to the wild upheaval of her life and lifestyle for a completely different kind of existence in a short period of time.

Wasn't it?

"There's the business with the pain reduction," Keir began. "One occurrence is unusual, but two in just over a week?"

"Couldn't it be that my bedside manner just offers some degree of comfort? Nothing unnatural, just a temporary reprieve or distraction from suffering."

"It could," he admitted. He stroked the hair on his jaw, a dark beard beginning to form after a few days away from the razor. "But there are other things."

"Like what?" asked Alison. "When were you going to mention it to me?"

Keir had some ideas about keeping things from Alison for her protection that she did not like. Especially since it was a flaw that she shared, having done the same to him and having suffered the consequences.

"I was not trying to conceal something from you," he said, reaching for her hand. She allowed him to take it. "I'm still not certain of it myself. But I'll tell you everything I've noticed. Starting with the garden."

They had reached Alison's gate. Beyond it, a large section had been cleared in front of the white cottage for a vegetable garden, which Alison had planted with the help of Gwenla and the farm boy Brytak, a young orc whose family managed the largest farm in Herot's Hollow.

Keir led her into the rows of vegetables. Most of the cool weather crops—lettuce, cabbage, spinach, arugula, and radishes—had been cleared after a very short first season, but there were still some kale, carrots, and garlic growing behind the newly planted summer fruits and vegetables.

"You see this row? This is a section Brytak planted."

It was an ordinary row of carrots. Alison did not see his point. "Those carrots are doing just fine. See, you can see a bit of their tops. Brytak said that means they'll be ready soon."

"They will be. But look at them in comparison to this row."

"I planted that row," said Alison.

Keir knelt to the ground and gently wiggled a carrot loose from the soil. It was fully grown. "I know you did," he said. "I watched you. You planted them a week after Brytak, just as he told you to, to allow you to stagger your harvest. And yet they produced before the ones he planted, and far more as well."

Alison didn't know much about gardening aside from what the locals had told her, but she didn't see anything sinister in the situation. "I imagine there could be one hundred explanations for that. Differences in the soil or water.

Differences in the seed. The heat, the light. There are so many things that go into growing plants. Perhaps the vine was particularly thick here, and the ground contains more ash as a result."

"All plausible," he said. "Again, maybe I'm making a fuss out of nothing. Can you see why I didn't think it was worth mentioning before?"

"What else?" asked Alison. "You said there were other things."

Keir led Alison from the garden into the cottage. The living room had been brightened considerably over the past several weeks through the addition of a number of decorative touches: new curtains in a bright yellow and green check pattern; new pillows on the sofa, hand-embroidered by Lydiach, the fairy tailor; a number of books added to the bookshelves along with Alison's pictures, including a particularly beloved portrait of Alison as a child with her mother and late father taken with what had then been an exciting new piece of dwarven technology, the picture-taker; and finally, a number of plants which thrived indoors, although Alison had to be careful of which ones to include as Dinah liked to eat the ones that made her sick. ("The trouble with city cats," Willow had said ruefully.)

Keir took his usual seat on the sofa, and Alison joined him in her usual spot as well, though she declined to recline against him as was her habit. "That plant over there, for one. It's particularly fussy. I've never kept it alive for long."

"It sounds as though most of your evidence relates to my green thumb. Are you truly concerned, or are you perhaps just a little jealous?" There was a teasing tone in her voice.

Any anger she had felt at him keeping things from her had passed.

"Maybe that's it," he said, not quite returning her smile. "Although there's also the dust that seems to vanish when you sweep, even though I've never seen you use a dustpan."

"My repair work on the flooring was, how did you say it? 'Inadequate, and possibly incredibly dangerous'?" Keir had insisted on redoing most of the repairs she had made to the cottage, which she had been quite proud of. The comments about "life-threatening infections resulting from rusty nails piercing the flesh" and "broken limbs resulting from falling through the floor and into the cellar" had seemed frankly unnecessary, and rather insulting besides. But she had allowed him to do it nonetheless, although he had only finished the flooring only recently. "There was ample space for the dust to fall through before you removed the excellent time-saving option of sweeping it into the little gaps."

This time, Keir laughed. "I don't know why I'm surprised. Very well. You've convinced me. I won't drag you to see the fairies to see if they can help you after all."

"I do want to see the fairies though," said Alison. "They may be able to help us with the dam situation."

"Gwenla must be so grateful to have you around to get involved in her schemes," Keir said lightly. There was no malice in his mockery. Alison knew Keir thought as highly of Gwenla and her schemes as Alison did herself. Gwenla truly loved the town, and they were both only too happy to help her preserve it.

"Of course she is. And I'll admit that I just want to meet the wild fairies for myself. My father read me so many fairy stories when I was a child, but he told me they were from long ago. I never imagined I might have a chance to meet them. Although, it's a pity what Aras said about the food. The city fairies of Arcas Dyrne make the finest meals of all. Or so I've heard. I never managed to try them for myself."

"Something we can bear in mind for future travels," said Keir. Alison liked to hear him talk about the future. It comforted her to imagine having him in her life for a long time. Maybe forever, though she wasn't ready to say that to him quite yet.

Keir continued, sensing Alison's hesitation. "It sounds like the fairies won't be easy to find, though. Maybe we can look for them while we're out with the korrigans."

"And the spriggan," said Alison.

"And the spriggan," said Keir. "Though I'm not in a hurry to meet him again. He did try to kill me."

"Only because of the old magic. Hey, there's our answer." Alison didn't know why she hadn't thought of it before. "If I do have the old magic affecting me, the spriggan will surely know."

"He'll know, and he'll try to kill you. Maybe I should go see him alone then." Keir sat upright, his brow furrowed in worry.

"Not a chance," said Alison. "But you will come with me, won't you? Just in case?" Alison doubted there was any reason the spriggan might turn violent as it had during their first encounter, but she had no way to bind it this time if it did. The only ash of the old vine that had been preserved belonged to Duncan Corbett, the town's archivist. And although he would give it over if asked, Alison agreed that it should be preserved for future research purposes.

"Of course I'll come," said Keir. He leaned over and kissed her gently on the lips. "After lunch, though. I'm starving."

A wonderful answer. Alison joined him in the kitchen, accompanied shortly by Willow and Dinah, who were never far away when the possibility of food was around. There, they prepared a hearty meal of vegetable stew for the humans and tinned fish for the cats, filling up for the adventures to come.

Chapter Five

THE IMPOSSIBLE SWORD

Rinka

"What are you doing? Where did you get that?" Rinka's eyes could not leave the sword in Drystan's hand.

It was like nothing Rinka had ever seen. From straight on, it looked like cold metal, likely the same kind of dwarven steel that her cleavers and butcher's knives were made from.

And yet from the side, the sword seemed to vanish. There was only the faintest shimmer where it should have been, as if the blade itself was a trick of the light.

"I'm getting ready," said Drystan, stowing the weapon at his side in a loop Rinka would have sworn did not exist moments earlier.

"Is it magic?" she asked. Rinka had never seen the old magic used before. But she knew from Alison's letters that it could be powerful and dangerous in the wrong hands.

She wished more than ever she knew who Drystan really was.

Drystan's attention was focused on the approaching boat. "Yes, magic," he said distractedly. "Can you see them? Can you tell how many there are?"

Rinka squinted into the distance. She could just make out three shapes—no, four—moving around the ship's upper deck. It was a motorized boat of some kind like the ferry, not a wooden boat with great big sails like pirate ships always had in the picture shows.

"Four, at least. They don't look like pirates to me," said Rinka.

"They're pirates," said Drystan.

"How do you know? Are you a pirate? Or a pirate hunter?"

"Neither," said Drystan. "I've just met their kind before." He turned to her, his face deadly serious. "Head inside and warn the captain. I'd like to be here to greet our new friends."

His entire demeanor had changed from his posture to the tone of his voice. He brimmed with an authority that felt practiced, as if situations like this happened to him every day, and he was usually the one in charge.

It mattered little to Rinka. One could hardly throw the weight of their authority around and keep their identity mysterious at the same time. "No," said Rinka. "I want to use my second question."

"Not right now—"

"Yes, right now." Rinka stood firm. She wanted to trust him, but before their game had been just that—a light-hearted way to pass the time during their journey. Now that danger was on its way—if it even truly was—she needed answers. "I want you to tell me if these pirates are coming here for you. Tell me the truth."

Drystan shifted uncomfortably. He glanced out to the approaching ship, which was close enough now that Rinka could make out its flag: black, with a white tree wreathed in red flame.

"Burning Ash," Drystan muttered.

"Burning Ash?"

"A mercenary group. Swords for hire. No, I don't think they're here for me."

"You don't think so? But you aren't sure."

"I can't be completely sure, no. It's possible. It would be best if you aren't seen with me, just in case." There was a warmth in his tone, a protectiveness that touched somewhere deep within Rinka, a vulnerable place she hadn't known existed.

"I'm not leaving you," she said.

Drystan's eyes widened, and Rinka felt the blush travel up her neck into her cheeks. She wasn't sure why she'd said it—he seemed to have a handle on the situation, and she wasn't likely to be much help in a sword fight.

But it had felt right, somehow.

"Alright," he said, the corners of his lips turning upwards in pleasant surprise. He placed a hand on her shoulder—then withdrew it, uncertainly—and then placed it there again, gently steering her into the cabin. "You're right. Let's go and warn the captain."

Just then, the ship's bells began to ring the alarm.

"I think they already know," said Rinka.

Several of the crew ran onto the deck, bringing the last few passengers who had been out watching the sunset back inside.

Rinka stole a glance back before she entered the door. The ship was almost on top of them now. Whatever they wanted, they would have it soon enough.

The interior of the ferry was crowded now with all of the passengers in one place. By the time Rinka and Drystan entered, there was nowhere left to sit, so they stood against a windowed wall. Rinka tried to look outside, but the 'lectric lights inside the cabin reflected off the glass and prevented much visibility into the rapidly darkening sky beyond.

"What's the meaning of this?" asked an older dwarven gentleman, his overgrown moustache furrowing with each muffled word. "Why have you brought us all in here? I cross this passage ten times a year at least, and I've never had this happen."

"Is there something wrong with the engines?" asked a Quarterling woman of a race Rinka did not recognize. "I'm an engineer."

A pair of human crewmen looked at each other, trying to get the other to take responsibility for speaking.

"There's another ship out there," said an orc when neither of them spoke up.

"Pirates?" exclaimed a fairy.

A panic rose from the crowd. Gasps, the clutching of children and valuables closer to the chest, a couple of skeptics voicing their doubt, and even a very human scream.

One of the crewmen finally found his voice. "Now, we don't know for sure if they're pirates. This is a passenger ferry, after all."

"So why put us all in here if you don't think anything is wrong?" said the old dwarf.

"Just a precaution. Let's all keep our heads. I'm sure if we keep calm and give them what they want, they'll be on their way, and we'll be just fine."

His voice wavered on the last words as the sounds of a commotion came from outside: boots on the deck and voices shouting.

Rinka looked at Drystan, who had rested his hand on the hilt of the sword. His forearm twitched with every sound from outside the cabin.

Then there was silence. A long, tense pause in which the very air within the room seemed to stand still, no one daring to draw a breath. Even the children were silent.

Then the door burst open. A member of the crew in a slightly different uniform than the others stepped in. She was human, middle-aged, and had the harried appearance of someone who had recently been in a tussle.

"'Evening, folks. We're in a bit of a situation here. I'd appreciate it if everyone could give us their cooperation to prevent further violence. The captain is assisting these—" She cut herself off, avoiding a word that would start a panic. "—ladies and gentlemen on their mission to lighten the load of our unarmed vessel."

A pair of people entered the door: a man and a woman, human and elf, respectively. Their clothes were well-worn and salt-bleached, their heads covered by red bandanas.

Pirates.

Drystan tensed. He and Rinka were only paces from the door, but there were several passengers between them and the pirates.

"Alright, here's how it's going to go," said the elf woman. She swiped her silver hair out of her face, revealing a huge scar that crossed from her left brow to the lower right of her jaw. "My friend and I here are going to come 'round, and you put your valuables in this." She held up a burlap sack nearly as large as she was. "Jewelry, rings, wallets, pocket watches. It all goes. You don't give us any trouble, there won't be any trouble. Any questions?"

The old dwarf who had been first to speak earlier leaned forward and opened his mouth but stopped short. There were few options. While there were a handful of men and women in the crowd who looked capable of defending themselves, there were far more elderly, children, and soft-looking folks who had likely never seen a fight, much less participated in one.

"Good," said the elf. "Let's go."

The room was quiet as they watched the pirates go from person to person. A human woman wept as she removed a locket. The old dwarf crossed his arms over his large belly when they reached him, defiant. But when the elf reached for the steel at her side, he handed over his pocket watch and wallet with the rest.

Finally, the pirates made their way around to the final group of passengers, the benches nearest to Drystan and Rinka and the group who stood with them against the windowed walls.

"The ring too, old man," said the human pirate. He stood in front of an old Halfling whose feet dangled from the bench. It was the man Rinka had helped board the ferry earlier, the one who had nearly been crushed by his own cart.

"No," said the old Halfling.

"Excuse me?" said the elf. She came around the bench to join her partner. "What did you say?"

The Halfling ignored the warning in her tone. "I said 'no'. I won't give it to you. It's worthless. Just brass."

"Must be worth something if you won't give it up," said the human pirate. The elf held a hand up to him, a smile twisting at the corners of her lips.

She had wanted this to happen. Rinka's eyes caught the movement of the elf's hand to her side and the flash of steel she produced.

The events that followed proceeded at such incredible speed, it was only Rinka's excellent vision that allowed her to track them. The elf's sword slashed towards the Halfling but was stopped with a *clang*. Drystan's impossible blade had met the elf's steel a moment before it could meet flesh. The human pirate, his reflexes poorer than the others, dropped the bag of stolen goods, and its glittering contents spilled over the floor, where the passengers scrambled to reclaim them. Rinka crossed the aisle in a bound and scooped the Halfling into her arms. Out of the corner of her eye, she saw the human pirate fumble for his sword at his side as the elf and Drystan clashed, the force of Drystan's large body shoving her backwards into a group of passengers who clambered out of the way of the fight.

The elf laughed.

The Halfling cowered behind Rinka for protection, but she was frozen in place. She had seen plenty of disagreements resolved with old-fashioned fisticuffs, but her normal course of action was to keep as far from the action as possible. The other passengers must have had the same instinct because they had begun to flee out the door at the back of the cabin.

"Eyes to the aft," yelled the elf to the floundering human. "You're losing them."

Drystan took advantage of her momentary distraction to charge her. She parried at the last possible moment—any later and Drystan would have finished the "X" across her face.

The cabin of the boat was half empty now, leaving a large open space for their duel, which they took advantage of. Steel met whatever strange material Drystan's sword was made from again and again with dizzying speed. Rinka felt the Halfling creep away behind her, but she stood still, mesmerized by the deadly ballet before her.

Drystan's sword was a remarkable thing in motion. The illusion of the blade, which seemed to vanish entirely from certain angles, confounded the elf.

"What the blazes is that thing?" she shouted as she ducked another of Drystan's attacks that she only saw coming just before it would have hit her. "I've never seen magic like it."

They separated for a moment, both panting. Drystan did not answer her.

"Tell you what," she said. "I'd love to have a sword like that. Give it to me, and we'll forget this whole thing. You'll be on your way, head still intact. Deal?"

She lowered her own weapon, a paltry curved blade of ordinary steel, and held out her hand to shake.

"No deal," said Drystan, and he dove to his left just in time to collide with the human pirate who had lunged for him while he was distracted by the elf.

There was a sickening slicing sound as blade met flesh. Rinka looked away, her stomach in her throat as the pirate began to scream.

"My leg! You took my bloody leg!"

"You idiot!" yelled the elf.

Rinka dared to peek, holding her hand up to her brow to cover her eyes if she couldn't take it. The blood ran along the floor, spreading in a strange pattern from the boat's motion.

Rinka retched. She had been a butcher by trade, sure, but there was a difference when the blood belonged to a living being.

The human had fallen onto a bench, clutching at his missing limb and trying in vain to stop the bleeding. The elf ran over, removing her belt and tying it around the wound.

"Quit your whining. It's your own fault. You're lucky it's such a clean cut." She looked at Drystan to assess his intentions.

He lowered his weapon. At least, that's what Rinka thought he did. She couldn't see the sword from this angle.

"What is the meaning of this?" The voice came from the door at the back, but it was not the captain she had been hoping to see.

The man who entered, a hobgoblin with a dozen piercings in his pointed ears, did not seem especially intimidating to her considering he only came up to her knees. Yet the elf immediately jumped up and to attention, and even the human attempted to do the same before realizing he could not stand.

"Sir, the passengers—"

The hobgoblin who must have been their captain held up a tiny hand to silence her. "No bloodshed. You had only one order." His voice was deeper than Rinka would have expected for someone his size, and the authority in it made Rinka stand up a little straighter as well.

"But sir, he started it—"

"What is the law of the sea? What were you meant to do?"

The elf kicked at the ground like a child unwilling to look into the eyes of the parent who was scolding her. "I was trying to capture him, sir, but he's got some kind of magic weapon."

"I see no weapon on his person."

Drystan stood still, arms crossed against his broad chest. The sword—and the loop on his belt—had vanished entirely.

The elf made a move towards him, but the captain raised a hand again, and she stopped in her tracks. "It was there! I fought him with it. You saw it, didn't you?"

She gestured in Rinka's direction. Rinka looked around to find out who she was talking to, but she suddenly realized she and Drystan were the only passengers left in the cabin. "Me?" she asked, dumbfounded.

"Yes, you. Who else? Captain, she's acting dumb, but she's with him. They were together at the start."

"Then you know what to do." The captain turned back to the door as half a dozen pirates filed in. He gestured over his head to Drystan and Rinka, and the pirates were on them. Rinka looked at Drystan, but he shook his head at her.

They were defeated.

"Yes, sir," called the elf after the captain. She turned back to Drystan as a pair of pirates tied his hands behind his back. "I don't know how you did what you did, but you're about to pay for it. Do you know the law of the sea?"

Rinka held out her hands to be tied in front of her, and the pirates, perhaps seeing her size, decided it was best not to argue with her. "Please—" she began, but Drystan shook his head again.

"Out at sea, you've got two choices: sink or swim," said the elf. She kicked the back of Rinka's legs and shoved her shoulders into her, pushing her forward. Rinka obeyed. She heard Drystan receive the same treatment behind her as they were marched towards the door at the front where they'd entered.

They exited into the cool night air, the sky having gone completely dark during their ordeal, Rinka and Drystan followed by their pirate captors.

"Sink or swim," repeated the elf as the pirates pushed Rinka and Drystan against the railing.

Rinka could swim, but she'd never tried with her hands tied before. And they were still miles from land at night with no boats in sight except the pirates' own ship. She turned to Drystan and voicelessly pleaded with him, tears in her eyes as the fear took hold.

"Trust me," he mouthed to her, winking as the pirates lifted them and flung them over the railing, into the inky black waters below.

Chapter Six

OLD FRIENDS

Alison

Willow hopped jauntily along the forest trail ahead of Alison and Keir, pausing on occasion to stalk a bug or bird and then trotting quickly to catch back up to them.

The forest path was wildly different from the last time Alison had taken it. The trees that were then just budding were now full of leaves, their heavily laden branches casting a welcome shade from the late spring sun. A number of birds had returned from their southern journeys, and they flitted through the branches and to the ground below in search of food for the hungry babies in their nests. The silence and stillness of the woods had been replaced by a world come to life with light, color, and noise.

"I doubt the Wildcat's awake," said Willow. The tabby cat had introduced Alison to one of her wilder brethren, a supposedly fearsome beast that Alison had found absolutely darling. "He likes to sleep in a patch of sunlight on a nice day like this one. I can't say that I blame him."

Willow yawned and stretched.

"You don't have to come with us," said Alison. "You can always go home and nap yourself if you like."

"And miss all the fun? Not a chance. Besides, you'll never find the fairies without me. I have better eyes for them."

This was true, at least as far as Alison knew. Willow frequently seemed to react to things Alison could not see at all, often by pouncing on them.

"Not at home, as suspected," said Willow when they reached the Wildcat's makeshift abode at the bottom of a tree. Alison wasn't sure how she was able to tell, but she trusted the little cat. "It's for the best. He's really quite rude."

Alison supposed that was true, but he was just so cute about it.

They continued on the trail to the north, Keir growing more tense as the forest began to shift from hardwood to evergreen. This was where the spriggan had tricked them and separated them, and where he had bound them and tried to kill Keir.

"Are you sure you want to do this?" he asked Alison. His brows furrowed as they often did when he worried for her.

Alison rubbed the line with her fingertip and then pulled his jaw to her, kissing him on the lips. She was pleased that the action still left him dazed as she pulled away, even though she had done it dozens of times over the past few weeks. "I'm sure. It's going to be fine."

"Are you sure you don't need the branches?"

Alison had summoned the spriggan in the spring with a bundle of branches the Wildcat had suggested, but Alison was nearly certain that it had caused him offense. "Worse comes to worst, we come back with them tomorrow."

There had been no need to worry. Alison heard a familiar creaking just moments later, and her eyes caught the movement as they came around a large spruce.

The spriggan walked forward from the grove in his ordinary form, which was much like a man made from a tree, his body the trunk and arms and legs the branches. Like the rest of the forest, he had grown a number of leaves since Alison had seen him last. "What brings you here, my friends?"

Alison gave Keir a pointed look on the word "friends." "Two reasons," she said. "No, three."

The spriggan gestured to them. "Come, sit in my shade and tell me your reasons three."

He walked onto the trail and planted his feet into the ground. And then he grew upwards, his body extending and curling over as his limbs grew down and out into the shape of a bench. Alison took a seat on one of his legs without hesitation. Keir took a little more coaxing, but he joined her.

Willow looked up at a little nook where the spriggan's shoulders curled over its body. "May I?" she asked it.

"Of course, little one."

Willow climbed the spriggan's body and rested in the nook, nearly beginning to sharpen her claws in its bark but stopping herself.

"Sorry," she said.

"Not at all," said the spriggan. "Now, the three reasons."

"The first reason is to see how you are and how the forest is," said Alison.

"Ah," said the spriggan. "This is not truly the first reason, but it is nice of you to say so. The forest is well. It has been a good spring with plenty of rain. Is it not a thing of beauty?"

The spriggan was not easily fooled, but Alison could see he was not offended that she had not come to visit him sooner, and that he knew they were there for more than just niceties. "It has been a lovely spring indeed."

"The second reason?"

"There is another threat to the town and to the land that surrounds it. The king is coming, and he intends to see that a dam is built across the river. These lands will be flooded, possibly for miles."

The spriggan bent forward more, his bark creaking as he considered. "A blow to the forest to be sure, but little compared to how much the people take already."

"True," said Alison. "But it would be an end to the town. The stone circle. All of it buried beneath the water."

"A town at the bottom of the lake. A strange thing, undoubtedly. But what would you have me do? I have not been able to keep the trees safe. There is only one of me and so many of you."

Alison didn't have much of an answer to this. "I don't know, to be honest. We aren't sure what we're going to do to stop it. But if there's a part for you to play, would you play it?"

"I will always come to the aid of those who protect the forest. What is the third reason you have come?"

Keir, who had been sitting as still as a statue on the spriggan's knee, turned to look up into its face. There was fear in his eyes, but also a fearsome protectiveness towards Alison that compelled him to speak. "You once felt the hold the old magic had on me. Do you feel any of it in Alison?"

Alison laughed at Keir's somber tone. The spriggan looked at her, confused by her reaction. "I promised him we'd ask, but the entire thing is preposterous."

"What part of it is preposterous? I told you when I met you that you had a whisper of the old magic in you as well. That whisper is louder now. It's more like a murmur, the difference between the wind blowing through bare branches and the wind through the leaves. The breeze is still light, but it's growing."

The spriggan moved its arm, causing Alison to jump in alarm. "No, child, I will not hurt you or restrain you as I did to him. The magic in you is not beyond your control, though it seems it may have been beyond your notice."

"Where did it come from?" asked Keir. Alison could see the guilt in his eyes.

"I suspect it was always there, but it was awakened by you."

"I knew it," he said. "I knew it all the way back when you recovered from the head injury so quickly. You could have died. You should have been unwell for weeks, yet you were on your feet and fine the very next day. I knew it then but couldn't admit it."

Alison could see that Keir had been considering this for ages. That his guilt had been weighing on him all this time. She thought back to the moments when he'd pulled away from her, moments she thought were connected to his trauma and to the isolation he had imposed on himself. And perhaps they were, but there was something else there all along.

"What does it mean for her?" Keir asked the spriggan. Alison had been so concerned for him she had not thought about what the revelation meant for herself.

She had the old magic in her.

The old magic, which had power great enough to imperil the entire town. The old magic, the maker of dream worlds and the same power that granted the spriggan his stewardship over the forest. The power wielded by the korrigans and the fairies and all the wild things left in the world.

It was her power too.

"It's for her to decide. Alison, the power that grows within you is your own. You can let it grow and learn to wield it, or you can squash it down and pretend it doesn't exist. But be careful—the things we try to ignore often become the things that haunt us the most. As long as you pose no threat to the forest, you will be safe in my company."

"If I wanted to learn to wield it, where would I turn?"

The old magic book Alison had bought a couple of years earlier had not worked. Alison had managed to make a glass bottle explode rather than create water within it as the book suggested.

But then, maybe the explosion was a sign of its own.

"There were once academies dedicated to its study. They took a great number of my trees to make their books, but they always planted more in return. I have not seen their kind in some time, though.”

“Most of the magic academies have been gone for a while,” said Keir. “There are still some scholars who consider magic alongside science, though.”

“If not among your own kind, there are other folk that still practice the old ways,” said the spriggan.

“Like the fairies?” Alison asked.

“Yes,” said the spriggan. “Although they can be temperamental. And they make a mess of my forest. Rings of mushrooms and doors in my trees and harnessing starlight for their evening revelries. They’re a wild folk, and I would expect lessons from them to come with a price.”

Alison knew she should be afraid. She had seen what the old magic was capable of, and she knew there were things in the world that did not share her notions of morality, that people like the wild fairies could not be trusted and should be feared.

But she trusted in herself. That even if she was faced with danger and hard choices, she would do her best to do what was right. And she trusted in Keir, that he would do his best to protect her. And she trusted in her friends, including the softly snoozing Willow, who admittedly wasn’t the most help at the moment as she had found a warm spot on the spriggan’s shoulder to nap after all, that they would help her whatever she asked of them.

“Do you know how to find them?”

Alison and Keir kept a lookout for the new signs of fairy activity the spriggan had shared with them: sounds of laughter or the tinkling of tiny bells on the breeze, flickers of light or floating orbs visible only in the corner of the eye, and the brush of something against the skin as if something had grown into the path that was absent upon closer inspection. But they made their way back to the cottage mostly without event, the one exception being a brushing against Alison's legs that turned out to be Willow.

Their plans to meet with the korrigans and continue their search for the fairies could not proceed immediately the following day. Keir was needed to evaluate the healing of an injury sustained by the innkeeper, and Alison's friend Rinka was due to arrive the very next evening.

Alison spent the day tidying up the cottage to prepare for Rinka's arrival. Brytak carried a new bed frame and feather mattress up the stairs into Alison's room, asking a dozen questions about Rinka. Alison gently let the young orc down—although Rinka was a bit younger than Alison, she was several years too old to be impressed by a teenager.

As she made her way through the cottage, Alison tried to use the magic the spriggan had told her of to make the work easier. She swept the floors and imagined the dust vanishing but was disappointed to find a neat little pile collected in the center of the room that certainly would have fallen through the cracks before Keir "fixed" them. She willed the pot to boil on the stove, but she was rewarded with only a bubble or two that seemed to come up a little early. She strained at the door handle, begging it to turn while her hands were full of linens up to hang on the line outside, but it did not so much as rattle.

"Maybe your powers aren't domestic," said Willow. The cat had slept through most of the chores, but she happily joined Alison outside in the afternoon sunshine. "Try setting something on fire."

Willow's face was so adorable and sweet that it was hard to remember that underneath her impossibly soft fur beat the heart of a killer. A most darling killer, but a killer nonetheless.

Alison pinned the linens to the line as she considered the cat's words. "Keir noticed the magic while I did domestic tasks, but I didn't. Maybe I'm focusing too hard." She attached two pins to a sheet that needed at least three and left it to dangle, turning her back on it.

Then she snapped back around, hoping to catch something happening.

It hadn't. The sheet slipped down from the second pin, forcing Alison to catch it just before it reached the grass below.

"Nope," said Alison.

Willow gave her a withering look, or as close to one as she could manage with her little cat brows. "Keir's magic came from a terrible pain he suffered. Do you really hate sweeping and gardening? Maybe it's that you need to be angry or upset."

There was a degree of annoyance or impatience in the tasks Keir had observed Alison doing. She liked the results of cleaning and gardening but found the activities themselves tedious. Perhaps her magic was the manifestation of a shortcut, her mind sparing her from boredom.

There were other tasks today that would enable her to test that theory. Washing the dishes, ironing the clothes, pulling the weeds from the garden. The tasks were never-ending.

Still, it would all be worth it once Rinka arrived. She had missed her friend dearly, and she could not wait to introduce Rinka to the aspects of country life she had come to love: the beauty of the landscape, the kindness and community she felt among the villagers, and the freedom from the burden of constantly worrying about having enough coin that enabled her to focus on her art and things that brought her joy. She did not know if Rinka would have the same experience, but she hoped her friend would find her own place out here.

"I'm not angry or upset much these days, Willow," said Alison. She gave the cat a scratch behind the ears as she knelt to carry the empty laundry basket back in. "I guess I'm just going to have to wait until we find the fairies. Can you keep a lookout for me when you're out at night hunting?"

"Of course," said Willow. "I've chased lights like the spriggan described into the woods before, but I always lose track of them. I suppose the trick has been to keep them in the corner of the eye all along."

"Don't chase them on your own," said Alison. "Wake me if you find something."

Willow stretched and scoffed. "I'll lose them if I let them go. You know I'm perfectly capable of talking to them if I need to."

Alison hadn't meant her offense, but she wasn't sure the cat would manage to resist "playing" with the fairies. There had been some tense encounters with Aras and his family when they flew too quickly within reach of the garden walls.

"I want to see them too," said Alison, attempting to smooth things over. "I need their help if I'm ever to get control of this."

"Fine," said Willow. "I'll come get you if I see them, and I'll do my best not to murder them in the meantime." She purred and rubbed up against Alison's legs, mostly joking.

Mostly.

Chapter Seven

ROW, ROW, ROW

Rinka

The fall was over in moments. The impact with the waves below came as a surprise to Rinka, who hadn't been willing to open her eyes to look.

The water was cold, far colder than she had expected considering what a warm day it had been. She thrashed her legs and thrust her bound hands out in front of her, pulling them back to her chest, a gesture she hoped would propel her towards the surface rather than deeper into the darkness.

She did not reach the air.

Panic began to set in as her lungs began to burn, the urge to take a breath where no breath was to be found overwhelming. She blinked her eyes open, feeling the sting of salt and struggling to orient herself in the blackened void around her.

She felt something reach for her before she saw it. A hand, pale and blue in the dim and distorted light under the surface, reaching for her shoulder and pulling her up, up, further up than seemed reasonable, until finally, she broke free.

She took a deep and gulping breath in, a glorious gasp of relief. She reached her bound hands for her eyes, trying to wipe the stinging salt away, but being thrust under by a wave before she could do so.

The hand reached for her again, and this time, it was joined by another. The hands pulled her up by the shoulders and into…something. A boat?

It was difficult to make out in the pale moonlight. Rinka could see nothing that distinguished the bottom from the waters she had been pulled from, but she could feel something substantial beneath her. She looked around, and what she saw frightened her even more than being thrown overboard.

It was a boat, that was for sure. Its build was identical to that of an ordinary two-seat rowboat, with curved sides and a pair of benches to sit on.

But it wasn't made of wood, or even metal.

It was made of water.

"What *is* this?" said Rinka. She was still bound, soaked to the bone, and she hadn't even gotten a look at whoever had saved her, but all she could focus on was the impossible vessel.

"Have you never seen a boat before?" Drystan turned to face her. He was as drenched as Rinka, but he looked no worse for wear. He had slicked his wet hair back, and as she watched him, he removed his shirt and began to ring it out over the side.

Rinka blushed and turned away, although she could not help taking one small peek at his bare chest, which gleamed with tiny streams of water in the moonlight.

It was not an unpleasant sight.

But it did not distract her for long. There were still the matters of her near-drowning, their dire predicament, and, most of all, the impossible boat to consider.

"I have seen boats plenty of times in the River Eabrun, but none that were made of water. Water." Where in the world was Drystan from that this was an ordinary thing? Rinka had never heard of anything like it, not in the picture shows or the papers or even the fairy stories and tall tales read to children.

"I'll admit it isn't ordinary, but there wasn't much to work from here," said Drystan. He had finished drying the shirt and was holding something even more impossible, a long narrow column of water that coalesced into something like an oar as Rinka watched.

"You made this?" Rinka asked, trying to point to him with her bound hands.

"Ah," he said, realizing she was still bound. He let go of the oar, and it pooled into the boat, lengthening it ever so slightly. Rinka felt dizzy watching it.

Drystan stood and climbed over the other bench to where Rinka sat on the boat's bottom. He reached for her hands and began untying the rope.

"How did you get free?" she asked him.

"A dagger. A smaller version of the sword I used against the pirate."

The sword, a dagger, and now the boat. All made from the old magic, somehow. All made by him.

"And why can't you use the dagger now?"

"I'm concentrating on this," he said, gesturing to the boat. "I can't do both at the same time, and water won't do much to rope."

"Oh, I see," said Rinka, although she didn't, really. She spoke her thoughts out loud, hoping they didn't sound silly. "The boat is made of water, and if you made a sword from water, it wouldn't cut. Is that right?"

He smiled. "Exactly."

"Then what was the sword made from?"

"Air," he said. "And this." He reached into his pocket with some effort (his trousers were still soaked, and he had not yet opted to remove them) and produced an ordinary silver coin.

"Incredible," said Rinka. She took the coin from him and turned it over in her hands, but she could spot nothing unusual about it. It was an ordinary silver emblazoned with a portrait of King Derkomai on one side and a pair of dragons, the arms of his royal house, on the reverse.

Rinka looked at Drystan. The mystery of him was so deeply appealing, even more so with each new revelation. And the magic that he wielded so effortlessly fascinated her.

And, if she was really being honest, she also simply enjoyed his company and was very glad to have met him.

And, if she was really, *really* being honest, she found him very easy on the eyes as well.

But yet here they were, stranded in the middle of the sea. She had put her faith in him, and it had landed her overboard in the middle of the night.

And sure, they were in a boat. But it was a boat made from water, and how could they possibly take it to shore?

Was Rinka insane? She heard her mother's voice in her head. *"In the middle of the sea. The bloody sea! I told you that you were a fool. A fool's fool. What are you going to do now, foolish girl?"*

She could have died on the boat, she realized. She could die out here on the sea and no one would even know it.

"Drystan," said Rinka quietly. "I'm scared. Why did you let them throw us overboard? They didn't seem to know you, but why did you think they might? I've had so much fun with our guessing game. But my life is in your hands now. I want to trust you. Please. I want to know who you are."

Drystan leaned back on the watery bench and drew a deep breath in. Now that Rinka's eyes had adjusted to the moonlight, she could see the seriousness of his expression, the tension in his shoulders as the adrenaline wore off and reality set in. "Of course," he said with a sigh. "I've gotten carried away. Rinka, in truth, it's been so long since I've met someone—that is to say…aw, bloody hell. Let me start over."

He shifted on the seat, a movement that would have rocked a normal boat but seemed to have no impact on this strange vessel. And then he leaned forward, looking Rinka right in the eye, and he took one of her hands in his. "I'm sorry. I was having such a good time getting to know you, and it had me in such good spirits. And maybe I was itching for a bit of excitement. I let things get out of hand with the pirates. But the elf wasn't going to let the Halfling go, and I just—"

"You don't have to explain that part," said Rinka. "You did the right thing."

He smiled weakly. "Is it right even if I was hoping for it to happen? Not for him to be hurt, of course, but hoping for the opportunity…Never mind. That doesn't answer your question."

He released Rinka's hand and brushed his hair back, leaning away from her once more. "I let them throw us overboard because I knew I could get us to shore, and I was afraid of what would happen in a fight with the numbers so against us. Of what might happen to you. Not that I don't think you could hold your own," he said with a wink.

"Oh no, I really couldn't," said Rinka. "You judged that correctly. The best I could have done would have been to throw them overboard first."

"I would have liked to have seen that."

Rinka smiled.

"Rinka, the truth is, if they had realized who I am, it would have changed things, and not in a good way. I couldn't take that risk. And if you truly want to know and end our game right here, I'll tell you. No guesses. No qualifications. Only the truth. I'll tell you anything you want. Is that what you want me to do?"

Rinka tried to read what he was thinking behind his furrowed expression. Disappointment that their game was over, or perhaps relief to finally be able to be honest with her.

And maybe a bit of fear of how the answer would change things between them.

Rinka feared that too.

"Don't tell me yet," she said. "I want to ask my final question. But once we're safely on the shore."

Drystan nodded and relaxed, fully breathing out for the first time during their conversation.

"Now," he said, helping Rinka to her feet. Only once she was standing did she realize that the boat moved far less than it should have among the choppy sea waters. It had an ability to ride the waves that seemed as if it wasn't moving at all. "Are you ready to row? It's going to take quite a while to reach land from this far out, and we need to hurry before the current takes us around to the eastern side of Wilderise. It'll be hard to come ashore there on account of the cliffs."

There was a comfort in his tone. He spoke about reaching the land as though it were a certainty.

"What about the ferry? The passengers on board? What if they throw more of them over as they did to us?"

"I'm afraid we're in no position to help them, but we'll follow the ferry's path as well as we can. Hopefully, the example they made of us will be enough to keep the others safe."

Rinka could just spot the light of the ferry fading into the distance in the direction of Wilderise. She thought of the poor Halfling on board, hoping that he'd just give up the ring the next time he was asked.

Drystan reached beyond the boat, producing another column of water that turned into an oar as it reached Rinka's hands. Like the boat itself, it felt wet and cool to the touch, but it did not slip through her fingers as she held it.

"Away we go," Drystan said once he had produced a second oar for himself.

When the oars hit the water, they seemed to lose their form for a fraction of a second, and Rinka worried his plan would not work. But they quickly regained their shape, and the impossible boat was propelled through the dark waves, floating with an unnatural smoothness towards Wilderise's shores.

◈

After hours of rowing, Rinka's arms were numb with exhaustion. It was still dark, the nearly full moon having crossed half of the sky during their journey.

Rinka's stomach growled. Drystan had been able to pull the fresh water from the air without breaking his concentration on the boat, collecting it into a disconcertingly round blob that somehow did not break when held but that still could be drunk from.

But he could not manage anything for them to eat, and it had been a long time since the sandwiches they had eaten on the boat, the pirates having interrupted what should have been dinner.

"We must be nearly there by now," said Rinka. "Are you certain we're going the right way?"

"Yes, I'm certain. We won't hit land at Sudport, but we're heading north."

The tone of Drystan's voice had changed, and his shoulders were slumped now, the effort of lifting the oar seeming greater and greater with every stroke.

Rinka was surprised. Having seen him bare-chested, he was not lacking muscle.

"Maybe we should take a rest," she said. They had taken a couple to drink and stretch their arms. What harm could a few minutes more do?

"No," he said. "If we drift much more to the east, we won't meet the coast at all." He took a couple more strokes and then slumped over.

"Is it the magic?" she asked.

"Yes," he muttered. "I don't know how much longer—"

The oar in Rinka's hands splashed over her dress and into the bottom of the boat. She leaned forward, catching Drystan before he fell overboard.

"Stay with me!" she said. The boat was holding for now, but it rippled alarmingly around them. "Drystan, wake up! You have to stay awake." She splashed some water on his face. He blinked his eyes open.

Rinka wasn't actually sure if he needed to be awake for the boat to continue existing, but it seemed likely to her. She searched the horizon. How far could they possibly be?

There it was. It was as far away as her eyes could see, but it was there nonetheless. Land.

"I can see land! Drystan, can you make me an oar? You can rest on the bottom of the boat. I can get us the rest of the way."

"You're nice," he said. "I'm just going to rest my eyes."

"Drystan, the oar—"

"Just a minute. Just need to rest for a minute." Drystan's eyelids fluttered. Rinka lowered him onto the floor of the boat, which rippled and wet his clothes as he touched it.

"No, no, no," she said. If Drystan fell asleep, would she be able to swim far enough and fast enough to get them to shore?

She was about to find out. Drystan's head fell to the side, and the boat collapsed beneath them.

Her head was pulled under the water by the fall, but she quickly resurfaced. She looked around for Drystan, but he was nowhere to be seen.

"You can't have gone far," she said, reaching out into the water around her. She dipped her head back under, forcing her eyes open again in the salty water, and she spotted him sinking beneath the waves.

She surfaced and filled her lungs with as much air as they could hold, and then she plunged down as far and as fast as she could.

His body was heavy, even in the water, or maybe it was just the exhaustion in her arms, but she managed to pull him up. At first, he did not seem to breathe, but she slapped his back hard, and he coughed up a bit of water.

He blinked his eyes open. "I'm sorry," he said. "Couldn't keep going."

"Hush," she said. "You got us this far. I'll take it from here. Can you hold on?"

He nodded weakly. "It won't take long to recover," he said. "Just need…a little rest…"

He was out again. Rinka managed to keep his head above the water. She wrapped her left arm around his chest, keeping her stronger arm free to swim.

It was slow going. Rinka was grateful for the times she had spent swimming in the River Eabrun as a young orc, her mother watching from the stairs as she splashed around with her younger brothers. But they must have been some miles still from shore, and while at least Drystan wasn't trying to pull her under, dragging him along took a ton of effort.

Yet Rinka didn't consider for a moment leaving him. He was a stranger to her still, but even if he were her worst enemy, she would never leave him, not even to save herself. It just wasn't who she was, no matter how foolish her mother said that made her.

Finally, when the dim light of dawn began to touch the sky to the east, she could see the coast clearly. They weren't near Sudport, that much was certain. Rinka could see little sign of civilization at all. There were great cliffs of stone surrounding a narrow strip of tan beach strewn with boulders, white waves crashing on the shore. The land stretched upwards beyond into a beautiful green hillside. Rinka's eyes spotted the motion of tiny white sheep on the hill.

It was magnificent, and not just because the very sight meant their salvation.

"We've made it, Drystan," she said to him. He had been asleep for at least the past hour, but he grunted in what Rinka imagined was appreciation.

She swam as hard as she could for the narrow strip of beach, but the ocean had other ideas. The current was faster here near land, and it pulled her so far to the east that she nearly had to swim sideways to counter it. As she was pulled off course, she spotted a narrow strip of rock near the horizon. At the end of it was a lighthouse painted with white and red stripes. It reminded her of candy they sold at a corner store in Arcas Dyrne, and her stomach growled.

"That must be where the land turns north," Rinka said to the half-asleep Drystan. "It's just cliffs on the other side of that."

Rinka redoubled her effort to make it to land, but the current was just too strong. It pulled her closer and closer to the lighthouse until finally she had no choice but to aim for it instead of the beach. The land surrounding the lighthouse was dangerously rocky, and she wasn't sure if she would be able to keep them from being dashed upon the rocks.

And yet still the current pulled. "Drystan, it would be a very good time for you to wake up now," she said. "We're coming around the point, and I can't seem to stop it."

At least the sea was relatively calm. There were clouds in the distance, but the wind was still over the water. The problem wasn't on the surface. It was far beneath, and Rinka was powerless to stop it.

She couldn't believe they had come all this way only to fail at the last moment. As they came around the lighthouse, she looked up and down the eastern shore for an answer.

There it was. A tiny little patch of beach tucked among the cliffs, a cave of some kind beyond. Rinka could not see if there was a way out of the cave, but if she could just get them to shore, they could rest long enough for Drystan to remake the boat.

Rinka swam for it, hard. She used every drop of energy left in her, thrashing with the current now instead of against it, and before long, she had made it. She dragged Drystan along the beach, his legs stumbling beneath him, and collapsed with him to the ground within the cave, hoping they were above the waterline.

"Welcome to Wilderise," she said to his sleeping figure and then passed out, exhausted.

Chapter Eight

INTO THE WOODS

Alison

Alison scratched out a line in the second verse of her poem about the spriggan. It was one of the most important poems in her book, a real tale of life in Wilderise that she hoped would capture the imaginations of the audience of nobles that would arrive in just a few short days.

It had also been one of the hardest subjects to capture. Alison found it difficult to depict the incredible sense of awe she felt in the presence of something so powerful, so magical, so much bigger than the life she had lived before. Weyland's illustration was miraculous, unfolding across two pages in a stunning depiction of the spriggan's incredible feat in helping to raise the standing stones.

But her own words just weren't doing it justice.

"Still not right?" asked Keir as he brought her a cup of tea and a freshly baked scone from the kitchen.

She shook her head. "I was hoping our encounter would have given me some inspiration, but I can't seem to figure it out."

"*The wise old one, the spriggan, follows.*" Keir read the scratched-out line. "That seems accurate to me."

"Accurate, but not majestic," said Alison. "I'll get back to it later." She stacked her papers together neatly on her desk and capped her pen. "Are you ready?"

"Almost," he said. "The cake is in the kitchen. I'll go get the horses and meet you at the gate."

"Oh, you got the cake already? You didn't say."

"I didn't want to disturb you at work," he said. "It's in the icebox."

He was so thoughtful. He'd gotten her the icebox when he heard her say how much she missed having one, and now he'd gone to pick up Rinka's welcome cake unprompted.

She could get used to this.

"Thank you," Alison whispered to him. She kissed him on the cheek as she went into the kitchen to check out the cake.

The baker had done a magnificent job. The cream was pale pink and impossibly smooth, and the strawberries on the top were deep red and mouthwateringly plump, picked fresh that very morning from the baker's own patch behind the store. It was very difficult to walk away without stealing one off the top.

But then, Keir had thought of that as well. There was a bowl of extra strawberries in the icebox as well, cleaned and ready to eat.

Gods, she loved him. She felt a little thrill at the thought. Would it be too much to say it to him right now?

"I'll be right at the gate in ten minutes," yelled Keir from the front room as the door closed behind him.

Her confession would have to wait. That was just as well. She had been waiting for the right moment for several weeks now, but it always seemed to slip away before she could work up the courage to speak. She had managed to steel her nerves once before, a couple of weeks earlier as they sat together on a beautiful candlelit evening. But her words had failed her, just as they'd failed her in writing the poem about the spriggan.

How could it be possible to capture a feeling so all-consuming into simple words?

Alison pondered the unfortunate circumstance of being a poet who couldn't express how she felt with her language as she took a bite into one of the extra strawberries. It was exactly as delicious as it had looked: juicy, fragrant, and wonderfully sweet.

If the greatest of her problems was either figuring out how to tell the incredible man she loved that she loved him or finding a way to describe the magic of the extraordinary town she called home, she thought she must be doing some things right.

She changed into her riding attire and met Keir at the gate a few minutes later. He helped her into her saddle— her romantic notions of sharing a single horse had been squashed weeks earlier when Keir had gone to fetch the horses from Fossholm. He had explained to her that two people could not possibly share a saddle, and that the weight of them together would hurt the horse.

And then he had suggested that if she wanted to be close to him, she needn't use the horse as an excuse. The memory of the encounter that followed set her heart racing as Keir climbed back into his saddle beside her.

"What's that look?" he asked her.

"I was just remembering when you bought the horses," she said.

The look he gave her told her he hadn't forgotten either.

"What time is Rinka arriving again?" he asked, glancing back towards the cottage.

"Soon," said Alison regretfully. She was excited to see her friend again, but she had to admit she wouldn't have minded delaying the trip for a moment if they'd had the time.

Keir led them up the lane towards Herot's Hollow. They traveled through the town, stopping to say hello to Gwenla, who was waiting at the post office for news of the arriving nobility. Then they followed the road along the river towards Fossholm, where they would meet Rinka when her carriage arrived a few hours later.

Alison had only taken the road to Fossholm a couple of times since she'd arrived in town. The town itself was about the same size as Herot's Hollow, but it was much newer, having only come up around the time Weldan House, the residence of Lord Ainsley and Keir's childhood home, was built. There were few businesses there that Herot's Hollow did not also share, but Fossholm did have a small printing press that published the *Hill Country Standard*, and they had agreed to print a first run of Weyland and Alison's poetry book as a pamphlet. With any luck, they'd make enough sales to raise the funds to cover the cost of binding in Sudport.

The road to Fossholm quickly entered the woods after they rounded the hill that concealed Herot's Hollow from the view of the wider Hill Country. It was only a few miles between the towns, but it felt longer in the isolation of the forest. The woods were so wild there, it was hard to imagine there were two bustling villages so close by.

"Be on the lookout for fairy activity," Alison reminded Keir.

"It feels absurd, listening for bells and looking for strange groups of mushrooms," he said. "The fairies I've known have been like Aras: sensible, practical, and hardworking. If we'd heard it from anyone but him or the spriggan, I don't know if I would have believed them."

"I also thought the idea of a giant angry tree person was absurd until I met him," said Alison.

"I still think that's a little absurd," said Keir.

Alison laughed. "It is, a little. But I'm still very glad to have met him."

"Hopefully we feel the same about the fairies after we find them."

Keir and Alison rode along in comfortable silence until they reached the turnoff to Weldan House. The forest opened, granting a view of the lane and the bridge over the river, the same river from the vine's dreamworld that pulled Alison over the falls again and again.

The same river where Keir's younger brother Danny had drowned years earlier.

"I've been thinking about it, and I'm going to stop by once we've gotten Rinka settled," said Keir. He slowed his horse to wait for Alison by the turnoff.

She came alongside, as close as her horse would let her, and took his hand. "Do you want me to come with you?" she asked.

"No. I need to do this alone. To have a conversation with him, man to man. It's long overdue."

Alison wished he could leave this place and all of the painful memories that came with it forever. That he could turn his back on his father for good, and that they could live out the rest of their lives in peace.

But Keir was born to be the duke of these lands, and over the past few weeks as he had begun to reintegrate into Herot's Hollow, Alison had seen a side of him she hadn't expected. A side of him that viewed his responsibility over the land as not a burden but an opportunity. A chance to do things better than his father had done.

Keir leaned to give Alison's hand a kiss. "Don't worry," he said. "I'm ready for this. I'll reach an understanding with him, one way or another. And then we can enjoy the summer's festivities here together."

"Enjoy them, and maybe ruin them a little."

Keir chuckled. "Maybe it won't have to come to that, although I would hate to disappoint Gwenla."

They continued down the road towards Fossholm, at last reaching the bridge into town. From the bridge, the falls were visible at a distance.

Alison felt the lurch of her body forward and the terrible drop, the sensation of losing the ground beneath her and hurtling into the churning waters below as she looked.

The past times she had been here in the company of her friends, she had looked away, willing the memory away and attempting to focus on the road ahead of her.

But this time, she stopped her horse on the bridge. She let the memory continue: the sensation of drowning beneath the surface, of being pushed down by the water again and again. The burning of her lungs. The pain in her arms, reaching for something solid but coming up empty.

And then, something else. Something pulling her upwards. Tugging her towards dying light and healing air.

The euphoria of feeling the air rush back into her lungs. A hand on her back and the sputtering of water.

A voice, singing, on the breeze.

The sensations were so real, so present, that she had not heard Keir's voice.

"Alison. Darling, are you alright?"

"What?" said Alison. She didn't want to break free from the memory, but Keir's voice had come like a hook, pulling her from it even as she fought to hold on.

He had gotten off his horse, and he was standing beside hers, reaching his hands around her waist to pull her down.

"I'm fine," she said, but the words were unconvincing.

"I shouldn't have brought you here," said Keir.

"Keir, I'm okay. I was okay. Something saved me, at the very end."

Alison stood next to Keir, leaning over the stone wall of the bridge and looking upstream to the spot at the bottom of the falls where it had happened. On the banks of the river, there was a dense thicket of reeds and rushes. Weaving into them was a little path that wound up to the road. A fisherman's path, perhaps.

It felt familiar, though Alison knew she had never traveled it before.

"I've been here. There, on the banks. I can feel it."

Keir's face was white as a sheet. "Let's get you inside," he said. "This is some lingering effect of the magic. We need to find those fairies and set this right."

Alison reached back out towards the bank, but the feeling had faded. She wanted to go over there, to see if there was something more to find.

But she looked at Keir, and she saw his fear and worry, and she turned away from it.

She allowed him to lead her and the horses into town. They hitched the horses at the stable and went into the inn for a light lunch of cucumber sandwiches, which they ate as they walked around the village, Keir's watchful eyes never leaving Alison.

"Really, I'm alright," she said. "Just a strange memory. Something I experienced in another world—of course it would leave a mark."

"We have a few hours before Rinka gets here," said Keir. "Why don't we go look for the fairies while we wait? Aras said they gather in the woods to the south of town."

Alison finished chewing her bite of sandwich—the cucumber was so wonderfully refreshing on this hot, sunny day—and answered. "Not quite so absurd now, hmm?"

"Maybe not," admitted Keir. "Do you feel up for it? We could walk through the shops like we planned—"

"No," said Alison. "I want to go."

And so they walked through the town, keeping out of the way of the locals who were busy washing windows and tidying up planters in anticipation of the royal arrival.

The river fed into a broad lake that ran most of the length of town before feeding into another stream to the south. The road to Sudport followed the stream into a dense hardwood forest, and this was the road Alison and Keir took.

Alison did not see or hear any of the things Aras and the spriggan had told them to look out for, but after walking a mile or so from town, she did spot a little trail off the main road that led into the woods.

It was narrow, only wide enough for one person at a time, and the way the light filtered through the trees had the effect of a spotlight on the entrance.

It was deeply inviting.

"Where are you going?" asked Keir. Alison had begun to make her way to the trailhead.

"Isn't this so lovely?" she said. "It seems to pull you in."

"It's not any of the things we were told to look for," said Keir. "And yet…"

"It feels right, doesn't it?"

Keir looked less certain, but he followed her nonetheless.

The path wound into the woods so perfectly, it felt as though it was put there just for them. Even the well-maintained roads they'd traveled earlier in the day had more obstacles to overcome—fallen logs to traverse, low-hanging branches to pull back—than the path, which seemed somewhat unnaturally clear. It was brighter than seemed reasonable too, considering how dense the woods that surrounded it were.

Alison couldn't tell how long they had been walking. The light didn't seem to move with the sun across the sky in this place. But before too long, they had reached what appeared to be the end: the entrance into a cave.

She turned to Keir. "What do you think?" she asked.

"I think we'd be insane to go in there."

The cave entrance was framed by moss-covered boulders, the woods growing up and around it, concealing it from view even just a couple of steps from the path. The air coming up from it was cool and damp and smelled a bit like a summer night: jasmine and campfire.

Alison hadn't doubted the path until this point. Aras had said something about fouler things lurking in the woods than fairies, although he did mention that happening at night, and it was definitely still daylight.

The cave didn't feel sinister—in fact, it felt just as inviting as the path had. But that aroused Alison's suspicions. There was something too perfect, too appealing about this place.

It could be the makings of something lovely and ancient and magical.

Or it could be a trap.

A breeze filtered through the trees around them, rustling the leaves and sending another sound through the air: bells.

It was unmistakable. The tinkling sound of tiny bells, pure and clear like water.

Keir snapped his head towards Alison. "Do you hear that?"

Alison nodded, and she led them into the cave.

Chapter Nine

ONCE MORE INTO THE SEA

Rinka

Rinka awoke to the smell of fried fish and the sound of a crackling fire. Her body was stiff from a night spent on the sand, and her arms ached in places she'd never felt before, but she was alive.

And she wasn't alone.

As she slowly pulled herself upright, she spotted Drystan. He was a few feet away, seated next to a fire he must have built at the edge of the cavern where smoke could escape.

"Good morning," he called over to her. It must have been late in the morning because the sun was nearly overhead as she left the cave's shelter to join him. "Are you hungry?"

"Starving," she said.

Drystan held out the skewer he'd made—there were two large, flat fish on it, and they looked reasonably cooked.

"Flounder," he said. "I haven't been fishing since I was a boy, but they're easy enough to catch."

Rinka looked around for equipment—he must have had a hook, at least—before realizing what he had done. "The coin?" she asked.

He nodded.

"Can you make it into a knife?"

The fire sputtered and went out as Drystan shifted his focus to the coin, producing from it a dagger.

"A little longer and narrower," said Rinka. She watched his face as he worked, but she could see little sign that he was performing magic. There were no magic words, no strange gestures. And yet he did as she asked, producing a much more appropriate knife for deboning.

Rinka made quick work of the fish. Although fish weren't her usual trade, she'd seen the fishmongers at work in the market, and she found it simple enough.

She handed a filet back to Drystan as she ate her own in just a few bites.

He pulled a glob of water from the air and handed it to her, the knife turning back into a coin as he did so.

"Thank you," she said.

He was looking at her strangely. Staring, almost the same way he'd stared at the coin as he worked his magic on it.

"Is it my hair?" she asked. "I bet it's a terrible mess. The first thing I'm doing when I get to Alison's cottage is having a bath. Which seems like an odd thing to want after spending far more time in the water than I'd expected, but the salt just clings to you—"

"No, Rinka. You look fine. Great, actually. The salt air suits you."

He couldn't quite meet her eyes on the last part, and that was just as well because she found she had to look down at the ground too.

"I—well, thank you," she said.

"No, Rinka. Thank *you*. You saved my life."

"I did my best," she said. "You got us most of the way there."

He shook his head. "We would have died. I was foolish. I overestimated my abilities, and it could have killed you. I hope you can forgive me."

"I don't think there's anything to forgive. I can't see another way for things to have gone—you weren't the reason the pirates were there, and I couldn't have let anything happen to the Halfling. In fact, if you hadn't been there at all, things would have likely gone far worse for me. I probably would have confronted the elf unarmed."

"You really would have, wouldn't you?" He was giving her the look again.

"Is that strange?"

"No," he said. "It's extraordinary."

Rinka didn't see how that was different from strange, but he didn't seem to be mocking her. She decided to change the subject. "Have you been awake long? Did you see if there's a way out of the cave?"

"I did look before you woke up, but it's no good. There's a passage, but it's collapsed. We're going to have to go back out into the water and look for another way onto land."

"Do you think there's an inlet somewhere?" And then: "Oh, no!" she cried as she realized something unfortunate.

"What is it?" Drystan stood and rushed over to her.

"My maps! My bag with my maps. And my trunk. It's all on the boat still."

Drystan laughed. "You know, I thought the maps were funny when you first showed them to me, but they really would have come in handy right about now." He put a hand on her shoulder. "Don't worry. I'll bet the pirates left anything that wasn't shiny on the ship. It'll be waiting for us when we get to Sudport."

"You really think so?"

"I do," he said. "Come on." He helped her to her feet. "I'll make the boat. With any luck, we'll be back to your maps and your trunk by nightfall."

"Can I help you?" she asked.

Drystan tilted his head, amused. "You know, I don't know if you could. I suppose it's possible. My mother used to help me, but then this particular gift was hers as well."

"Oh, I'm sorry. Is she…?"

"Oh, no, she's alive and well. Just far away. As far away from my father as she could get."

Rinka nodded. "My parents are the same. Well, the reverse, actually. My father was the one lucky enough to escape."

"Would you like to try? To help me make the boat?"

"I would. What do I do? What do *you* do?"

Drystan held up his hands. For the first time, Rinka noticed that Drystan held his left arm a little funny, as if he couldn't quite bend it the same as the right.

He made a gesture of pulling into him. As he did so, water droplets appeared in the space between his palms. "My mother described it as a pull. A request you put out into the world for it to change its shape. My father's magic is different—harder, violent. I never quite grasped it. But my mother's magic feels natural to me. It's a negotiation. A dance, almost. A give and take. May I?"

He reached for her hands, and she gave them to him.

"Close your eyes and imagine the rain. Imagine asking the sky to give you the water. Don't push it. Just ask, and see if it answers."

At first, Rinka felt nothing but the tension in her wrists and the feel of his smooth skin, the light stroke of his fingertips on the back of her hands. She was close enough to him on their little patch of shore to hear his breath over the waves. Paradoxically, it was both calming and exciting at once. His breath and the waves fell into an almost meditative rhythm, but the feel of his presence so close to her was also invigorating. Exhilarating.

And then she felt it. Her mind turned to the rain, and she let a question enter her thoughts: *may I have some water?* There was nothing at first, just the gentle sounds of the waves and his breath, but then she felt a pulse flow between them.

It snapped and hummed with 'lectricity. It flowed back and forth between their hands and through their bodies, and Rinka almost let it go out of fear, but she held on. She wanted to open her eyes to see his response, but she resisted the urge. What should she do with the power? Was he waiting for her to act? Should she take it from him and try to wield it?

No, that didn't feel right. It was a dance, he'd said. She imagined his hand around her waist, imagined their feet in motion, moving together across the sand.

She did not move, but she felt the rhythm of the 'lectric flow between them pulse and change. Heard the rhythm of his breath quicken.

And then she felt the water. It welled between her hands, and in her surprise and delight, she let go.

The droplets fell to the ground at their feet and sank into the sand.

"I felt that!" she said. "Was that it? Did I help?"

Drystan's eyes were wide, his mouth not quite closed. "I'm not sure what happened. It wasn't like when my mother taught me. But yes, I think so. Here. Hold my hand and think of the sea. Look out at the waves and imagine them taking shape. Imagine the boat."

Rinka looked at the waves. They were relatively calm here on this tiny stretch of beach, but they crashed with much more force on the cliffs that surrounded them. She struggled to hold the image of the boat within her mind—it was so peculiar; her mind resisted the thought. Or perhaps it was the sea that resisted.

Then Rinka felt a surge of power again, this one far stronger than before. It was odd, but she felt the question in it. Not the words themselves, but she felt the ask in the 'lectric pulse between them. It was humble, almost apologetic.

As if Drystan was conveying to the sea itself what a strange request this was.

The sea responded, or at least that's what it felt like. The boat began to take shape in the shallow water at their feet. Each tiny crash of wave added to it, giving it form, until it was there before them, gently rocking in the waves and waiting for them to board.

"I don't know if I did anything, but I could feel it," said Rinka.

"I felt it too," he said softly. "What did you think?"

"It's wonderful!" Rinka beamed at him. "Can we do it again? Let's make the oars. What about a sail? What's that thing they use to steer—a rudder? Do you think that would help?"

Drystan smiled at her, dropping her hand. "Let's keep it simple for now. I can't let go—I have to keep holding onto the question or I'll lose it like I did last night."

"I'll help you," said Rinka. "Maybe it will make a difference."

"It already has."

They made the oars and took to the sea once more. The new boat maneuvered just as well as the old boat, and soon they were out far enough to avoid getting beaten back into the cliffs.

"Which way?" asked Drystan.

"You don't know?"

"We know south will take us back towards Sudport. But we also know the current runs in the opposite direction. So maybe our best bet is to keep going further north and hope we find a break in these cliffs."

"Didn't you say it was all cliffs on this side?"

"Well, I knew there were cliffs here, but I didn't exactly pay much attention to my geography tutor."

A geography tutor, not a geography class. He had grown up well-off then. Rinka had been so distracted by their perilous situation and the thrill of experiencing magic firsthand that she hadn't noticed all the information he had given her about himself.

"Let's see where the current takes us. I doubt we have much choice about it anyway. Besides, worse comes to worst, we'll just go all the way around the island and come across Sudport from the other side."

Unfortunately, that wasn't the worst-case scenario. The worst-case scenario was what actually happened: the current began to take them out to sea.

"We're getting further out," said Rinka a little over an hour later. The cliffs were still visible, but they were definitely shrinking, and quickly.

And in the distance to the east, storm clouds were beginning to gather. Lightning flashed between them ominously.

"I know," said Drystan. She could hear the exhaustion and fear in his voice. "Let's strike directly towards the shore and see if we can't get out of this current."

They began to do so, but it seemed to have little effect.

Rinka wasn't sure how much longer she could keep going. Her arms still hadn't recovered from the night before, and she had only slept a few hours at best. And she was even more concerned about Drystan, who had to both row and maintain the magic holding the boat together.

How much more could he endure?

Rinka laughed. It was an odd response, and it elicited a puzzled reaction from Drystan.

"What's so funny?"

"Just…everything," she said, setting down her watery oar and gesturing broadly. "My mother always said I was a fool for wanting to leave Arcas Dyrne, for having my head stuck in the clouds and at the picture show, and she was right. She was actually right."

She laughed again, and this time, another laugh joined her.

But it wasn't Drystan's.

"What was that?" he asked.

More giggling. High-pitched, girly giggling, to be precise. And a lot of it. At least two girls' worth of giggles.

"Where is that coming from?" asked Rinka.

She looked around, but there was no one in sight. She heard a small splash and turned towards the sound, but all she could see were a few bubbles on the surface.

"Is someone there?" asked Drystan.

A splash again, and more giggles.

Rinka reached for the oar on the bottom of the boat, and then she screamed.

There was a face there. It was distorted by the boat's watery bottom, but it was a young woman's face.

"Under the boat! They're under the boat!"

The face burst into a huge smile and another fit of giggles that left bubbles attached to the bottom of the boat.

It vanished into the dark water below, and then a second later, another face appeared above the waves right beside Rinka.

Floating right at the surface, it was apparent what the giggling girls were.

Mermaids.

Chapter Ten

A DINNER, ENCHANTED

Alison

The cave was cool and damp, but it wasn't dark, not completely. There was a shimmer in the air and on the walls, a glittering flicker of light that stayed in Alison's peripheral vision with no discernible source. The glow was faint, but it was enough to illuminate the path, which wound through the narrow passages into the ground.

The only sounds were their footsteps and a faint echo of dripping water from far off.

"How far do you think it goes?" Keir asked from close behind her, his hand on her waist in case she lost her footing.

"Not far," said Alison. Even as they spoke, the passageway ahead grew brighter, the craggy rock of the walls becoming more defined as the ground began to climb once more.

They rounded a bend, and suddenly the bright light of the exit flooded the final chamber. Alison walked towards it, Keir so near to her now that she almost stepped on his foot.

Emerging into the light, Alison realized they were no longer in the woods. The land that stretched before them wasn't bare—it was heathland, a gently sloping open landscape covered in low-growing shrubs tinged with purple.

"It's early," said Keir, bending to observe the spires of lilac-colored blossoms. "The heather on our lands is just starting to bud."

"No," said Alison. "I think it's late. Maybe not the season, but the hour."

The sky, which had been bright with midday sunlight before they started on the path into the woods, was tinged with pink and gold, the hour before sunset.

Behind them, there was a strange churring sound: a high, fast strum, almost like a door creaking open or a chain pulling against stone. As Alison turned to see, the motion of a bird in flight caught her eye.

"A nightjar," said Keir. "What a rare sight."

It was nearly silent as it flew over their heads, its small, brown body swooping low into the heather and vanishing from their view.

"An omen of death, according to some," said Keir.

A chill shuddered up Alison's back.

Keir squeezed her hand. "Superstitious nonsense. I've also heard that they're the spirits of lost children or the mortal enemies of goat herders."

"Most of the superstitions I'd heard turned out not to be true," said Alison, convincing herself as she spoke. "It's easy to blame all sorts of ills on things you know little about."

The bird took flight again, heading away from them into the heath. Alison tracked its flight, noting a path through the heather that led downhill towards a wood.

"Shall we follow the omen of death and see where it takes us?" she asked Keir, letting out half a nervous chuckle.

"We've come this far," he said. "I feel something of a pull towards those woods. Can you feel it too?"

"Yes," she said. The path seemed to have its own gravity. The pull of it was familiar—it was not unlike the pull that existed in the vine's dream world, the compulsion that propelled her again and again into the river. "But let's hurry. I don't want to miss Rinka when she arrives."

They followed the path through the heather—again, it was unnaturally clear and easy to follow—and as they did, the sky turned from pink and gold to a deep and vibrant red as the sun slipped behind a hill, and then to a rapidly darkening blue as it vanished completely.

Around them, fireflies began to take flight, the flashes of their light synchronizing as they, too, followed the path towards the woods.

As they approached, they heard music and laughter and the murmur of voices in conversation. The voices were much too deep to be those of fairies, and the shadows that stretched from the light of the woods into the last of the heather were long. Fulling shadows, or Halfling at least.

Keir stopped Alison, tugging on her arm. "I'm not sure this is right—" he started, but just then, something began to fly up the path towards them.

It *was* a fairy, or at least it looked just like one. It had the ordinary features—a human face, brightly colored hair (blue, in this case), and white feathery wings, which it used to hover a few feet above the ground.

It was dressed ordinarily as well, in a finely made white tunic with matching trousers that seemed to glow in the light of the rising moon.

Everything was perfectly ordinary, except for one thing…

"You're enormous," said Alison before she could stop herself.

The fairies of Herot's Hollow barely came up to Alison's knees when standing. This fairy was easily as tall as Keir, maybe taller.

They laughed. "I never get tired of hearing that. Come on," they said, gesturing with their hand and wing simultaneously. "You're late for your own dinner."

"Excuse me?" Alison was still trying to make sense of it. She looked around the landscape, guessing that maybe they had been made smaller in this strange place. But the heather was the appropriate height, and although the trees loomed large ahead, they appeared no larger than usual.

"Your dinner," they said, as if they could not believe she had forgotten. "It's started."

Alison looked at Keir. He was uneasy, his brows furrowed into their signature worried expression, but he shrugged as if to say, *it's up to you.*

Alison looked back up the path towards the cave where they had come from. It was still there, still clear and obvious behind them. If this was some sort of trap, wouldn't it have vanished by now?

Alison wasn't sure, but they had been told to take this path by beings they had trusted, and although she wasn't ready to abandon all caution, her curiosity propelled her forward.

She took Keir's hand. Whatever lay ahead, they would face it together.

They followed the fairy into the woods. The fireflies filtered into the trees, joining a thousand tiny fairy lights that hovered and danced, illuminating the darkness.

Alison gasped. What she had expected to see based on the shadows she'd glimpsed beyond the wood was a campfire with a handful of fairies gathered around it.

And there was, indeed, a fire.

But it was a great, roaring bonfire in the middle of a clearing, and around it arose a city in the trees. Dozens of buildings wrapped around the tree trunks, a vast web of ropes and boardwalks extending between them. They were made of raw, natural materials—tree limbs that were still covered in bark, purple heather woven into a latticework, mossy roofs with chimneys of river rock—but they weren't crudely made. There was an intricacy to the structures, an artistry finer than anything human hands could craft. An artistry that rivaled the finest of the elvish structures Alison had known in the city, as skilled as the carvings in stone the dwarves were known for, if perhaps less enduring.

Beside the bonfire, there was a long table carved from the trunk of what was once a mighty tree, a hundred-year-old oak, maybe. There were dozens of benches and stools pulled up to it, all uniquely made, and on its surface was the largest banquet Alison had ever seen.

There were many things Alison recognized: platters of meats, fish, and sausages; great loaves of bread and pretty plaited buns with a sticky-looking glaze; cheeses in many colors, some with delicate veins and others with thick red rinds; steaming bowls of bright vegetables gleaming with broth and butter; and bottles of wine and dark spirits in all shapes and sizes.

But there were also many things Alison had never seen before: strange-looking fruits in shades of sparkling blue, some of them covered in what appeared to be rabbit fur; pie dishes that seemed to hum with energy; goblets of golden liquid that fizzed and bubbled; and flowers braided into pastries, including the poisonous foxgloves Aras had warned them about.

"Come, friends," said the fairy that had greeted them to the revelers gathered near the fire. They weren't just fairies, Alison realized. There were all sorts of people here: humans, elves, dwarves, and even orcs and some of what she guessed were smaller folk based on their features: pixies, hobgoblins, and sprites, although all were around the same size in this space. "Our guests have arrived at last."

A number of people came over to meet them before taking their seats at the table: a young dwarven man with red hair and a lazy smile; a pixie or maybe a korrigan (it was hard to tell without the height difference) with iridescent wings and a haughty laugh; a pair of human women, drunk on love or something like it; and several more fairies, their hair in all the colors of the rainbow.

Alison and Keir approached the table, unsure of where to begin.

"Much of it is poisonous," Keir whispered to Alison.

"Ah, of course," said their fairy host. They took a seat at one end of the table, gesturing to Keir and Alison to take the bench nearest to them. "Mab, if you wouldn't mind."

The fairy gestured to another. She looked much like their host, her hair a similar shade of blue, but she wore a long, white gown with beads that twinkled like starlight. "Of course, Genn," she said simply, and then she flitted over the table and stood behind Keir and Alison, placing a head on each of their shoulders.

They froze, staring at each other in alarm. But Alison felt nothing unusual, and in another moment, the fairy had taken the plates in front of them. She half-walked, half-flew around the table, taking from various dishes until both plates were full.

"These should be to your liking," she said when she returned. "And there's nothing there that will harm you, through poison or otherwise."

Alison's plate was full of all the things she loved the most, and Keir's was as well, although they were quite different.

"That's an incredible gift," she said to Mab. And then to Keir: "I didn't know you liked blue cheese."

"You made such a fuss about it that time, I didn't want to admit it," he said sheepishly.

Alison took the fork and knife before her—they were mismatched, like most things here—and dug into her plate. Although it had seemed like far too much at first look, she found that everything was in the perfect proportion for her appetite and preference. When she'd finished, she felt impeccably, pleasantly full.

There was conversation at the other end of the table, but on this side, they had eaten in silence, the fairies watching Alison and Keir closely while they ate their own dinners.

"Is it all to your liking?" the host—Genn—asked.

"Yes, thank you," said Alison. "Perfectly so. Do you know why we've come? I'm afraid we can't stay long; I'm due to meet with a friend in town."

"All in good time," said Genn. "First, we dance."

They clapped their hands, and the table was clear in an instant.

"Come, friends. It's time for the dancing," they said to the gathered crowd.

As the table emptied, Keir asked Genn how they'd known they were coming.

"How does a moth know to follow the moon?" they said. "How does Jenny Greenteeth know who to drown?"

They did not elaborate further, and Alison was frightened to ask them to clarify.

Alison studied the crowd gathered around the bonfire. They were two dozen, maybe three, but the city beyond them must have held many, many more. She wondered how these guests were chosen and what was happening in the strange world beyond her limited view into it.

She was pulled from her wondering by Mab, the fairy who had made their plates. She came along beside Alison and closed her eyes, listening with a smile on her lips.

Alison listened too. The band had not begun to play again, but the air was filled with song: crickets, cicadas, and the nightjar from earlier, churring and chirping on its own.

"A wonderful chorus," said Mab. "Gennet, play with them."

Genn took a seat on a log, raising a fiddle into the air. They began to play, and at first, it was an odd little tune. The notes jumped around in rhythm with the night creatures until a melody began to take shape. It wasn't like the melodies that Alison knew, nothing like the rowdy music of Mr. Smalls, the bard who was still hanging around the inn of Herot's Hollow despite his repeated claims that he would be leaving any day now. It was organic and earthy, almost indistinguishable from the sounds of nature.

At least, it started that way. Several others joined Gennet, and as they added their instruments to the tune—a flute, several drums, and some sort of large stringed instrument played with a bow that Alison had never seen before—the tune grew into a lively dance.

Alison was concerned about the delay, hoping she wouldn't be too late to meet Rinka, but they had come this far, and it seemed a shame to leave before they had any answers. "What do you say?" asked Alison, her hand held out for Keir. The others around them had begun to dance in a dozen different and wild ways, no set of steps alike.

They had never danced together before—there hadn't been the occasion—and Alison worried for a moment that Keir would decline.

But he took her hand and led her to an empty space, and he placed the other hand on her waist and began to lead her around the bonfire with a surprising grace.

"I've successfully avoided having to do this for years," he whispered to her. "I always hated it, not least because at court, it's less of a fun bit of exercise and more of a dangerous political game. Dance with the wrong person in the wrong order and it's a wild scandal. I'd rather face the king's armed forces in open battle than go through all of that again."

"And yet," whispered Alison back, "you're just so good at it."

Keir moved so well that it didn't matter that Alison didn't know the steps. He made up for any awkwardness happening below Alison's ankles, leading her round and round as the fairies looked on.

"Perhaps I was just waiting for the right partner," he said and lifted her hand to his mouth to kiss.

"May I cut in?" asked Genn. They had left the fiddle behind, but the band played on.

Keir looked at Alison, who nodded. He let go of her hand.

"No, no," said Genn. "She's lovely, but I meant with you."

"Oh," said Keir, his face flushed in the firelight. "Sure, I suppose."

Chapter Eleven

THE LITTLE MERMAIDS

Rinka

The second mermaid surfaced nearer to Drystan. They were young in appearance—the same as teen-aged humans or orcs—with bigger, rounder eyes than any of the peoples of the land. One was fair-skinned and blonde where the other had dark brown skin and black hair, but there was a similarity between them, both in their full figures and their attire, which appeared to be made from an iridescent material similar to the scales of their fish tails.

"You're getting nowhere fast," said the darker-haired girl, and both girls started giggling again.

"Our mother said we shouldn't talk to humans, but you're not human, are you?" said the other girl.

"No, we're not. Are you mermaids?" asked Rinka.

The girls laughed and then said in unison, "Obviously."

Rinka had seen a picture show with a mermaid, but she was certain they had just used an elf in a costume. There were rumors that ships encountered them from time to time, but there were rumors about all kinds of things that almost certainly weren't real: kraken and giant squids and creatures with mouths so big they formed whirlpools.

Unless…

"Oh Gods, they're all real," said Rinka.

"What?" asked Drystan.

"They're all real. All the creatures. The kraken, the sirens, all of it."

"The sirens are mean," said the girl with dark hair. "They took Cordy's seahorse."

Cordy, the blonde one, looked sadly into the water. "He was my pet, and his name was Randy. I'm Cordelia, by the way, but you can call me Cordy. And this is my sister Maisie, but you can call her Em."

"No, they can't."

"Yes, they can!"

The girls lunged for each other. Rinka shot Drystan a helpless look.

"Hey!" he shouted. "No fighting."

Rinka waited for the girls to laugh at him, but they didn't. They stopped in their tracks, somehow impressed by his authority. Cordy stuck her tongue out at Em, but she retreated back to a safe distance.

"You're going out to sea, you know," said Em. "This is a strange boat you have. It doesn't seem like it's very good."

"It's the best we could do," said Drystan, a hint of actual hurt crossing his face.

Kids. Their honesty could be brutal.

"Say," said Rinka, seeing an opportunity. "Could you help us? I'll bet you can swim way better than we can row."

"Of course we could," said Cordy. "But it's gonna cost ya."

"Cordy, don't be mean. They seem nice, and they might be a little stupid."

"I'm not being mean. You're being mean. They can hear us, you know."

"I didn't say anything mean. I just called them stupid, and I mean, look at them—"

"Girls!" Rinka tried the authoritative voice Drystan had used, and to her surprise, it got their attention. "We need to get back to land, but we can't climb the cliffs. Do you know a place we could go? Could you help us get there?"

"Oh, you want the river," said Em. "There used to be land people there, but they all left on account of the pirates."

Rinka looked at Drystan. She didn't want to encounter the pirates again, but at this point, they had to take their chances. If they couldn't find a way back onto the shore, they wouldn't make it.

"Yes, the river," she said. "Can you take us there?"

"One story each," said Cordy. "That's the price. We'll take you to the river, but you have to tell us one story each about being on the land. And it better be a good story, too. Is that nice enough for ya, Em?"

Em nodded thoughtfully. "It's a fair price."

Drystan smiled at Rinka. "I think we can manage that," he said. "I think my friend Rinka here would like to hear a story too."

"Rinka? What kind of name is that?" asked Cordy.

"It's an orc name," said Rinka.

"An orc!" shouted Em. "I've never seen a real orc before. Where are your fangs? We saw a human boy with his dad once, and he said orcs have vicious fangs."

Rinka opened her mouth a little, happy to oblige.

"Cool! Look, Cordy, fangs!"

The girls swam over closer to get a better look. "Rinka, tell us your story," said Em. She grabbed onto the side of the boat and began to kick her tail.

"Hold on!" said Cordy. "I'm coming."

Cordy swam under the boat—stopping to pull a silly face through the bottom at Rinka—and then grabbed onto the opposite side and started kicking.

The boat rocketed into motion once more. Their tails were incredibly effective: they were moving at least twice as fast as they had before, and the current seemed to have little impact.

Rinka searched through her memories for a story that would be interesting to girls who had spent their lives underwater.

"Have you heard of the city of Arcas Dyrne?" she asked them.

"Yes," said Cordy automatically.

"No, you haven't," said Em.

"Yes, I have!"

"No, you haven't."

"Do you want to hear the story or not?" asked Rinka.

"I do!" said Em. "We don't know what Arkish Deer is though."

"Arcas Dyrne," said Rinka. "It's the biggest city in Loegria." She paused, and seeing no recognition, added: "The big island to the south of here."

"Oh, the dragon island! You're from the dragon island? Can you fly?" asked Em.

Rinka laughed. "No, I can't fly. Only the king can fly, and his family, I guess."

"Have you met them?" asked Em.

"The royal family? No," said Rinka. "I can't say that I have."

"We know the king of the ocean. And his husband too," said Cordy. "They're really nice."

Rinka was previously unaware that the ocean had a king, but she nodded politely and didn't admit it.

"So Arcas Dyrne was built by the dwarves first. They built it underground, a great city beneath the surface. But when they allied with the elves, they allowed the elves to build upwards, and when the dwarves created the manufactories, the humans and orcs moved in too. And even some of the smaller folk, fairies and hobgoblins and pixies, left their homes to come live where the action is. So Arcas Dyrne is for everyone, all kinds of people living together."

"It's like that where we live too, only everyone we know can breathe underwater," said Em.

"It sounds really great," said Cordy. "Why did you leave?"

"It is pretty great, but I'm not the only person that thinks so. So many people want to live there that it's really expensive. I lived with my human friend named Alison in a tiny flat on the seventh floor of a building that needed a lot of work, and even then, we could barely afford it. And once she left, I couldn't afford it at all. But she's made a home for us in Wilderise—the land just over there. That's where I'm going."

"What's the seventh floor?"

With Drystan's help making models out of seawater, Rinka explained to the girls the concepts of floors, stairs, lifts, and a number of other ideas she had taken for granted but which seemed exotic and fascinating to the little mermaids.

Fascinating for a time, at least. By the time Rinka had finished explaining underground rail-wheelers to them, they had grown bored of Rinka's admittedly shaky explanations of modern engineering.

"It's your turn, Mister?"

"Drystan."

"We're almost there, Mister Drystan," said Cordy. "Tell your story, quick."

Rinka could see no change in the cliff-lined coast, but there was an area jutting deeper into the water near the horizon. The river must have been on the other side.

"Alright," said Drystan. "I'll tell you a story about the school where I worked—"

"No!" shouted Cordy.

"We hate school!" cried Em.

The girls had stopped kicking.

"You hate school?" asked Drystan. "I had no idea."

He smirked. Rinka could see it—he had known he'd get this reaction. He was teasing them.

"Tell us a love story," said Em. She looked between them, her big brown eyes flashing back and forth. "Are you two in love?"

Rinka looked wide-eyed at Drystan, who was also caught off guard by the question. "We've only just met," she said.

"Oh. That's too bad," said Em. "Tell us a love story anyway," she said to Drystan.

"All my love stories ended in heartbreak," he said. He looked at Rinka.

He was being sincere.

"That makes two of us," she said.

He smiled.

"Did you cry? Tell us a story where you cried," said Cordy.

"Cordy! That's so mean."

"I'm not telling him to cry again. I just want to hear a sad one. Don't you?"

Em reluctantly nodded. "I do want to hear a sad one," she said.

"Okay," said Drystan. "But we've got to get to shore before it's dark. Can you listen and kick at the same time, like before?"

"Yes, sir!" said Em. She made a silly little salute and resumed, her sister not far behind.

"I was seventeen the first time I fell in love," said Drystan. He looked at Rinka, and she wasn't sure how to react. She wanted to listen, wanted to hear more about him, but she was worried, too, about what she might hear.

"Was she pretty?" asked Em.

"Beautiful," he said. "To me, at least. I was wildly in love with her the way you can only be when you're young, when you're so excited that it's finally happening for you that you don't notice all the things that are wrong. When you're blind to everything that isn't exactly how you wanted it to be, how you pictured it your whole life. It was a deep, all-consuming love that almost drove me mad."

Rinka flushed. She had never felt anything like that. There had been men, but it truly had been one disaster after another for her. Her own childhood sweetheart had been a young orc her mother had encouraged her to see who kept her from her friends and treated her more like a slave than a partner. She had never loved him, and although she'd felt the promise of it once or twice since, it had always ended in disappointment.

The girls were entranced. "How did you meet her?" asked Em.

"Did you get married?" asked Cordy.

"Almost," said Drystan. "We were engaged. We met at a ball—she wasn't the girl I was supposed to go for, but she was from a good family, and my mother wanted me to be happy, so she helped broker the engagement after we'd spent the season getting to know each other."

"Why didn't you get married?" asked Rinka before she could stop herself. The girls nodded at her. It was a good question.

Drystan sighed, looking out over the water. "I got so swept up in it all—I went from barely speaking to any girls other than my sister to engaged in a few short weeks. I didn't notice how she felt. Or if I did, I wrote it off as nerves. Gods know I had plenty of them myself."

"What was wrong? She didn't like you?" asked Em.

"She did, but not because of who I was. She liked me because of what I had. Because my family was rich, and she liked beautiful things. It took me a while to see the difference. It was ultimately when I saw a pair of servants together—they were really, truly in love—that I realized she didn't love me at all. And I didn't love her, not the person she really was. I didn't even know her."

"What did you do? I thought you said it broke your heart, but it sounds like you broke hers," asked Cordy.

"No," said Drystan. "I broke my own heart. The love was real, and it was intense. But the person I loved didn't exist. I told my mother I couldn't marry her. She was furious, but she understood in the end. My father, on the other hand…"

"My father would skewer me if I did that," said Cordy. "But what about the girl? What happened to her?"

"She was humiliated. Angry. She avoids me to this day. But she went on to marry well, and as far as I can tell from a distance, she's happy. Happier than we would have been together."

"That's sweet," said Em. "You're holding out for your true love."

"That's stupid," said Cordy. "You hurt that girl for no reason. What if she would have grown to love you?"

"I guess I'll never know," said Drystan. "But I don't regret it. And I don't believe in true love, but once I'd realized the woman I loved wasn't real, I couldn't stay with someone else. It wouldn't have been fair to her either."

Rinka had watched him closely during the entire ex-change, and she could tell there was more to the story, something he wouldn't say. Maybe it was because of the girls, or maybe it was something he didn't want to admit to her, but there was something left unsaid.

The girls asked a few more questions but were disap-pointed with his responses as they finally rounded the cliff, bringing the river into view.

"Well, I've heard better stories, but we're here," said Cordy.

"You're so mean, Cordy," said Em. She turned to Drystan and Rinka. "I liked your stories. If we swam up the river, could we come visit you someday? Our mom doesn't like for us to go too far inland, but I bet she'd let us if she could come too and meet you."

"I'm not sure how far the river is from where I'm going to be, but I'll come back one day," promised Rinka.

"Look, Cordy, there's a whale!" said Em.

Rinka leaned over the side of the boat to get a better look. In the distance, a dark shape broke the surface, send-ing a burst of water into the air.

"It's Charlie. Can you make it the rest of the way on your own? We want to go see our friend," said Cordy.

"I'm sure we can manage from here," said Drystan. They were only a few hundred feet from the river delta now. The land to either side of it was relatively flat, gently sloping up to cliffs on one side and mountains on the other.

"Thank you for your help," said Rinka. The girls were already beginning to swim away. "I'll call on you when I make it back to the sea."

The girls waved behind them, too interested in the whale to give a proper goodbye.

As they rowed towards the river, Rinka could see a few small wooden structures on the side nearer to the mountains, boarded up and long since abandoned. If pirates had been here before, there was no sign of them now.

The river was wide and slow, the current weaker and easier to traverse than the rocking ocean waves had been. As they approached the abandoned town, they saw the ruins of a bridge and a disused dirt road leading out of town uphill and into a forest.

"What do you think?" asked Rinka. "Up the river or into the woods?"

"I vote for the woods," said Drystan. "I've had enough of the water for a while."

Rinka agreed. The road must have led somewhere once. Chances were, it would still. And although she was ready to help Drystan with the boat in whatever way she could—perhaps there was some energy within her he could tap if nothing else—she didn't want to end up in the same situation as the last night, his body so weak he couldn't stay awake.

"Would you mind if I took a moment to rinse the salt from my skin and out of my clothes?" asked Rinka. They were still damp anyway, but at least the cool blue water of the river would get them a bit cleaner.

"I'll do the same," he said. He moved to the other side of the broken bridge out of view.

As she pulled the tangles from her red hair loose beneath the surface, she thought of Alison. She was due to meet her friend that very night, but she had no idea how far she was from Sudport, let alone Herot's Hollow. She hoped she'd make it somewhere in time to at least send a pigeon before Alison began to worry.

The sun was still high in the sky, the air warm and breezy as Rinka donned her yellow dress once more. She caught Drystan stealing a glance as they met on the road.

He carried something in his arms—a folded sheet.

"I found it stuck under a rock," he said. "I thought it might come in handy if we're caught out at night."

They made their way along the road and into the woods, walking for miles without meeting another traveler. The road was poorly maintained, covered in places with so many branches and so much debris that it was hard to see where it continued.

At last, just around sunset, the road left the woods into a clearing. There, it met another road, and this road had a signpost.

In the direction they'd come, *Gull Bay—8* had been scratched out.

To the left, it said *Sudport—32.*

"Well, we're not making it back to pick up our things tonight," said Rinka.

Drystan gestured to the signposts to the right.

Fossholm—7.

Herot's Hollow—12.

"Seven miles. That's doable," said Rinka. "My friend Alison will be waiting there."

But Rinka had not considered the terrain. The road up from Gull Bay had been mostly flat through the valley, but as they met the main road, it climbed into the aptly named Hill Country. Their progress was slow, slowed further by the encroaching darkness, the light of the full moon obscured by clouds that had rolled in from the sea.

Rain began to fall off and on, and yet Rinka pressed ahead.

"We have to keep going," she said. "I'm supposed to be there by now. Alison is going to worry."

"Rinka, you can barely walk," said Drystan. He'd been trying to get her to stop for over an hour now. "You're exhausted. I'm exhausted. We can barely see, and it looks like the road is never going to level out. We can make it there in the morning once we've rested. A carriage could even come by and get us there sooner. But I don't think we can make it further tonight. Let's rest for a while. Alison will worry for a night, but I'm sure she'll be relieved when she sees you tomorrow."

He was right, as much as Rinka didn't want to admit it. Her feet hurt so much—her shoes had been gone since she went overboard—she could barely move them. But they were so close. Just a few hours away…

"Fine," she said. "But only for a quick nap. Then we're back on the road."

Drystan led her from the path a few feet until he found a low-hanging branch. He draped the sheet he'd found over it, using rocks to anchor it to the ground.

"I don't suppose you could magic us a feather bed?" asked Rinka.

"I'm afraid not. Or I could, but it would be gone the moment my head hit the pillow."

Rinka understood.

The makeshift tent was small, too small for even one of them to lie down without their feet hanging out the end.

Drystan cleared the ground as best as he could with a magic burst of wind, and then he removed his shirt and placed it down to give Rinka something better than the dirt to lie on.

"Thank you," she said as she collapsed to the ground.

He lay down beside her, careful to keep a few inches of distance between them even as it forced him to lean against the sheet.

The nearness of him awoke her in spite of her exhaustion. They had touched before—his strong arms pulling her from the water, his hands holding hers as he showed her the force of his magic—but this was different. Facing him in the dark, she felt as if the energy still flowed between them, invisible and powerful. A vital pulse, something both careful and wild, that was in the tent with them and that was them, together.

"Rinka?" he whispered. There was no one around, not for miles as far as they knew, but he kept his voice low all the same. "Are you still awake?"

She nodded, not daring to speak, knowing he could feel the movement.

His hand moved at his side, fumbling in the dark for her. It reached her shoulder and then her ear and then moved to cup her cheek.

She sighed even as her body tensed.

And then he traced the line of her jaw to her chin and then up to her lower lip, his fingertips brushing the soft skin impossibly lightly.

She drew in a breath, her lips parting under his touch. Her heart raced, the pulse so loud in her own ears that she thought he must have been able to hear it too.

And then there was a laugh—bright and clear—but it didn't come from Rinka or Drystan.

It came from outside the tent.

Rinka snapped upright. "What was that? Girls? Did you follow us here?"

That wasn't possible. They were miles from the water now, and the laughter wasn't the same as the sweet giggle of the mermaids, anyway. It was musical, melodic, and it went round and round the tent in an impossibly fast circle.

Drystan's hand was in his pocket, and in a moment, Rinka's eyes caught the glimmer of a dagger as the coin changed shape once more.

He tore back the sheet. A light floated in the darkness, a glowing orb as large as a fist, a shimmering yellow and green that laughed as it flew.

"Fairy fire," he said. "A will-o'-the-wisp."

"Can it hurt us?"

"No," he said. He pocketed the coin and retrieved his shirt from the ground. "It wants to help us." His eyes were aglow in the light of the strange creature, his face awed and filled with childlike wonder.

"Come on," he said, taking her hand. "We might manage to get that feather bed for you tonight after all."

Rinka was uncertain—all of the stories she'd heard about following lights into the woods at night ended in death or disappearance—but Drystan knew things about the magic of this world beyond even her wildest imaginings.

And she trusted him, she realized. She knew he would not bring her into harm's way. Not intentionally, at least.

So she followed behind him as the light led them deeper into the woods, hoping there would be a bed wherever it led them.

Only one bed, ideally.

Chapter Twelve

SOURCES OF POWER

Alison

Genn smiled brightly at Keir, their teeth white and sharp. "Wonderful!" they said. "You're such a marvelous dancer, I had to ask."

Alison drifted back towards Mab. She wasn't insulted by Genn's rejection—Keir truly was the superior dancer. The pair of them moved beautifully together, Keir leading the fairy, who mimicked his motions perfectly.

"They're a shameless flirt," said Mab as Alison approached. She stood near the bonfire alone, the tap of her foot to the music sending ripples through the twinkling silk of her dress. "Don't mind my sibling. Keir only has eyes for you."

"How do you know who we are?" Alison asked. "How did you know we'd come?"

"There are many eyes and ears in the forest and the fields. We've known of you for a while—of him for even longer. We kept close watch on the situation with the vine, preparing to move the city if we had to."

"Are we not in a different place? The light seems different here." Alison wasn't sure how the vine could have threatened this world, as different as it seemed from her own.

Mab's eyes widened. They were the same deep blue as her hair, but they seemed to have a light of their own that flashed as she spoke. "Yes, this place is different, but it is connected to your world in a thousand different ways. You took one path, but there are many others."

"And you were afraid the vine would take one of those paths," said Alison.

"Not exactly. The vine's magic was just a twisted bit of Keir's mind. Easy enough to dispel, at least for us. What we feared was him. What he could have become, what it could have done to your world and ours. We were very glad when you came, Alison Lennox."

She gestured to a pair of chairs from the banquet table, and they flew over. Alison took the smaller chair—although this place made the smaller races roughly Fulling height, it had done nothing to address her limited stature.

Even fairies were taller than her here.

"I have the answers you're seeking," said Mab. "About your magic and his, about how it came to be and what you must do to control it. Do you want to wait for him? Or would you prefer me to tell you alone?"

Alison knew this was a sensitive area for Keir, that much of his pain and trauma was tied to the old magic and that it caused him a great deal of distress. She certainly wanted him to hear whatever the fairies had to say, but she also didn't think it would hurt to have her as a buffer, allowing her to share the information in a way he could process while causing him the least harm.

"I want you to tell me," Alison said. "But what of the cost? We were warned your help would come with a price."

"It does," Mab admitted, "but the price is something you're already planning to pay. We know the king is coming, and we know what they're planning to do to this land. It's the greatest threat we've ever faced. We know that many of our kind—your neighbor Aras and his fine children, for example—prefer to live among the peoples. They prefer to live without our gifts, and we don't blame them for wanting all of the innovations that make life bearable without magic. But we hope there's a way to preserve this land, as much of it as can be spared. That's all we ask of you. Use the knowledge we give you to protect our home. I believe that's what you're already planning?"

"It is," said Alison.

"Good," said Mab. "Although I dare say, the entertainment your lover is providing is possibly payment enough."

Alison looked back to the bonfire, and several fairies and a dwarf were all taking turns dancing with Keir.

"Oh, dear," said Alison. "I hope he doesn't need rescuing."

Mab laughed, and the laughter was bell-like, clear and bright. "I'm sure he'll manage for a bit longer. Now, let's begin with that magic of yours. What do you want to know first?"

"Where did it come from?" asked Alison. "Did he cause it, as he suspects?"

"Yes and no," said the fairy. Alison suspected many of her answers would be like this. If there was one thing she'd learned of magic, it was that it did not like to fit into neat little boxes or within clearly defined lines. "Magic belongs to all peoples of the world, and to some of the creatures too. But it comes to some more naturally than others, whether through birth or experience.

"Imagine that all people are born with a reservoir of magic like water and a well with which to reach it. Some reservoirs are larger than others, and some wells are deeper than others. As the peoples of the world have turned from magic, most have found their wells too shallow to reach the reservoir within. But with time, exposure, and practice, one can dig a deeper well. This is what happened to you. Your experiences with magic have led you to break into your own reservoir, but the magic within was always yours."

"Then Keir still has magic, too?"

Alison knew the old magic had worked through Keir, but Keir believed it had abandoned him after the incident with the vine.

"Yes, although in his case, he sought to fill in his well. But magic, like water, has its way of working through the cracks."

"If he can use magic, why didn't it work for him? Why did the vine happen?"

"Magic, as you may have noticed, has a will of its own. There are many theories as to where that will comes from. Some say the Gods above or the Devils below, others say the elements of the world or nature itself, and still others say from the hearts of the people and creatures who live in it. The fairies of this wood believe it is all of those, and that they, like magic itself, are one and the same, although they may appear quite differently at times. But one thing is certain: the will must not be denied. Keir sought to twist something into being that could not be. He, like many before him, tried to conquer the magic and control it to do his bidding, and it transformed into the vine."

It was similar to what the spriggan had told Alison when she had first learned Keir was responsible for the vine. "So is Keir right? Am I doing magic without realizing it, and if so, how do I learn to control it? After I spoke with the spriggan, I tried to do magic again, but it didn't work."

"May I see your hand?" Mab asked.

Alison gave it to her without hesitation.

Mab examined the lines on Alison's palm without comment. Then she laced her long fingers with Alison's, and Alison could feel a bit of a pulse travel between their palms.

"Oh," said Mab. "That's interesting. Let me go get Keir."

Mab left, breaking in on Keir's dance with the dwarf as Alison contemplated what she had learned. It didn't seem that far-fetched, although it was difficult to imagine that all people had magic, though perhaps there had never been a time in which all people were willing to use it. There seemed to be so many reasons to turn from magic—the difficulty of knowing how to follow its will, the unpredictability of the results, and the scale of the negative consequences, among others.

Was it really worth it then? Was it worth the cost, if one could even determine what the cost was in advance?

Alison had to admit that there was something alluring about it in spite of everything. The mystery and the power of it, the communion with some kind of eternal force, even if she was unsure what that force was.

Mab returned with Keir, his face flushed red from the exertion and his spirits higher than Alison had seen in a long while.

"Did you see any of that? That dwarf I danced with last had spent time with Lady Sibba's people on the Rock. If we go there, we'll need to do some stretching first. I've never seen people move that way."

"I did see that. I told you that you were a great dancer," said Alison, caught up in her thoughts and not quite matching his excitement.

"I'm sorry that I left you," said Keir. "Mab tells me she's teaching you about magic?"

He looked at Mab, who took one of each of their hands and placed them together.

Alison felt a pulse again, but it was far stronger than when Mab held her hand.

"Yes, I thought so," said Mab. "Alison, did you ever notice any sort of magic going on when Keir wasn't around? Even in hindsight, once you knew to look for it?"

Alison thought about the things Keir had pointed out and realized he had been present for all of them. "No," she said. "I don't think so."

"It's the bond between you," said Mab. "It's the source you've been drawing from. As Keir fills his well, some of the water escapes, and that's what you've been drawing from Alison, at least in part."

"I'm sorry, a well? What are you saying?" asked Keir.

Alison caught him up, watching his reaction closely as she explained that he still had magic too. He didn't seem surprised.

"I could feel it sometimes. Not as powerful as when we were within the dream world, but I could feel the echo of it," said Keir. "I tried to ignore it, but I guess it doesn't work that way."

"You could continue to fight it, and after a time, it would stop troubling you," said Mab gently. "But if you wanted to learn to wield it, you could do so. Together. You draw strength from each other. You can use that to dig your wells deeper, to combine and share the water within. In time, it could be as though there was only a single reservoir. That's how it is for Genn and me."

"So the bond doesn't have to be between lovers?" asked Alison.

Keir's eyes darted from Mab to Alison. There was that "love" word again, sneaking its way into conversation just as it snuck into Alison's mind over and over.

"Not at all," said Mab. "There are as many sources of power as there are people. For many, it could be a lover. But the bond could just as easily exist between family or friends. Sometimes, even passing acquaintances can experience it. And for some, the source is something else entirely—a connection to nature, a pet or familiar, even art or music."

"Can it change?" asked Keir. "If Alison wanted to pursue but I—" He squeezed Alison's hand. "If I couldn't."

"It can," said Mab. "It might take some time for you, Alison, to find another way to dig your well, but you could do so if you wanted to."

Alison looked at Keir. Both of them wielding magic together—it could be something incredible. Maybe it could be enough to save Herot's Hollow.

But she couldn't ask it of him, not if he wasn't ready for it.

"We'll find another way," said Alison. "If you don't want to…"

"No, I didn't mean that. I just need some time to think," said Keir.

"I'm sorry to interrupt," said Mab, "but I think our final guests are arriving."

There was movement in the trees beyond the bonfire. Two figures approached—a tall man Alison mistook for Weyland at first based on his size alone, but as he stepped into the light, she saw his dark hair and tan skin and realized she didn't know him after all.

Behind him was a woman. An orc with red hair.

It couldn't be. Could it?

"Rinka?"

Chapter Thirteen

REUNIONS

Rinka

The path the will-o'-the-wisp followed through the woods wound up and down, left and right, twisting and turning dozens of times. Rinka sighed with relief once they finally made it into a clearing—her bed awaited.

Or so she thought. In the clearing, there was a roaring bonfire, a dozen or more figures dancing to a lively tune played by a band of…fairies? Except they were large, Fulling-sized, and was that a Fulling-sized hobgoblin too?

Rinka turned to Drystan, whose attention was being sought by one of the very large fairies. The fairy appeared normal, so could they have shrunk? Rinka was looking around, trying to get her bearings, when from across the clearing, she heard her name in a familiar voice.

"Rinka?"

There she was. The very person Rinka had been traveling to meet. Her former and future roommate, Alison.

Alison rushed towards her, arms outstretched. Rinka ran to meet her, her exhaustion temporarily forgotten in the joy of reuniting with a dear friend.

"My Gods, Rinka, are you alright?" asked Alison as she pulled away. "You look…"

"Terrible?" offered Rinka.

"No, no, I wasn't going to say—"

"But you were thinking it," said Rinka. She laughed, and Alison did too.

Alison looked well—her dark hair was longer than when she'd left Arcas Dyrne, and she had maybe put on a little weight, making her appear stronger and healthier than when she'd left. Her blue eyes were as bright as ever, although they were now full of concern. "What happened? Where is the carriage? How did you get here? What time is it? Did you miss us in town? How long have we been gone?"

"We didn't quite make it to the carriage," said Rinka. She shivered in the cool night air. Alison looked at her wrinkled dress and bare arms and removed her overcoat, a well-made tweed number that was too tight for Rinka but felt nice draped over her shoulders, and she led Rinka closer to the bonfire.

"We?" asked a man who had followed them. He wore a riding outfit that nearly matched Alison's with the colors reversed, and Rinka recognized his handsome face from the sketch Alison had sent her.

"You must be Mr. Ainsley," said Rinka, offering her hand to shake.

"Keir," he said. And then he spoke over her shoulder to someone coming up behind her: "Ah, here comes trouble."

Rinka turned to see Drystan approaching. She looked between the men and there was no doubt about it—they knew each other.

"Ainsley. I was wondering how long it would be before I ran into you."

"Come here, you old knocker-waffle," said Keir. He held out a hand to shake, which Drystan took and pulled him into a hug which was half hug, half hitting each other on the back repeatedly.

"Knocker-waffle?" asked Alison.

"A story for another time," said Keir. "Alison Lennox, allow me to introduce you to His Royal Highness Prince Idris of the Kingdoms of Loegria and Wilderise, Duke of Whatsits and Earl of Wherefores, Lord over all of us peons, and heir to the throne."

"Oh," said Alison, hearing the joke in Keir's words but reading something in his face that Rinka did not understand, "you're serious."

She curtsied to Drystan.

Rinka laughed.

Keir looked from Rinka to Drystan, seeing something in either their relation or attire. "Oh no," he said. "Don't tell me you've been Drystan Droswyn again." Keir's eyes were sympathetic when they returned to Rinka. "I don't blame you for not realizing. Who would look at this wanker and think *prince*, after all?" He slapped Drystan's arm playfully.

Drystan turned to Rinka, his expression sheepish. "Well, I guess the game is up. I'm sorry I didn't get to hear your third question—"

"Wait," said Rinka. "You're joking. All of you are joking with me, right?"

"Friends, a toast to our royal guest!" The fairy who had greeted Drystan clapped their hands together, and several other fairies brought around trays filled with glasses of various sizes and shapes holding a variety of liquids.

Their royal guest.

"I can explain," said Drystan—Idris? *Prince* Idris—softly. He took a pair of glasses from a tray and offered one to Rinka.

Rinka stood still. She was so tired. Could this be a dream? Maybe she'd fallen asleep during their walk.

"Rinka?"

Did Loegria have a prince? Yes, she seemed to remember it did, but… "Didn't you abdicate the throne or something?"

"Not yet," he said. He took her hand—she was still too dazed to respond—and pressed the glass into it, seeing their host waiting.

"To the prince! *Slàinte!*"

"*Slàinte!*" the crowd responded. Rinka took the glass to her lips reflexively and took a sip. It was strong, dark whisky, and it felt like fire in her throat.

She looked it at the drink and then at Drystan—no, Idris.

And then she downed the entire glass.

"Easy," said Idris. "They make it strong in this part of the world—"

"It puts hair on your chest!" said Keir. He was laughing, his arm around Alison, who was looking at him as if he was the greatest thing in the entire world.

"*I told you,*" came a familiar voice in her head. "*I told you that you were a fool, girl. A prince! A common orc and a prince. Isn't that a laugh?*"

"No," said Rinka out loud. "It's not funny."

"Rinka? Who are you talking to?" asked Alison. Then she pulled another fairy to the side. "Can we get something to eat for my friend? And perhaps a place for her to lie down?"

The fairy flitted away, careful to keep its wings close in the crowd.

"*You like him. Don't try to deny it, girl; I know how your foolish heart beats. Now what are you going to do?*"

The fairy returned in mere moments with an incredible-looking plate of food. Rinka took it and allowed the fairy to lead her to a small table off to the side.

There, Idris joined her with his own plate.

"Fairy food," said Idris. "Wonderful stuff." He dug in immediately, starting with a little cup with red and white layers of some kind of jam and cream. "Cranachan," he said. "It must be raspberry season already. Here, give it a try."

He took Rinka's spoon and dipped it into the cup. "The fairies know our tastes, but they don't know if we'll like something we haven't tried yet. You'll love it," he said. He held the spoon out for her to eat from.

A few minutes earlier, she would have let him feed her. They had gone through something together that had broken down most of the usual boundaries she felt with strangers, although Rinka wasn't prone to strong boundaries anyway, if she was being honest.

But now…this man before her wasn't the same man she'd followed into the woods. He couldn't be.

"If you're the prince, what were you doing in a third-class carriage?"

Idris put the spoon back into the cup. "Drystan Droswyn makes it easier for me to travel. I didn't want to travel with the rest of the family—in fact, they don't even know I'm coming—so it's easier if I just pretend to be someone else."

"No one recognizes you?"

"No, not usually. It's amazing how little people notice someone down on their luck. Most people, at least." He raised his eyes to meet hers, a smile tugging at his lips.

Rinka considered it. Few people had so much as looked at Idris during their voyage together.

The pieces fit together. The ticket-taker who let him stay on the train—perhaps an arrangement he'd worked out if he truly did regularly travel in disguise. The pirates who might have been there for him, and why he wouldn't let them capture him—he would have made a valuable hostage, that was for sure. He'd told her he was well known once, but not anymore. And it was true; Rinka hadn't heard anything about the prince in years. "Your family—they're coming here, too? The royal family?"

"Yes," said Idris. "My father, my sister, and the rest of the court. It's all part of some plot of his to develop Wilderise. A fool's errand, I'd say. The people here are tough as nails. He'd have an easier time negotiating with a brick wall. But yes, they're coming, and I wasn't invited per se. I've been out of courtly life for a long while, and I've been cooped up in my office at the University for even longer. But I decided I wanted to see it. Wilderise, my father's pitiful attempts at diplomacy, and most of all, my sister. We're not exactly on the best of terms, but I've missed her nonetheless."

"And you're all dragons," said Rinka. It explained the ears, at least, and the other non-human traits. The magic. "Wait—can you fly? Could you have flown to shore?"

She wasn't angry at Idris for the deception in general: after all, he'd admitted to being someone else early on, and he'd even given her an opportunity to know the truth outright. But if he could have flown them to shore and didn't, and they nearly died...

"We are all dragons, yes. My mother as well, although what I told you about her—about her leaving at the first opportunity—was true. She's from a land in the Far East, and she's a different type of dragon. My sister and I inherited our father's form. I can still take that form at will, but no. I can't fly. Not anymore."

Rinka could hear a wound in his voice, and then he held up his arm to show her another one.

"The Curse of the Air," he said. "An enemy of my father's gifted me with it on my twelfth birthday. It doesn't look like much in this form, and it doesn't stop me from doing much either. Except the one thing I loved: flying."

On his elbow, there was a series of small scars. "My father hired every healer and doctor and cleric in this land and many others. But no one could set it right. Over time, he grew to resent me. The heir of his house and his throne, and the first ruler in generations who would not be able to take to the skies. Then the situation happened with the girl I was engaged to, and he began to show an interest in my sister, Ceri; started talking about her taking the throne. I went to university—it was there that I got to know Keir, although we'd known each other for years from court events—and I decided to stay on as a professor. It was easier to stay out of the way. My father and I had it out at the Winter Feast two years ago. He explained that he expects me to abdicate the throne, and while I have no interest in being king, I do have an interest in remaining a thorn in his side as long as he lives, so I refused. I haven't seen anyone in my family since."

Rinka understood strained family relations. Her mother's voice haunted her every thought, after all. And she could understand his desire for a different life than the one he'd been born into; she felt that way often as well.

Maybe there was something of the man she'd gotten to know in him after all.

"So you're here for the summer, then?" she asked as casually as she could manage.

"Yes, and I have an idea about that," he said. Rinka suppressed a yawn, but it didn't escape his attention. "But it can wait until the morning. Come, try a bite of this cranachan. It will give you sweet dreams."

He held out the spoon again, and this time, Rinka let him feed her a bite.

It was lovely—toasted oats soaked in honey and cream layered with the sweet raspberries. At the end of the bite, she felt the slight burn of the same whisky she'd drunk earlier.

"You were right," she said. "I do love it. My father loves to sneak booze into as many recipes as possible too."

"Rinka is quite a chef herself," said Alison, coming over to join them. "Did you get enough to eat?" she asked Rinka. "Mab has gotten us some rooms ready for the night, and there's a hot bath and clean clothes waiting for you if you're done."

"That sounds wonderful," said Rinka.

"Come," said Alison, "and you can tell me how you came to be here, and how you managed to meet a prince. Good night, your highness. Keir will bring you to your room, if you can manage to tear him away from the other guests, that is."

"Good night, Idris," Rinka said, catching herself before she misspoke. There would be no sharing of a bed after all, but that was for the best. How could she dream of sharing a bed with a prince?

"Good night, Rinka," he said. "Sweet dreams."

Rinka put her the foolish desires of her heart aside and followed her friend. The promise of a hot bath and a warm bed was enough, she told herself.

She could live without the look he gave her as she walked away, the regret and hope and longing that kept his eyes on her until she'd finally slipped behind a tree and out of view.

Chapter Fourteen

MAGIC AND MAYHEM

Alison

Alison awoke to a kiss.

It was a good kiss, soft and sweet, the lips that met hers warm with a taste of honey.

There was a strange lack of facial hair, though. No hair or stubble at all. Had Keir already gotten up and shaved?

"Good morning," said Rinka as she pulled away.

Alison screamed.

"What are you doing? What's going on? Where's Keir?"

The orc in Alison's bed yawned and stretched, the white lace of her borrowed nightgown peeking out from under the sheets. Her long, red hair tumbled into her face as she propped herself up on the pillow. "Come back to bed, my love," said Rinka.

Magic. It had to be. Some kind of fairy magic, maybe in the food that they ate? Alison wasn't certain, but whatever it was, she needed to find a way to stop it.

Alison leaned out the door into a hallway. There were several rooms in this treehouse. The girls had been given two on this side of the hallway, the boys right on the other side.

"Keir?" Alison called at his door, knocking lightly. "I need some help. Something's wrong with Rinka."

The door burst open, sending Alison falling forward into the room.

"Rinka?" called Keir. "My darling, what's wrong?" He ran from the room into the hall, leaving Alison to pull herself up from the floor.

"Oh great," muttered Alison. "You too."

She gathered herself and ran back into her room.

Keir was trying to get into the bed with Rinka. "Are you hurt? Rinka, sweetheart, talk to me."

"Who the hells are you? Alison! It's not what it looks like. I don't know this man. Don't worry; I'll get rid of him."

Alison watched, horrified, as Rinka in her lacy nightgown lifted Keir by the waist and threw him over her shoulder.

He didn't fight back. "Really, Rinka? Right here in front of your friend?" he said, laughing.

"Rinka, no!" shouted Alison seconds before disaster. Rinka had made her way to the glassless window and was about to throw him through it and to his death several stories below.

"Oh, I'm sorry. Do you know him? Did you bring him here for us? A little unconventional, but I'm open to new experiences—"

"No, Rinka. Something has happened to both of you. You're not being yourselves. Put him down so we can talk."

"Good idea," said Rinka. "Let's discuss boundaries—"

"What is the meaning of this?" came a voice from the hallway.

"Prince Idris," said Alison, giving a small curtsy and pulling up her chemise. "Your highness. Rinka told me you are an expert with magic. Perhaps you can help us sort out this mess."

"Anything for you, my little chipmunk," said Idris. He draped a large arm around her.

"Chipmunk?" She sighed, removing his arm with some effort. "Not you too."

"What did you just call her?" asked Rinka.

"Alison, why are these people in your room?" asked Idris. "Would you like me to get rid of them?"

"No," said Alison, and then she turned to see him holding a sword. "Stop! Where did you get that? Put it away. They're my friends."

"Friends? Is that really what you're going to call us?" said Rinka, tears in her eyes.

"Everyone stop! Sit still and don't kill each other. I'm going to try to find the fairies."

Alison snapped the door closed behind her, hoping they could keep it together long enough for her to find someone to help.

She raced down the hallway to the ladder they had climbed to get up here. She pulled on the hatch, but it wouldn't budge.

The door creaked open behind her. "Rinka, please," came Keir's voice. "Don't do this."

Alison rushed down the hall as Rinka shoved him into it. "Your services are not needed here," she said and slammed the door behind her.

Alison watched Keir in his pajamas as he knocked on the door, and it dawned on her.

This was a test, she realized. A chance to use her magic, to learn to control it.

She approached him, placing a hand on his shoulder.

"What are you doing?" he asked.

"I have an idea to make Rinka jealous," she said. She tried to feel something between them that she could latch onto, something like what she'd felt in the vine's dream world or when they had raised the standing stones with the spriggan. Maybe in this state, he wouldn't resist it.

"I wouldn't want to make her jealous," said Keir. "I love her."

Alison tried to ignore the sting of hearing those words from him, words he hadn't said to her yet himself. But to her surprise, the pain did something else—it revealed a place within her, a spot right in her chest where she felt a surge of…something. Power, perhaps.

She hoped it was power.

"I understand," she said. "I have another idea. Come close so I can whisper it to you—they can both hear better than we can."

As Keir leaned towards Alison, she grabbed the collar of his pajama top and kissed him.

At first, he tried to pull away, but Alison concentrated on the spot of power, willing it to rise from her chest into her throat and finally to her lips.

He relaxed and then melted into the kiss.

"Alison," he said when he finally pulled away.

And then he pulled her in again, lifting her off the ground into his arms and pushing her against the door, kissing her like he'd been away from her for years, not hours.

It was hard—really hard—to pull away from him, but there were other issues to address. "We need to help the others," she said, gasping as he lightly kissed her neck. "Soon. Later. Maybe a few more minutes would be—"

There was a loud crash from within the room.

"Oh, bloody hell," she said. She pulled on his arms, which reluctantly lowered her to the ground.

"What are you going to do?" asked Keir. "I was still in my head. It was like I was watching myself say and do things, and when you kissed me, I broke free. But I'm not sure kissing them would work."

It was a good point. "No," said Alison. "I'm pretty sure it wouldn't." Alison reached for the doorknob, trying to come up with an answer, but it twisted on its own accord and then pulled back into the room.

Alison let go this time before she could fall to the floor.

"What's going on out here?" asked Rinka. Her hair was pulled into a messy bun and the strap of her nightgown was torn.

"Are you alright?" Alison asked as she looked past Rinka into the room.

She could see what had crashed to the ground: Prince Idris.

"Oh my Gods," she said, rushing to his slumped figure. "Please say you're not dead. We can't have killed the prince."

She attempted to push the magic from her chest into her fingertips, but before she could do so, Idris stirred awake and then snapped upright.

"Alison, get behind me. There's a wild woman on the loose," he said, putting himself between her and Rinka.

"I told you to stay down," said Rinka, moving to charge Idris once more.

He dodged a mean right hook aimed directly for his nose, pushing Alison down and out of the way. Alison crouched back towards Keir, who was still standing by the door.

"What do we do?" she whispered to him as they watched Rinka attempt to topple Idris once more.

"They say passion burns like fire," said Keir. "Maybe we dunk them in water?"

It was an absurd suggestion, which meant in this silly fairy land it just might work.

"The wash basin is over there." Alison gestured to a little carved stand near the bed.

Keir went for the basin, flinging its contents at the other pair as they fought.

He missed.

Thankfully, Rinka and Idris didn't even notice. Rinka was too busy trying to pull Idris's hair out, and Idris was trying to tie her wrists together with some odd sort of fabric that seemed to vanish at certain angles.

The water pooled onto the handwoven rug.

"Maybe…" said Alison. She grabbed Keir's hand.

She felt for the source of power and grabbed onto it faster this time. Then she searched Keir for something like it.

"What are you doing?" he asked.

"Trying to pick the water up again from the rug. Can you help me?'

"How?"

She kissed him.

"I don't know how that's meant to help, but I'm happy to do it—"

"Hold on to how that feels, and pull on the water with me," she said.

It felt genuinely insane but also right, somehow.

Which is to say that it felt like love itself.

The water vibrated on the floor as if the room was shaking and then began to rise into droplets.

"That's it!" said Alison. "Can you feel it?"

"I—I think so," said Keir. He looked anxious, so she kissed him again.

"Anything?" she asked as she spun to look.

The water was still rising. Their attention to it caught Rinka's and Idris's attention.

"Quick, before he stops it," said Alison. She imagined the water crashing into their faces and then flicked her wrist.

She didn't know if the gesture would help, but it felt like a good idea, and sure enough, the water splashed right onto them both.

Rinka squealed, and Alison watched as she looked around the room in confusion. "Oh Gods, what happened to us?"

"The fairies," said Alison. "I think this was their way of helping me—"

"Step forward and face me, you rogue," said Idris.

He had a sword in his hand again, and he was pointing it at Keir.

Alison screamed.

"I guess that makes sense that it worked for Rinka but not him," said Keir. "Dragons are pretty much made of fire, so I guess the water couldn't do much—"

"Are you going to fight me or just keep talking?" asked Idris. "There's a fair maiden's honor at stake."

"Fair," perhaps, but "maiden," well…

"Drystan, stop this," said Rinka. "I mean, Idris." She held up her hands in surrender.

Idris smirked. "It seems at least the orc has come to her senses. But this rogue that stands beside you, Alison, that dares to steal kisses from your lips. He must pay the price for his treachery."

"Very well," said Keir. "I accept your challenge."

"What are you doing?" asked Alison.

He held a hand up to her, then turned to address Idris. "But I haven't brought my sword."

"Do you have a silver on you?" asked Idris.

"Alison, we've got to stop this," said Rinka. She climbed over the bed to join them. "You broke me out of it with water. How can we break him out of it?"

"With a cut," said Keir.

"No!" cried Rinka.

Alison was surprised by the strength of Rinka's response. Was there something between them?

"Not to him, to the bond between him and Alison. I can feel it. Can you?" Keir asked them both.

"I don't know what you're talking about," said Rinka.

"I don't either," said Alison. She searched around with the newfound sense that she'd used to locate her own power within her. She couldn't see anything, but she did feel something there: an invisible string tying her to Idris.

"Wait, he's right," said Alison. "There is something there."

"That's the bond of fate, my little hedgehog. You can't fight it," said Idris.

"Give him a silver," said Rinka.

Keir had nothing in his pockets, but Alison found her coin purse on the stand where the water basin had been.

"Here," she said to Idris.

"Come here and give it to me, sweet starfish," he said. "And then get out of the way. I will defend your honor for you."

"Starfish? My honor?" asked Alison, unable to stop herself from snorting with laughter. "I'm very sorry to disappoint you but—"

"It matters not," said Idris. "What matters is this fool that thinks he can claim you."

"I mean, 'claim' is a bit much, don't you think?" asked Keir.

There was a man—a future king—in this room holding a sword, but it was difficult to take him seriously.

At least it was until Alison handed him the coin.

They watched as he turned it over in his hand and stretched it upright, turning it from an ordinary silver into an extraordinary weapon.

"My Gods," said Alison. Was her own magic capable of such a thing, or was this some kind of dragon magic unique to the prince and his family?

"Still playing at the old parlor tricks, are we, 'Dris?" asked Keir. He crossed the room and took the sword from Idris.

"And now," said Idris. "We dance."

It *was* like a dance, Alison realized as she watched them. Keir moved with the same grace, the same elegance in a sword fight that he did while dancing by the bonfire.

But he was outmatched—either because Idris was simply the better fighter or because he was trying to kill Keir and Keir was trying only to disarm Idris. It made for a deadly imbalance, and Alison began to truly fear for their lives for the first time during this ordeal.

"Watch out!" she shouted as Idris feinted to the left and struck a blow to Keir's side that slashed open his pajama bottoms, leaving a scraping wound on his leg.

"It's just a scratch," said Keir, breathless. "Stay back."

Rinka and Alison moved to the doorway as Idris jumped onto the bed, swiping at Keir's ear but losing his balance temporarily on the soft mattress.

Rinka saw her chance and lunged for Idris's ankles, sending him careening face down onto the bed.

"Keir!" yelled Alison, holding out her hand. He ran around the bed and took it with his left, and she sent a surge of power through them.

Rinka leapt backwards to the wall as Keir raised the sword.

"Now!" Alison shouted, and Keir brought the sword down into the empty air between where Alison stood and where Idris was pulling himself upright on the bed.

Alison felt a slice through something; a clean, cauterizing wound that caused her no pain. It felt as though her hair had been cut, and she found herself touching the dark end of her plait to make sure it was still intact.

Idris turned over in the bed, propping himself up against the wall. His chest heaved from the exertion. He was remarkably handsome, Alison realized, shooting an approving look at Rinka for her good taste and good fortune as her friend went over to check on him.

Alison stumbled towards the bed and took a seat down on the corner, suddenly feeling as though she had been running and jumping around the room herself.

"It takes it out of you, doesn't it?" asked Idris.

Alison felt as though she might fall asleep again despite only having woken an hour or so earlier. "This is what magic does?"

Keir took a seat beside her. "Are you alright?" he asked. "I feel a bit dizzy myself."

"Well, I feel fine, but what in the world just happened to us?" asked Rinka as she reached for a towel to dry her face and hair.

"The fairies," said Idris. "One of their games, no doubt. They always are good for a bit of fun."

"Fun?" asked Rinka. "You call that fun?"

"I think you're right," said Alison. "I asked them for help understanding how to use my magic, and I think this was their lesson."

"A harsh lesson," said Rinka. "We could have killed each other!"

"I'm not sure we could have," said Idris. "I felt restricted while under the spell. I couldn't change form. I suspect there were invisible railings to prevent us going too far."

If that was what Idris was capable of while restricted, Alison feared what he could do unbridled.

"How is your wound?" Idris asked Keir, who had fetched the washbasin from his room to clean it.

"It's nothing," he said. "A pity I never got the hang of the healing spells I researched, but perhaps I was missing an important element." He looked at Alison.

"It's a good thing you knew what to do," said Alison. "All I could remember from the fairy stories I've read was true love's kiss."

Alison heard her words the moment after they left her mouth. Keir blinked, his lips parting as if to respond, but then closing again.

Alison's thoughts began to spiral, but then she felt a pulse in the spot of her chest where her power came from. It was warm and tight, almost like an embrace. She looked at Keir and his eyes were soft, his smile stretching to wrinkle their corners.

"I read a lot about the old magic when…" He paused for a moment, a shadow falling over him, but he regained his composure. "A while ago," he continued. "It's often metaphorical, sometimes clever, sometimes built on a bargain. I doubt my ideas were the only answers, but at least they seemed to have worked."

"Well, I'm grateful," said Rinka. "Should we get going soon? I'm not sure how we're meant to get back to the road. We followed a fairy light to get here."

"Hold on, let me see if the way down is open again," said Alison. She left the room and went into the hall, already knowing the answer before she arrived at the hatch, which was indeed unlocked once more. "Fairies," she muttered under her breath.

Idris had risen from the bed by the time she returned to the room. "Rinka, may I speak with you before we depart?" he asked. Rinka nodded, and they left the room together.

Alone with Keir once more, she felt the warm pulse as he crossed the room to her. "'True love's kiss,' eh?"

He took her hands as she held her breath.

"Alison, these past months have been some of the hardest of my life."

It wasn't what she'd expected him to say at all, and she felt the same sting she'd felt minutes earlier when he'd said he loved Rinka.

"Wait," he said, seeing her response. He released one hand to lift her chin. "Let me finish."

Alison nodded, the pounding of her heartbeat filling her ears as she looked at him.

"When we left the vine's world, I felt triumphant. Like we'd finally fixed some broken part of me for good, like all the bad days were in the past. But unfortunately, that isn't what happened. And at first, I was terrified to let you see it. I didn't want to hurt you and disappoint you after what you risked helping me. I didn't want you to see the pain I still felt, to know the dread and guilt and shame I battled as I tried to make amends with the town, to come back from my isolation and to take responsibility for the harm I caused. And as much as I wanted to be a good partner to you, I worried that I just wasn't able to. Not while a part of me still felt so damaged. Not as I realized that a part of me might always be damaged, might never be whole again. How could I be with you? How could I give you the life and the love you deserve when I am not a whole, healthy person? How could what I have to give possibly be enough?"

Alison wanted to respond, wanted to tell him that he was enough, that even without having experienced the same pain, she felt the same fears, the same doubts that she was worthy of his love. It was what, she realized, had kept her from speaking. Kept her from telling him the truth of how she felt.

But instead, she let him finish.

"But as much as I tried to hide it from you, I know you saw it. And the way you responded—your infinite patience, your empathy, your kindness—it made me fall deeper and deeper. And as much as I wanted to be better, I woke up one day and realized that even if I never quite became the man I was before again, the man I felt you deserved, you would stay by my side anyway. And that you were happy there, and safe. And it made me feel safe to be exactly who I was, too. And maybe that's enough. It's not perfect, but it's ours, and it's enough."

He pulled her closer, resting her hands on his waist as he held her head and looked deep into her eyes.

"I'm in love with you, Alison," he said. "I will love you until the end of my days, and I am yours for as long as you'll have me. I will never stop wishing I could be more for you, and I will always worry I'm not doing enough. But whatever comes our way, I want to face it together. If that's what you want as well."

Alison could hear the question in his final words, could feel the doubt that she knew would never fully leave him.

It didn't matter.

"I love you, Keir," she said. "Exactly as you are. You are more than enough."

She held her hand to his heart.

"You are everything."

He took her in his arms then, and they picked up from where they left off earlier in the hallway, keeping as quiet as possible to avoid embarrassing their friends.

Chapter Fifteen

THE SECOND GAME

Rinka

Rinka's eyebrows lifted as she heard rhythmic sounds coming from across the hall.

"I'm glad to see him so well," said Idris. He had settled on the bed with his back against the wall, just as he had been in Alison's room. "He was always a dour sort. Too serious by a mile. I think they just make them that way up here."

He gestured for her to sit beside him, but she didn't trust herself with him on the single bed, so she took a seat in a chair that looked to be held together by living vines.

"I thought you were a bit of a dour sort when we met," said Rinka.

"Did you really?" asked Idris, leaning forward. "I thought I came across as dark, handsome, and mysterious." He played with the loose laces of his shirt, drawing attention to his muscled chest.

He was entirely too sure of himself.

"Perhaps one out of three," said Rinka.

"Handsome?"

"Mysterious," said Rinka, tossing an embroidered throw pillow at him.

He laughed. "I suppose I can't argue with that. I was disappointed to have our game come to such an abrupt conclusion, and before I was able to hear your third question. I don't suppose you'd tell me what it was."

In truth, Rinka still hadn't settled on her third question, and there was no chance it would have led her to his royal status anyway. "I think I'd rather save my third question for another time," she said. She could think of nothing to ask right now, but she could see no reason to sacrifice a question with a guaranteed honest answer.

"I see," said Idris. "A good move, but I would have expected nothing less. I have another bargain to propose, if you'd be willing to listen."

Rinka's mother's voice sounded off a warning in her head once more. *"Run, stupid girl. What are you doing getting tangled up with royalty? You don't belong here. He doesn't care about you. You're just a game to him."*

"Go on," said Rinka.

"When we get into town, I'll have no choice but to admit who I am. And once I do so, they'll make sure I have good accommodations, likely in Weldan House—that's Keir's family estate. And I'll have to go along with all the usual court nonsense: the parties, the luncheons, the balls.

Dreadful waste of time, but I thought you might like to see it all. You spoke of your love for the picture shows, and I thought you might enjoy seeing all the glitz and glamor of court firsthand."

"I would," said Rinka. It was true—she'd never truly allowed herself to dream of a posh life like Alison did, but was there any little girl that hadn't dreamt of going to a ball with a prince?

"The court is rather old-fashioned. Since neither you nor Alison are nobility, you'll be denied access to all but the public events. Ms. Lennox might get some invitations since she's courting Keir, but her beau is generally allergic to a good time and probably won't want to go anyway. I, on the other hand, have no choice, and if I must go, I'd rather it be with you."

Rinka tried her best to ignore the rapid acceleration of her heartbeat. "How am I meant to attend?" she asked.

"If we were courting—or if we were to say we were courting—if we were to *pretend* to court, you might get invitations as well. And if you were to pretend to be a noble of some kind, you might be allowed anywhere. Perhaps you could even stay in Weldan House too."

"I told you. You thought he was asking you to court him, didn't you? You hoped. I told you, but your fool heart didn't listen."

Rinka put her hands over her ears to block out her mother's voice. It was a pointless exercise; the woman's voice was not truly in the room with her. It was in her mind, and it wasn't going anywhere.

"Are you alright?" asked Idris.

"Sorry," she said. "Water in my ears from earlier. I think I must have misheard you. Did you say 'pretend to court'? 'Pretend to be a noble'?"

"I did. It wouldn't be so bad to pretend to court me, would it? You'd get the attention—and the pity—of the entire court. People would be lining up to rescue you from me."

That part made a lot of sense, Rinka had to admit. As much as she enjoyed his company, she would never be able to marry a prince. But Alison was a commoner, and she had landed a future duke. There would be many nobles to meet, and some of them had to be low enough status to consider her.

"What about…this?" She gestured broadly at herself.

"The sea-bleached dress? I'm certain we can get you some nice clothes made once we arrive, especially once we share our tale of how the pirates took all of our things," said Idris.

"No, not that. Me. I'm an orc."

"I had noticed that, yes," he said. "I'll admit the court is a bit behind the times on notions of race, but they have been trying to reform that image. One of my sister's ladies-in-waiting is an orc, the young widow of an elvish earl. The Ainsley family are human, and they've held a duchy for generations due to their service in the Great Wars."

"The Great Wars are what I'm talking about. Times may be changing, but not everyone has such progressive views on things. It took me ages to find a position after I lost my job as an office cleaner. I hated butchery, but when people look at me, they see violence, chaos, bloodshed. They don't see beauty, grace, elegance, any of the things I think of when I think nobility."

"If someone looks at you and fails to see beauty, then they're blind," said Idris quite sincerely.

Rinka blushed, speechless.

"And truly, those things are not inherent to the nobility. Just wait until you meet the Duke of Penmond. But I understand your meaning," Idris continued. "I can't promise that you won't face that kind of treatment, and I understand if you'd rather not deal with the entire thing. You should visit the University one day; there are wonderful things happening there that might give you some hope for the future. But if you do still wish to give it a go, I can promise you this—anyone who dares to say anything to you that you don't like in my presence will live to regret it."

Rinka was worried less about what they might say to her—she had heard it all before—and more about what they might do if they found her out. "Don't most nobles travel with servants? Won't they think it odd if I show up alone?"

Idris couldn't help but smile that she was still entertaining the idea. "I travel alone. Perhaps they'll think it's just a quirk we share. Or you could invent some story—say your lady's maid caught a fever during the journey, and you sent her home to recover."

Rinka could think of a dozen other objections, but the truth was, she was curious. "Alright," she said simply.

"You'll do it? You'll join me for the summer?" His face— his dark and handsome face, she had to admit, although he was no longer as mysterious—was so hopeful, so joyous at the prospect, she couldn't help but getting excited herself.

"I'll join you for as long as we can keep up the charade. Can you protect me if something goes wrong?"

"It won't, but of course I'll protect you. Just keep clear of my sister. She schemes even worse than my father."

"Even worse than you?"

"My games are child's play compared to hers, believe me," said Idris. He slapped his thighs and stood once more. "Come, let's give Keir and Alison the news."

"We'll tell them the truth," said Rinka. "I can't possibly keep something like this from Alison."

"Of course," said Idris. "But once we're in town, we'll have to play the part. I hope you can handle it, Lady Rinka." He held out his arm.

She looped her arm through his, holding the elbow upright as she had seen in the picture show. "I'll do my best, your highness. It's like my father always said. 'Fool them once, shame on you. Fool them twice, and they're the fool.'"

"I don't—you know what. That one actually works," said Idris through his laughter.

"Though I wouldn't mind a lesson or two on our journey. Just in case."

"With pleasure," he said, and he led the great Lady Rinka from the room.

Chapter Sixteen

HAVE YOU SEEN THESE HUMANS?

Alison

Alison led the group from the treehouse back to the clearing. The bonfire was reduced to embers, and the great banquet table was mostly empty even though the sun had nearly made it overhead.

They bid goodbye to the fairies, thanking them for their "lessons" and their lodgings. Then they made their way back across the heath, through the cave, down the path, and onto the road to Fossholm.

By the time they reached the town, it was midday. With growling stomachs, they approached the inn for a bite to eat before continuing on to Weldan House, where Idris and Rinka were hoping to retain accommodations, Keir was hoping (and dreading) to have the opportunity to speak with his father, and Alison was hoping to meet with the korrigans and enlist their help.

The town had been amazingly spruced up in just the single day they had been gone. The thatching on the roofs had been repaired, the signs had been repainted, red buntings had been hung across the lane to honor the king's royal colors, window boxes had been planted with cheery summer flowers, and the cobblestones had been swept and washed until they gleamed under the sun like pebbles in a stream.

A familiar dwarf with grey hair was barreling down the street towards them, fliers in hand.

"Hello, Gwenla!" said Alison, waving to her. "What do you have there? Can we help?"

Gwenla shrieked and broke into a run, sending the fliers tumbling into the air in her wake.

"My Gods! Alison, you're alive! And Keir. You're alive. You're alive!"

She hugged them both fiercely. As she let go of Alison, Alison reached to the ground and retrieved one of the fliers she had been carrying.

MISSING:
Have you seen these humans?
Alison Lennox & Keir Ainsley
Please send a pigeon to Gwenla, Number Three Orchard Lane, Herot's Hollow, with any information.

Below their names was the portrait Weyland had made of the pair of them a few months earlier. The fliers had been printed recently—they were still warm from the press.

"Gwenla, what is this?" she asked.

And then she realized.

"How long have we been gone?"

"Eight days!" said Gwenla. "At first, I thought you might be held up in Fossholm, or that you'd gone to visit Lord Ainsley at Weldan House. But then we heard the news of the pirate attack on the ferry, and I worried you'd gone after your friend—hello, you must be Rinka." Gwenla had noticed Rinka and Idris for the first time. She pulled Rinka into a hug. "Weyland told me not to worry. He said you knew how to take care of yourselves and that you were probably just delayed dealing with the constables in Sudport. But when a week had passed and we still hadn't heard anything, he agreed to help me with the fliers. Oh, he'll be so happy to hear that you're safe!"

"I'm so sorry to have worried you both. We've only been gone a day from our perspective."

Alison recapped their recent adventures, and Gwenla nodded along, but the part she was most curious about was not the part Alison expected. "Idris? Why, you're not the wee *Prince* Idris, are you?"

"I'm not exactly 'wee' anymore, but yes. I am he."

Gwenla bowed. "Apologies, your highness. I thought the royal entourage wasn't arriving until tomorrow."

"I suppose they might be," said Idris. "I wouldn't know. I traveled on my own."

"On your own? Well, aren't you brave? I've seen you once before, when you were just a wee lad. My love Lady Willana, Gods rest her soul, she'd lived in the city, and we went to visit some of her friends there. And they were having an event at the castle for your fifth birthday, a great big festival on the castle grounds. And oh, you were just such a precious little thing. Your little red cheeks and your cute little dimples—oh! And your dragon form—so tiny and red. And when you took to the sky, Lady Willana was so worried for you. But you flew so well! You landed right on top of the highest tower, and you didn't want to come down. Gods, that must have been twenty-five years ago."

"A bit more, actually," said Idris. He smiled politely, but Alison, who had been reminded of the curse on him by Rinka, could see the strain.

"Come on into the inn," said Gwenla. "Sit down. I'm sure Ms. Morrison—she's the innkeep here—will be pleased as punch to know you're here. I'll get the drinks, and then you lot need to fill me in on this scheme of yours."

Alison caught Gwenla up on the plan to pass Rinka off as a noble, which Gwenla thought was wise on account of the reputations of Keir and Idris. "Not that you aren't both quite charming gentlemen, but you tend to be on the fringes a bit, don't you? We need someone who will really get in the mix if we're going to convince these folks to save our town—and Rinka, you seem like just the type," said Gwenla, and Alison agreed. Rinka had a natural friendliness and ease to her that few were blessed with. It had come as no surprise to Alison to learn that Rinka had made a friend during her voyage, and Alison would not be surprised if Rinka made it to the end of the summer with a dozen new friends, regardless of whether or not they were successful in their town-saving efforts.

Gwenla filled them in as well on the upcoming events. "The royal arrival is tomorrow; we'll all be here to see them fly in, of course. Then the Midsummer Festival is the next day, and that's where they'll be having the dam demonstration. It would be good if something were to go wrong during the demonstration, but of course we'll need to be careful so that no one gets hurt. If you don't mind, I'd love it if you'd ask the korrigans if they have any ideas."

"I can do that," said Alison. "I'm sure they won't be pleased to see their streams dammed up. And if they can't or won't help, there's always magic."

"Not my magic, I'm afraid," said Idris. "My father knows what that looks like. He'll probably suspect just about any kind of magical interference was me."

Alison guessed that Idris had probably ruined more than one occasion that way before from the way he spoke of it.

"You'll need a good alibi then," said Rinka.

"And miss all of the fun?" said Idris.

Gwenla smiled at him. "I'm sure we can find something important for you to do. It's so good of you to want to help us."

Alison suspected Idris's help was born less from altruism and more from a desire to make Rinka happy, but she kept her suspicions to herself.

They said their goodbyes to Gwenla, who promised to bring the good news of their reappearance to Weyland since they wouldn't be back in Herot's Hollow until the evening. Then they set out on the path to Weldan House.

Alison peeked back to watch Idris and Rinka joking and chatting as Keir led them through Fossholm. In truth, she'd been surprised to hear of their idea of pretending to court. She had suspected the feeling between them was genuine, at least on Rinka's side of things, and she worried that her friend was in danger of having her heart broken.

But Rinka seemed in high spirits, and Alison wasn't one to interfere without good cause. Still, she resolved to keep an eye on the situation and to be prepared with a hot cup of tea and a clean handkerchief should things change.

They reached the bridge near the falls, and Alison again felt the pull of the path near the water. "I think I'll turn off here," she said. "I'll follow the path up from the falls to see if there are any signs of activity."

"Are you sure you don't want to stay on the side of the river closer to Weldan? It's easier going on the west bank," said Keir.

"All the more reason to avoid it," said Alison. "The korrigans are seldom seen, probably because they stick to places that are more difficult to tread."

Keir looked from Alison to Idris. Idris seemed to understand his hesitation. "Go with her," said Idris. "I know how to handle showing up at a manor house unannounced. I'll do my best not to give your father's butler a heart attack."

"Mr. McKnight has little patience for nonsense," warned Keir. "Although he's far too respectable to let someone like you know it. I'll meet you up there soon."

"Good luck, Rinka," said Alison as they departed. "If the ruse doesn't work out, you can always stay with me for the summer." She gave her friend a meaningful look with a glance at Idris to say, *if it doesn't work out for any reason.*

Rinka nodded that she understood.

Alison led Keir across the bridge as Rinka and Idris continued down the tree-lined path to Weldan House. The water at the bottom of the falls was so lovely and blue on that cloudless day that it was almost possible to forget the tragedy that had taken place there.

Almost, but not entirely. Alison shivered as she remembered the feeling of the icy cold water on her skin. She brushed the sensation aside, focusing on the warmth she felt when looking at the riverbank.

On the other side of the bridge, the road back to Herot's Hollow curved up into the woods, but there was a footpath off to the left that led down to the water. Alison was grateful for her riding boots, which allowed her to take the steep descent with minimal hassle. Keir followed closely behind her, offering his hand to help her balance as she clambered over rocks to reach the smoother path she'd seen from the bridge.

There was something to this path that spoke to her in the same way the path into the fairy woods had, and that gave her pause. "I really hope this doesn't lead to more fairies," she said. "As fun as they were, I don't really want any more of their lessons at the moment."

"Do you want to turn back? You can come with me to the house. I'm sure we can find another way that doesn't involve the korrigans."

"No," said Alison. "I'd like to see Nolwynn again." And so she pressed on.

The path wasn't much like the fairy path had been. It was steep, climbing over rock and through dense woods to the higher ground above the falls. But the warm feeling was there, and Alison realized what she was feeling was magic.

At last, the path stopped climbing. It crossed two tiny streams, which they carefully navigated by crossing steppingstones, and when it turned to follow a larger brook, Alison heard a splash of something hitting the water.

Alison stopped, holding her hand up to signal Keir to do the same. "Did you hear that?" she whispered.

She saw movement on the opposite bank of the brook.

"Hello?" she called. "I'm here to see Nolwynn. Do you know her?"

There were several more splashes from just around the bend, and then large streaks of silver and gold came into view as they swam through the water and emerged on the bank next to Alison and Keir.

There were five of them, all just below waist-height, all with long hair of silver or gold and thin gowns or tight breeches in shades of silver, gold, and blue. The one in the middle wore a simple golden diadem, and Alison recognized her at once: Nolwynn, their leader and Alison's companion during her journey to Herot's Hollow in the spring.

"Greetings again, Alison. You are welcome here," she said, the others bowing slightly to their guests. "He, however, is not." Nolwynn looked up at Keir with unmistakable contempt.

Alison looked at Keir, who was as puzzled as she was. "I don't understand," said Alison.

"He isn't welcome. If you'd like to speak with me, he'll need to leave."

Alison opened her mouth to protest, but Keir stopped her with a hand on her forearm. "It's alright," he said. "I'm sure they know who my father is. We're not far from the road back into Fossholm. I'll go up to the house, and I'll meet you back at the stables in a few hours. I trust you'll help her find her way?"

"We will," said Nolwynn. She stood as tall as her diminutive stature would allow, making it clear she wouldn't say another word in his presence.

Keir gave Alison's hand a parting squeeze and returned along the path they had taken.

Nolwynn and the korrigans led Alison along the stream and over another steppingstone path to their encampment, which seemed to be constructed mostly of salvaged goods: sheets and curtains in varying colors, discarded and broken bits of furniture, and a small campfire over which a crooked spit turned a dozen or so salmon. It was a small camp, which came as no surprise to Alison considering their size, but there were several Fulling-sized tents among the group, and there seemed to be quite a few Fullings moving about as well, although they had the same dress and hair as the korrigans themselves.

"You could keep better company, my dear," said Nolwynn as she led Alison to a large tent near the campfire.

"What do you mean?" asked Alison. "Why isn't Keir welcome here?"

Alison wondered what grave offense Keir could possibly have committed against the korrigans. The town had resented his absence, but Alison had never met anyone that had a real quarrel with him. He could be standoffish and a bit rude when cornered, but she'd never seen anyone send him away on their first encounter.

"There's little good to say about any of them up at that house, but he is the worst of the lot," said Nolwynn.

Alison followed Nolwynn's gaze to a group gathered near the stream. They were mostly korrigans, but there were two Fullings with them. One appeared to be an older elf, although his silver hair might have had something to do with the korrigans' influence rather than age. The other was human, her hair a very pale gold that matched a long gown that clung to her thin figure.

But her eyes. They were dark and wide as they caught Alison's before quickly turning away.

Alison had seen them before. They were Keir's eyes. His father's eyes.

"Who is that?" she asked Nolwynn.

"Don't mind her," said Nolwynn, but Alison was already walking around the campfire towards the young woman.

Alison's mind reeled. Keir had never mentioned a sister, but who else could she possibly be? She looked a bit younger than Alison and taller, not as tall as Keir or his father, but not far from it either.

"Leave me alone," said the young woman as Alison approached. "I don't wish to speak with you."

"Who are you? Are you Keir's sister?"

The young woman winced at the name as if Alison had slapped her across the face. "Stay away from him too. You don't know him."

"Alison, you don't need to do this. I know this isn't why you've come," said Nolwynn, fluttering upwards on iridescent wings to come between them.

"I appreciate your concern, Nolwynn, but I need to know. Keir and I are together. If there's something I need to know about him, I need one of you to tell me."

She looked up at the korrigan, defiant. She did not doubt Keir, but there was clearly something about him she didn't know, and she intended to find out what it was.

Nolwynn sighed, flying beside the young woman to place her tiny hand on her shoulder. "I think you should tell her, love. She deserves to know who the man she's with truly is."

The young woman composed herself, her features returning to neutrality in a way that was alarming familiar. It was exactly the same face Keir made when he regained control over his emotions.

"My name is Charlotte Ainsley, but I was born with a different name," she said. "I lived there in that house with him as a child. I am his sister."

Alison could not, would not, believe that Keir would have concealed an entire sibling from her.

And then she realized that he hadn't.

"Danny?"

Chapter Seventeen

RULES MEANT FOR BREAKING

Rinka

As Rinka and Idris made their way up the lane to Weldan House, Idris offered her advice on passing as nobility.

"First, confidence is everything. Courtiers are not accustomed to being questioned, and while it can be good sport to put particularly unpleasant folks on the defensive, it's best to just smile politely at whatever nonsense is said to you. Then as long as you say your nonsense with conviction, they'll do the same in return. You can openly contradict yourself in conversation, and as long as you say it with gusto, no one will dare to reveal you."

"But they'll gossip behind my back, won't they?" asked Rinka. She was starting to get nervous about this entire idea. What if she said or did the wrong thing and they threw her in the dungeon like they often did at the picture show?

"Of course, but they'll do that no matter what you do," said Idris. "Remember that no matter what they have to say about you, it won't be as bad as what they say about me."

"A small comfort," said Rinka. "What else?"

"Second, you mustn't speak with the servants unless absolutely necessary. You don't need to be cruel to them, but they have a lot of work to do, and you'll get them in trouble if you take up too much of their time. And be careful of what you do say to them—they're liable to gossip as much as the people they serve."

"I really don't need or want anyone waiting on me hand and foot," said Rinka. "I've taken care of myself for years. I can light my own fires and clean my own chamber pot and cook my own meals."

"You absolutely will not do any of those things unless you want to be discovered immediately," said Idris. "You will not dress yourself or wash yourself or even comb your own hair. Because you're not traveling with a maid, one from the house will be assigned to you while you stay. Let her do her job without any trouble, for both of your sakes."

"Can't I just tell them not to bother?"

"No!" Idris sighed, stopping in the middle of the gravel lane. "If you don't want to do this, you don't have to, you know. We can still see each other some. As long as I attend the most important things, I can get away without doing the rest."

Rinka did want to see what it was like, she had to admit to herself. She felt uncomfortable with being waited on, especially knowing how hard the work must be, and she felt nervous about the deception, but as Weldan House came into view in all of its glory, she could not resist the opportunity to find out what it was like to live inside its opulent walls.

"Fine," said Rinka. "I'll let the servants do their work. What else?"

Idris listed out a number of other etiquette lessons: who to curtsy to and when; which titles and styles to use in greetings; which cutlery to use first at meals; when to wear a hat; which doorways and stairwells were to be used, and which were for the servants only; and many others, but Rinka was distracted by the manor house before them. It was enormous; the façade was at least as large as the central rail-wheeler station in Arcas Dyrne, the largest building Rinka had ever seen.

But unlike the central station, there were no great towers surrounding it. It sat alone, a marvel of tan stone at the end of the looped lane, the rows of windows like dozens of eyes looking out on the landscape. Rinka could not fathom that people actually lived here. That Keir had grown up here, and that all of this would be his one day.

"Are you even listening?" asked Idris. "Don't tell me you're taken with this monstrosity. It's ridiculously large. A monument to human arrogance, an insane overcompensation for being overlooked in high society…you love it, don't you?"

"It's wonderful," said Rinka.

Idris sighed, but she caught a brief smile flash across his face before his features settled on vaguely disapproving once more.

"One final thing for us to discuss before we make our grand entrance," he said. "Regarding our…courtship."

Rinka willed the blood to stay out of her cheeks. "Go on," she said.

"In public, the nobility is still quite traditional regarding etiquette between romantic partners. We must give the appearance of caring for one another without causing a scandal. It's expected for people who are courting to display small tokens of affection, but there are limits."

He winked at her, and she wondered just where those limits lie, but she was too afraid to ask.

"All these rules," said Rinka. "Why do I have the feeling that none of them apply to you?"

"Oh, they all absolutely apply to me," said Idris. "If the rules don't apply to you, they aren't very fun to break, now are they?"

"What exactly is expected of me? In a courtship arrangement," said Rinka. She tried to affect a casual air.

"Nothing too serious. Just a bit of flirting. Holding hands. An extraordinary amount of dancing—I'll need to arrange for someone to come teach us the steps. Promenades around the grounds. Perhaps a stolen kiss or two under the moonlight."

She tried to hide her surprise at the last part, but she was unsuccessful.

He held his hands up in surrender. "If you want, that is. I, for one, don't see any harm in having a little fun for the summer. Do you?"

For once, her mother's voice was silent. Perhaps that part of her was too shocked to know what to say.

Rinka considered it. She did find him very handsome. And charming, if a bit arrogant. She admired the sincerity underneath his humor, which she also found enjoyable. And most of all, she enjoyed their games together. Things had been pretty fun so far, mortal peril aside. What was the harm in letting it continue?

And besides, she couldn't possibly marry a prince. There was no future for them, not even if she'd wanted it. So why not enjoy each other for the summer? She had no real reputation to ruin. No one knew who she was, and once the summer was gone, it was doubtful she'd see anyone but the locals ever again.

"I don't see any harm in it, no," said Rinka with a coy smile.

Perhaps he'd expected a bit more of a protest.

"Right," he said, half choking on the word. "Good. Very good, then. That's settled."

"What the matter?" she asked, her tone teasing. "I thought it was a bit of fun."

He smiled at her, pursing his lips a little. "I did say that, didn't I? Ah, look." He pointed to an approaching man coming down the drive dressed in a navy livery coat. "Our welcome party has arrived."

It wasn't much of a party. No one's nose was bleeding, after all, and there was only the one guest from the manor.

The footman took one look at Rinka and Idris's basic attire and said, "I'm sorry, sir and madam, but the grounds are closed until the festival in two days' time."

"Not closed to guests, surely?" asked Idris.

"Sir, the accommodations within the manor have already been reserved for the royal family and their closest companions. There are lodgings available in town for folks of your…persuasion."

How rude, thought Rinka. "Don't you know who you're speaking to?" she asked him.

"I'm sure I do not," said the footman. "You'll need to be on your way now—"

"This is your prince," she said. "Prince Idris of Loegria and Wilderise."

The footman, who was human and perhaps a few years younger than either of them, looked at Idris doubtfully. "If this is the prince, why has he arrived a day before the rest of the royal family by foot and with no staff in tow? Now, you've had your fun, but really—"

The footman could not finish his sentence, and Rinka couldn't blame him.

There was a loud *crack,* and the smell of a thousand struck matches filled the air.

Rinka felt a gust of wind just beside her before she saw it.

Standing next to her, in the exact same spot where Idris had been moments before, was a large red dragon.

Chapter Eighteen

MAGIC AND MEMORIES

Alison

"I no longer go by that name," said Charlotte. "But yes, Danny—Daniel—is the name I was born with."

Danny was Charlotte, and she was alive.

She was alive.

Alison cried out and ran to her, pulling her into her arms. Charlotte was stiff beneath her. "You're alive. You're alive. You're alive," said Alison over and over until Nolwynn gently pulled her off of the young woman.

Alison wept openly and without shame. Charlotte looked at Nolwynn with the same furrowed-brow concern that Keir so often did, and it made Alison weep even harder.

"Have you been here all this time?" she forced out between sobs. "Is this where you went after you went over the falls?"

She could see it clearly now. The coming up for air at the end of her experience in the vine's world was real. Charlotte really had resurfaced after the fall. And the sound of singing: it must have been the korrigans. Nolwynn had told Alison when they met that korrigans didn't drown people, they saved people from drowning.

"You saved her," said Alison to Nolwynn. "Oh, thank the Gods. You saved her."

"He told you about me?" asked Charlotte. "What did he say?"

Alison thought through all of the things she'd heard about Charlotte as a child. All of the stories Keir had told her, of all the times he'd tried to shield her from their father's wrath. Of all the times he'd taken the blame to protect her. Of the times their father had blamed Keir to drive them apart.

She understood why Nolwynn had told him to leave.

"It wasn't him, Charlotte. He loved you—loves you—so much. It was your father. He lied to you to keep you apart. But he was cruel to you both. He hurt you both. Keir did everything he could to help you—"

"No," said Charlotte. "They were in it together. You don't understand. They were happy I was gone. I was alone in that house."

"You weren't," said Alison. "Let me bring him back here. He can tell you—"

"No!" said Charlotte, taking a step back away from Alison. "I don't believe you. I think you should leave."

Alison panicked. She had to find a way to make Charlotte believe her, had to find a way to convince her that Keir had only been trying to protect her. He deserved to have her back. They deserved to have each other again after all these years apart.

"Show us," said Nolwynn. "I can feel the old magic on you now. Show us what you know."

Alison had no idea how to do that. To share her memories with them—it wasn't the same as moving some water around the room.

Was it?

"I'll help you," said Nolwynn. "Give me your hand."

Nolwynn took one of Alison's hands and placed it on Charlotte's. Then she placed her own small hand on top of them both.

Alison felt a surge of power from Nolwynn into Alison and then into Charlotte. It felt different from the power she'd felt from Keir or Idris, more akin to the fairies' magic. It was the same power she'd felt drawing her to the path, and Charlotte shared it too. Alison could see in the connection how the korrigans shared their magic with the other races who came to live with them, how it shaped and changed their bodies to adapt to life in and near the water, how it had transformed Charlotte into her feminine shape as she grew.

The power pressed against something within Alison. It felt like a knock against a door. A request for entry into her thoughts and memories.

Alison didn't know what would be shared if she answered, but she did it anyway.

For Keir's sake. And Charlotte's, too.

She allowed the door of her mind to open wide. Out spilled a thousand hopes and dreams and wishes, memories of good times and bad. The joy of meeting Rinka and the pain of losing her father. The boredom of her old job and the peace she felt in the garden. The love she felt for the town, for Gwenla, for Weyland, for Lady Sibba, for Willow and Dinah.

And Keir.

"Focus it," said Nolwynn. "Close it down to what we need to see."

Alison focused on Keir, closing the door until only he remained.

She brought them to the memory of her first conversation with Keir about his sibling. The memory from several months earlier was hazy, with the only clear image being Keir seated at the kitchen table. Charlotte shifted uncomfortably as the memory focused in on Keir's words.

Alison's memory of the conversation did not play out like a picture show. Instead, it existed in fragments, but the gist was clear: their mother had given Danny a doll named Charlotte, the name she would have given Danny if he had been born female. The name Charlotte had taken for herself once she'd known who she was, Alison realized.

"I remember that doll," said Charlotte. "I loved it so much."

Their father had broken the doll and blamed it on Keir, who was too afraid of what his father would do to him to defy him. Though her memory of his words wasn't exact, Alison could remember exactly how Keir had sounded as he spoke, the pain and regret in his voice.

She moved then to other memories: tales of Charlotte climbing trees and riding horses and making friends in town. She let Charlotte see Keir through her eyes, all of the joy and love and sorrow and longing he felt as he spoke of the sister he had no idea still lived.

And then she brought Charlotte to the memory of the vine. Those memories were crystal clear. She allowed Charlotte to watch the picture show of the loop they were caught in, how they'd tried over and over again to come up with a way to save her, and how finally, after exhausting every other option, Keir had accepted that she was gone and let her go over the falls.

"But I wasn't gone," Charlotte said. Alison let go of Charlotte's hand and opened her eyes once more. Charlotte's rosy cheeks were streaked with tears. "I was right here for all those years. I saw him sometimes. I'd see him riding with Father, and sometimes I'd see him reading alone up near the house. I kept my distance—I was terrified of him. I was terrified of what he'd do if he knew I was still alive."

She took Alison's hand again. "Is this truly the Keir that you know? I want to believe you, but it's so hard. It's been so long."

Alison could not imagine what Charlotte must be going through. To have the entire story of her life rewritten, to realize that everything she believed about her family was wrong. To find out that she had been loved and wanted and missed after years of believing otherwise.

"This is the Keir I know," she told her. "This is the Keir I love. I am certain that the thing he regrets most in this world is not doing more for you. I know that he would do anything to go back and change things and that accepting that he can't has been the most difficult thing he's ever had to do. I know that finding out you're alive is going to be the greatest thing to ever happen to him. I know this must be so difficult to hear and understand, and I don't blame you a bit for doubting it. But I hope you can find it in yourself to forgive him. You both deserve the chance to know each other again."

Alison knew these things not just because she knew Keir, but because she knew how they felt in her own heart. She knew what it was to long for just one more day with someone; she knew what it was to relive every one of their final moments, seeing the mistakes that were made and the things that she missed so clearly in hindsight. She had watched her father's final breaths, and still, all these years later, she'd wake up some days hoping to hear his laugh just one more time.

But for Keir, it could happen. And while she felt a tiny bit of envy, what she felt the most was elation that this impossible wish could come true for him.

Charlotte wept quietly as she listened to Alison's words. Alison took her in her arms again, and this time, she returned the embrace.

"I can't believe I've wasted so much time," she said. "I've spent most of my life blaming the wrong person. I don't know how to come back from that. You said you hope I can forgive him. But how can I ask him to forgive me?"

"There's nothing to forgive," said Alison. "You were a child, and you were scared. You both were."

Alison held her for a good, long while until Charlotte stopped weeping and let go.

"Thank you," said Charlotte. "Thank you for sharing your memories, and thank you for your patience and your comfort. I'm sorry. I don't even know your name."

"I'm Alison." Alison held out her hand to shake.

Charlotte chuckled. "It's nice to meet you, Alison."

Then Charlotte turned to Nolwynn. "I've had a good life here. I don't regret staying with you, and I appreciate everything you've done for me. You saved me. You made me who I am."

"We let you be who you are," said Nolwynn. "You did the rest."

"And I thank you for it. But I want to see him again. I hope you understand."

"Of course," said Nolwynn. She wrapped her small arms halfway around Charlotte's torso. "There will always be a place for you here if you want it. Go. Be with your brother."

"I'm just going to take a moment to get some things and collect my thoughts. Should I meet you in town?" asked Charlotte.

Alison told Charlotte to meet them back at Keir's house in Herot's Hollow. She thought a more private location would be better for their reunion, and Charlotte agreed.

"Now," said Nolwynn once Charlotte had gone into her tent to pack. "What was it you actually came here for?"

Chapter Nineteen

THE PICNIC

Rinka

Smoke poured off of the red dragon sitting in the middle of the drive before the manor house in thin wisps that filled the air with the smell of brimstone.

He was sitting upright like a cat, his forearms reaching the ground where great claws at the ends of his talons scratched deep grooves in the gravel. In this position, he was only a couple of feet taller than in his human form, but the draconic body that stretched behind him was at least twice as long, and the tail that swept the gravel side to side was longer still.

He held his wings close to his body, but the left wing did not seem to fold all the way in to mirror the right. *The Curse of the Air*, Rinka thought.

Perhaps the most peculiar thing of all was his clothes, which were still on him, stretched and adapted to his new figure. At some angles, they seemed to be less visible, the shiny red scales visible beneath. His magic, Rinka realized. The same magic that he used to stretch the coin beyond its usual shape.

The footman bowed and backed away, stumbling as he went. "Your royal highness. I'm te-te-terribly sorry, sir."

Idris huffed, a cloud of thick black smoke coming from his mouth.

"I'll fetch the others. We'll get your rooms ready at once. Please, sir. Right this way," said the footman. He remained bent at the waist, unwilling or unable to look Idris into his eyes.

Rinka was not frightened of him. Perhaps she should have been, but what she felt was more a sense of awe than fear.

He turned towards her, and she instinctively reached out for him. She pulled her arm back, unsure, but he held one of his scaled forearms out to her to touch.

She stroked the red scales. They were smoother than she'd expected, polished like river rock, with many bumps that felt like the sequins on a fine dress.

"Incredible," she whispered. She traced the line of his forearm over his ragged shirt and onto his back, where his broken wing emerged.

It was smoother still, stretched like satin over bones that weren't quite in the right configuration. It was a terrible thing, what had been done to him as a child.

"I'm sorry," she said.

He leaned his long neck towards her, nuzzling his head against her shoulder. Then he gently pushed her back, and there was another loud *crack* as he returned to his ordinary form.

"After you," he said to her, gesturing for her to follow behind the footman.

"Your highness," said the footman. "May I inquire about the young lady accompanying you? Will she be joining us as well?"

"This is the Lady Rinka, heiress to an earldom in the principality of Paistos. We met on the ferry when we were besieged by pirates. She'll be staying for the summer as well. She's had to send her lady's maid home early, but I'm sure a house as fine as this one has one to spare to attend her."

Rinka had never heard of Paistos. Did they speak the common tongue there? Did they have an accent?

"How do you do?" she said, affecting her voice just slightly to mask the recognizable accent of the working class in Arcas Dyrne. She curtsied to the footman and then immediately realized her mistake.

The footman looked at Idris, puzzled.

She wasn't meant to curtsy to the servants, only her superiors, including royalty and the highest-ranking nobles. "Are you not the duke?" she asked, feigning ignorance. "In my land, it is customary for the head of the house to greet guests."

The footman laughed. "I'm afraid not, my lady. The duke is away receiving more of our visitors. He'll be sorry to have missed the opportunity to greet you."

When the footman turned his back, Idris winked at Rinka.

Perhaps all those hours spent watching picture shows had been good for something after all, despite what her mother said.

The footman led Rinka and Idris through a great wooden door into the entrance hall. It was two stories high, with magnificent paintings lining the walls all the way up to the ceilings, which were themselves painted with scenes of humans and elves in dramatic poses and ancient attire. At the end of the room, a grand marble staircase with gilded railings led up into the house beyond.

The footman pressed something on the wall, and somewhere deep within the house, a bell rang. A pair of humans emerged from separate doors, one of them which had looked like a section of wall until it opened.

The butler was a severe man with salt-and-pepper hair and an impeccably tailored coat and tails. An older woman in a black dress and white apron joined him. They spoke quietly with the footman, and then they pressed a different lever on the wall, which rang a different bell.

"Your royal highness," said the butler, bowing to Idris. "My lady," he said, bowing to Rinka. "Welcome to Weldan House. I'm sorry we weren't able to greet you. We'll have your rooms ready at once. Would you like to take a tour of the home while you wait?"

Rinka didn't know why he was apologizing—it wasn't as though they had been expected.

"Yes, thank you," said Idris. "A tour would be nice."

Another woman in a maid's uniform arrived through yet another door. She curtsied to them and then spoke to the housekeeper.

The housekeeper brought her over to Rinka. "My lady, this is Ms. Murray. She will attend you while you stay."

"Right this way, your royal highness. My lady. We'll start in the drawing room."

Ms. Murray was young, barely more than a teenager, and human. Her hair was nearly concealed by her white bonnet, but it was red like Rinka's, and Rinka felt a kinship with her immediately. She, too, had been a young woman working in service, although she had cleaned offices, not houses.

But Rinka remembered what Idris had said, and not wanting to get her in trouble, she kept quiet and followed Ms. Murray as she led them through room after extraordinary room. First was a series of rooms used for entertaining: a drawing room with a number of plush couches and chairs arranged for conversation, a game room with tables set up for cards and a large billiards table, and a music room with a grand pianoforte. Next, they visited a pair of galleries with portraits and busts of previous dukes and duchesses alongside art collected from all over Loegria and the continent. Then they entered the library. It took up an entire wing of the house.

"There are over twenty-thousand volumes here," said Ms. Murray.

"Quite a collection," said Idris.

"Yes, your highness. The Marquess has a particular love of books."

"That sounds like him," said Idris. "Keir," he whispered to Rinka.

Ms. Murray led them then into the gardens. There were formal gardens with elaborate hedges arranged in a symmetrical design, casual gardens with tables meant for dining al fresco, and a great green lawn that sloped all the way to the river. There were dozens of people there erecting a great white tent on its banks, undoubtedly for the upcoming festival.

"We'll take our tea out here," said Idris. "Picnic style, if you wouldn't mind."

"Of course, your highness."

"Oh, and can you have someone send into town for the tailor? Our trunks were absconded by pirates. Lady Rinka and I have need of new wardrobes."

"Yes, your highness. Right away, your highness."

Once she was out of earshot, Rinka turned to Idris and curtsied. "Yes, your highness," she said. "Whatever you say, your highness. Don't you ever get tired of hearing it?"

"I've heard it all my life," he said. "I barely notice it at all."

He led her to a flat bit of lawn in the shade of an oak that was as wide around as a rail-wheeler car. "This will do," he said.

A group of servants came over to them with a quilted blanket and several trays of sandwiches, bowls of fruit, and a beautiful tea set made from delicate porcelain. They laid it all out for them, even pouring the tea.

Rinka had to stop herself before she thanked them. Idris told her it wasn't necessary—she'd have to thank them dozens of times a day, and that would get tedious in a way that hearing "your highness" apparently did not.

"Well," said Idris. "What do you think?" He sat down on the blanket, lounging back to lean his head into the sun.

Rinka joined him, tucking her legs to the side in a way she hoped looked elegant. "It's beautiful, and it makes me feel a little sick," she said.

He leaned towards her and took her hand, concerned. "Are you alright? Should I send for…well, I suppose Keir's the doctor around here."

"No, I'm not physically ill." Apart from her racing heart now that he was holding her hand. "But seeing all of this and knowing how people live in Arcas Dyrne. How *I* lived in Arcas Dyrne. Well, it's just a bit depressing."

"Oh, that," he said. "Like I said. A monument to human arrogance. Not that this house is unique by any means. And compared to the castle, well, it's positively provincial. Although I don't think Father ever bothered to add a billiards table; I'll admit I'm envious of that."

"Doesn't it bother you?" asked Rinka. Idris had started eating a sandwich that had been cut into a neat triangle, and he looked frankly unbothered by anything at all. "Don't you feel any guilt for living this way while others struggle?"

"I don't live this way," said Idris. "There are staff at the University who take care of things there, but not nearly as many, and I only have a handful of rooms there."

Rinka frowned and sat her teacup down.

"Rinka, this is the way the world is. It's unfortunate, but there isn't anything I can do to change it."

"That's not true at all," she said. "You will be king. You could change all of it if you wanted to."

"First off, as I explained to you, I have no intention of being king. And second, do you know what happens to kings that take away the rights and privileges of their subjects? They don't tend to keep their heads attached to their bodies very long."

She leaned away from him, looking out at the workers below. "I'm not talking about taking something away, but rather giving people the opportunity to rise above their birth."

"Oh, I'm all for that," said Idris. "It's one of the reasons I work at the University. Education is power."

"I suppose it's one path," said Rinka, although she had further questions about how people were given access to education in the first place. Her parents were unable to send her to university, after all. "I just don't know how you could be born as one of the few people in the world who could actually change it and then turn away from that possibility so easily."

He sighed. "I'm not opposed to changing the world, and I'm not opposed to using my station to do it. Come on now, you haven't even been part of society for a day. I've spent a lifetime with these people. I'm not trying to be callous, but I know the rules. I know what can be done."

"Didn't you say something about the fun of breaking the rules?"

Idris smiled wryly. "Well, if you're just going to use all my words against me, I suppose I'll have to be more careful what I say. You know, you're rather charming when you're indignant. The line that forms beside your nose—just there," he said, touching the spot. "It's rather becoming."

Rinka was dubious. "You find a line on my face attractive? Are you trying to distract me, your highness?"

"Don't you 'your highness' me," said Idris, and he reached to her sides and tickled her.

Rinka shrieked and rose to her feet. "What are you doing?"

"I'm breaking a rule," he said. "Isn't that what you wanted, my lady?"

Rinka giggled and ran for it.

Idris chased her across the lawn. The warm summer breeze lifted her hair, and the sun warmed her grey skin as she ran from him, laughing all the while.

She flew past the formal gardens and a large fountain, past an orchard and the stables, and kept going until she reached an outbuilding of some kind near the woods, running around the back of it as he finally caught up to her.

He grabbed her hand and shot an arm out in front of her, trapping her. "Got you," he said.

She wiggled and tried to escape from the other side, but he held his other arm out and walked her back to the wall, pinning her there with no way out.

She squeezed her arms tightly to her sides, trying to conceal the ticklish bits from him. "Mercy!" she cried.

"Mercy?" he asked. "Are you sure?"

He darted one hand into the space between her arm and her side, tickling his fingers against the sensitive spot there.

She squealed. "Mercy!" She was panting from both the laughter and the run, barely able to breathe the word out.

"Mercy?" he said again. His chest was heaving too from the exertion, and Rinka thought for a moment that he might go for her other side, but instead he lifted his fingers to her cheek.

He stroked her jaw, and then her chin, and then her lips, brushing them exactly the same way he had in the tent.

She trembled. He was so close to her she could feel the pull of his gasping breath on their shared air, could smell the sunlight on his skin.

"Mercy," he whispered. "Gods know I'll need it."

Then he kissed her, grabbing her hands and pinning them up over her head against the wall, their bodies rising and falling in time with each other as they regained their breath and then lost it once more.

Summer fun, indeed.

Chapter Twenty

REUNIONS, PT. 2

Alison

Alison tried to catch Nolwynn up on the situation with the dam, but Nolwynn was already aware: her people had spotted the construction of the demonstration dam on a different stream to the west of the manor.

She agreed to send some of her people to help "liven up" the demonstration a bit. "I'll watch from a distance," she said. "My last encounter with the king was…tense. I don't want to draw his ire again."

Alison advised that everyone should keep their distance. "We need him to believe that the dam has failed because of its own design, not because of magic."

With a plan in place, Alison bid farewell to Nolwynn and headed back into Fossholm to meet Keir, following a path the korrigans showed her that avoided the worst of the climbing and bouldering.

He was there at the stables already when she arrived. "They're settling in nicely according to the staff, off on a tour of the grounds by the time I got there. My father wasn't home—he's on his way back from Sudport with most of the royal staff and attendants. They'll get here just before the king and princess fly in. Alison, what's wrong?"

She had known she wouldn't be able to hide her feelings from him—he was far too perceptive. "Come," she said. "Let's talk while we ride."

Alison led them, urging her horse forward as fast as she could handle. She debated what to say to him and how to say it. Would it be better to let him see Charlotte for himself?

No, she decided. She'd tell him herself once they reached her cottage to give him time to come to terms with it so he could meet Charlotte on even footing.

They rode as quickly as they could back into Herot's Hollow, crossing the river at the bridge south of town to avoid most of their neighbors and traffic. Keir was terribly worried, but he trusted her enough to allow himself to be led.

From the gate, Alison could see that the cottage and the gardens had been visited, likely by Gwenla and Brytak, in her absence. She would thank them later. There were more important things at hand.

"Do you remember when I told you that it felt like I came up for air at the end of our time in the vine's world?" she asked him once they were inside. "And that I felt it again when I was looking at the falls when we came into town."

"Yes," he said. "I remember. I suppose it was a path back to normalcy, back from the experience of being someone else into your own skin."

"Keir, it was real," she said. "I...met her. Just now. She survived."

Alison took his hand and led him to the couch.

"Who are you talking about?" he asked. His expression, the tone of his voice. He was so much like Charlotte it brought tears to Alison's eyes.

"Danny," said Alison. "Her name is Charlotte now. The korrigans saved her. She's been with them all this time."

"I don't understand," said Keir. "Alison, did the korrigans do something to you? Danny died. I saw it myself. We searched the river and the lake beyond for hours. Days. He was a child. He couldn't have survived long on his own."

"She wasn't on her own. The korrigans save people from drowning. They saved her. They helped her become who she had always been. Charlotte. Your sister."

Keir froze. In the memories Alison had shared with Charlotte, there had been signs of who she was, signs she was sure Keir had noticed as well. "You met someone who claimed to be my sister?"

"No, Keir," she said gently. "I met your sister. She's alive." The tears fell down Alison's cheeks.

Alison watched the thoughts cross Keir's face. Disbelief, anger, doubt. Concern for Alison—had they done something to her? Was this some effect of the magic still confusing her mind and making her say things to hurt him?

"Alison, I believe that you believe what you're saying is true. I know you wouldn't lie to me, and especially not about this. But I don't think I can believe it until I see her for myself."

Alison nodded. "She's coming here. That's why I wanted to get back here so quickly. She'll be at your house soon."

Keir sat back, rubbing his jaw and staring off into the distance, deep in thought.

"She didn't believe me either," said Alison. "She thought…she thought you were like your father. That you hated her. All the times you took the blame, she thought that's how you really felt."

His eyes were haunted when they met Alison's again. Some part of him was beginning to believe it. "What did you say to her? How did you convince her to come here?"

"I showed her," said Alison. "My memories of you and what you'd told me about her, what happened to us with the vine. Nolwynn showed me how."

Alison felt around using that extra sense, but she couldn't find the door anymore. "I don't think I can do it on my own, or I'd show you myself."

"That's alright," he said. "I don't need to see into your private thoughts. I'll go and meet her, this woman who claims to be my sister. And then I guess I'll know."

∽⊙⊙⊙∾

Charlotte wasn't there yet when they arrived at Keir's house. Alison privately began to worry she wouldn't show at all as she fetched the water and put the kettle on.

It had just begun to boil when there was a knock at the door.

Alison hurried into the front room in time to see Keir standing there, deciding whether or not to open it.

She gave him a moment.

He shook his head and reached for the handle.

On the other side, with a small golden bag draped over her shoulder, stood Charlotte.

"Keir?" she asked, her voice high and strained with emotion.

Alison held her breath as she waited for Keir's response.

He said nothing.

Instead, he took Charlotte into his arms, clutching her to him, his body heaving with sobs.

Alison felt the tears start again.

"Charlotte," she heard him whisper. "You're home."

After a nice—if somewhat awkward—tea, Alison left Keir and Charlotte to catch up on their own, returning to her cottage to get some chores done before heading back into Fossholm for the royal arrival the next day.

She tried once more to wield her magic around the house. And it worked, sort of. She couldn't manage to remove the mold from the strawberry cake in the icebox—a devastating loss—and she couldn't get the dust she swept up to disappear, but she was able to get the broom to move around the floor on its own.

A little.

She sighed. Knowing where her power came from was a step forward, but she was still a long way from being able to consistently control it, at least without Keir around for the connection between them and his guidance on how the old magic worked.

And without the pressure of a life-or-death situation to motivate her.

After tending to the vegetable garden the next morning, unfortunately without the aid of magic, she stopped by Keir's on the way to Fossholm. She knew he had little interest in seeing the royals arrive, not when his father would be among their entourage.

"Charlotte's still asleep," he told her when he met her at the door. "We stayed up late talking. I think she's going to stay here for a while. With our father around much more than usual this summer, she wants to steer clear so he doesn't see her."

"Of course," said Alison. "Are you still coming to the festival tomorrow?"

"I wouldn't miss it," he said.

He hugged Alison tightly when it was time for her to leave. "Thank you for bringing her back to me."

He looked so content as she left it brought tears to her eyes once more. To finally know peace after all that time— it was everything she'd ever wanted for him.

Alison headed next to Gwenla's house so that they could walk over together. She found her in an argument with Willow over Willow's attendance.

"Gwenla thinks I need to stay here because dragons eat cats," said Willow. "You've met a dragon. Did he eat any cats in your presence?"

"Not that I can remember," said Alison, not wanting to pick a side. "It's a long way to walk down to Fossholm though. Are you sure you want to go down there?"

"Oh, fine," said Willow. "I'll just stay here and nap then."

"We'll be back in the evening. If we're late, Keir's sticking around. He can feed you and Dinah," said Alison.

"Keir isn't coming?" asked Gwenla.

Alison explained to Gwenla what had happened with Charlotte as they made their way from the stables.

"It's wonderful," said Gwenla. "I have half a mind to say forget about the royals; our sweet Charlotte has come home!"

"Let's give them a bit of time together," said Alison. "They have a lot to make up for."

"Of course you're right," said Gwenla. "But I can't wait to see her again. She was so mischievous, so wild, so clever. I can't believe she's been right down the road all this time."

The stables at Fossholm were entirely full, so Alison and Gwenla were forced to leave their horses at a new hitching post in the high street. It seemed the entire population of the Hill Country had come to greet the royal family, and most of the nobles had already arrived or were arriving. The streets were full of well-dressed elves and humans, many of them wearing red to honor the king.

Gwenla and Alison followed the crowd to the lawns of Weldan House. Some filtered in behind the barricades lining the drive, while others headed to the stands that had been erected on the hillside. Down by the river, a white tent had been raised for the court. Alison had not been invited to join them for this occasion, not that she would have in Keir's absence anyway.

Gwenla spotted a group from Herot's Hollow in the stands, and she and Alison went over to join them.

It was most of the town aside from Keir and Weyland: Lady Sibba, Duncan Corbett, Nigel Smalls, Strelka, Brytak, and even Alison's fairy neighbor Aras and his adult children, Mezec and Lydiach.

"I met your friend Rinka yesterday," said Lydiach. "Sorry, I mean the Lady Rinka of Paistos."

The fairy was a tailor, and she explained that she had been brought in to make a dozen new dresses and outfits for Rinka within the week. "The tailor in Fossholm was overwhelmed with making an entire new wardrobe for the prince. Apparently, they lost all of their things in the pirate attack on the ferry."

"Yes, I heard about that," said Alison. She didn't mention that Rinka's trunk had already made its way to her cottage in case someone were to overhear her. "They were very fortunate to survive."

Lydiach winked a tiny eye at Alison, who nodded her appreciation for her discretion.

A set of trumpets began to sound from somewhere in the distance.

The crowd hushed. There were voices shouting military orders from up the drive in Fossholm, the tinny sounds of a band playing from far away and the clearer sounds of drums reaching them long before they could see the procession that had begun.

The parade that followed was as elaborate as any Alison had seen in Arcas Dyrne. There were marching bands and military regiments, their officers riding behind on horseback; troupes of dancers and choirs of elves; dwarves arriving in horse-drawn carriages with geometric filigree; and, at the very end, a single motor carriage, the first that most in Wilderise had ever seen.

"It's the duke," someone in the crowd said. "Our Lord Ainsley arriving in style!"

Alison snorted. Trust the duke to arrive in the most expensive and impractical fashion he could manage. How would he even begin to maintain such a vehicle in this part of the world?

The procession looped along the drive and returned to march up the river as the crowd cheered.

"Lords and ladies, gentlemen and gentlewomen, people of the Hill Country and beyond. Rise for the arrival of your king," yelled a man in a red uniform who stood between the stands and the tent.

No one had been seated, at least not in the stands with the commoners. The nobles began to file out of their tent as those from the procession joined them. Alison spotted Rinka with Idris at the very front of the crowd.

They were holding hands.

"Aww," said Gwenla. "Aren't they sweet together?"

"Shh," said Alison. "We're not supposed to know her."

The trumpets flared again. Alison watched as Rinka pointed into the distance. Strelka and Brytak, both orcs themselves, pointed too. "There they are!" said Strelka.

The royal family had arrived.

Chapter Twenty-One

THE ROYAL ARRIVAL

Rinka

The kiss lingered on Rinka's lips and in her mind as she went about the rest of her day.

It was there with her when the tailor—Lydiach, a friend of Alison's who thankfully did not give away Rinka's true identity—arrived to measure her for her new dresses and gowns. It was there when Ms. Murray dressed her for dinner in a hideous frock left by a former guest of Weldan House, the only garment they could find suited for the occasion that would fit her broad shoulders. It was there at that very first dinner in the manor when she was seated among the distinguished guests who had already arrived, dukes and viscountesses and lords and ladies whose names she would not be able to recall because there was only room for one name in her mind: *Idris*.

It stayed with her the next day as she joined him in the tent where he had been seated as the guest of honor for the arrival of the royal family, his family, a table apart from the others in a tent apart from the others.

"How did you sleep?" he asked her. "Were your quarters to your liking?"

Rinka had gone from a room shared with her mother to a tiny closet of a room in the flat she shared with Alison to one of the most opulent guest rooms in Weldan House, a room with an enormous four-post bed, a private dressing room, and a balcony that overlooked the central courtyard. The dressing room alone was larger than Alison and Rinka's entire flat.

"I barely slept at all," she said truthfully. It wasn't because of the unfamiliar surroundings though, and it certainly wasn't due to a lack of comfort. "There was something occupying my mind that kept me tossing and turning in bed."

"Oh?" said Idris. He shifted in his seat, his eyes wild with mischief. "Care to share it with me?"

"I think you already know what it was," she said, casting her eyes downward demurely and then glancing back up at him, a picture of feigned innocence.

He moaned, lowering his voice so that only she could hear it. "Lady Rinka, I do believe you are a tease."

A duke approached, bowing to Idris and starting a conversation about the pirates that had attacked the ferry. The duke was disappointed to get little from Idris, who seemed rather distracted, until Rinka shared her version of the tale, which fascinated him and brought others around as well.

The only thing that caught Idris's attention was a retired admiral's mention of an increase in naval spending to secure the waters once more.

"I wouldn't be surprised if my father hired Burning Ash himself," said Idris to Rinka once the crowd had dispersed.

"The king would hire pirates?" asked Rinka. It sounded insane.

"He would, and far worse than that as well," said Idris grimly.

By the time the trumpets sounded the beginning of the procession, they had been served a four-course lunch, and more than a dozen other courtiers had come by to discuss some matter or another. Idris had grown increasingly impatient during their exchanges, although Rinka was having a decent time. They seemed nice enough so far, at least.

Rinka and Idris walked along their elevated platform to a window out of the tent overlooking the drive. Rinka peered out of the window as Idris came up along beside her, gently pressing his thigh against her hip and resting his hand on the small of her back.

"Careful," said Rinka, holding back a sigh. "How am I ever meant to sleep at night if this is how I spend my days?"

"If I had my way, you wouldn't be sleeping at all," he murmured. "Everyone is watching the procession."

Rinka looked to her left, and indeed the rest of the courtiers were gathered by the open wall of the tent, all of their eyes fixed on the parade beyond.

She dared to lean back into him, feeling him against her.

He groaned softly, brushing his lips on the bare spot between her neck and her shoulder. "You'll be the death of me," he whispered in her ear, his breath tickling her and reaching some part low within her that hadn't awakened in a long time. "If I could fly, I'd take you far away from here right this very moment."

She turned to face him, keeping her body close. "And then what?" she asked.

"And then—"

The trumpets blared again. "Pixie's britches," said Rinka as they parted.

Idris laughed. "Don't tell me you don't swear."

"Give me something to swear about, and you'll find out," said Rinka.

Idris let out a low whistle. "Damn," he swore.

Rinka wasn't sure exactly what had come over her. Maybe it was the heat, which was considerable inside the tent, maybe it was the freedom she felt whilst pretending to be someone else, but whatever it was, she liked it.

She took the hand Idris offered her as they reluctantly followed the crowd from the tent and onto the lawn.

"Just over here, your highness," said a man in a military uniform, leading them to a spot at the front of the crowd nearest to the riverbank. "They'll be arriving from the southwest."

Rinka peered into the sky. Fluffy white clouds were making their way across the sun, their shadows lazily traveling over the hills and forest as a warm breeze whipped up the sides of the tent behind them. Rinka searched the landscape for winged creatures but noticed only a large bird of prey, possibly an eagle, soaring over the lake to the east.

Then she saw them. There were a dozen or more dragons approaching, their silhouettes tiny as they crossed the sun.

Idris followed the direction of her pointing finger, staring for a long moment before he could see them too.

"That's Ceri out front. You can barely see her against the clouds."

Rinka hadn't noticed the white dragon until Idris pointed her out. The others, in shades of red, black, blue, and green, stood out better against the sky.

The crowd had noticed them now. There were scattered cheers that joined together into a continuous yell as the flying party approached.

The dragons grouped into formation as they began their descent. They formed a great vee in the sky, a large dragon that was such a dark red it was nearly black at the front.

King Derkomai. Idris's father.

The king led the others down to the manor grounds so suddenly that some of the crowd in the stands moved out of the way to avoid them. The dragons swept low, performing a close pass over the crowd before ascending once more to make one final circle.

One by one, the members of the royal family landed on the open lawn to the north.

"My aunts and uncles. That little one there is my cousin, Nik. He's only nine," said Idris. "He's the last in the line of succession that's allowed to change form."

"I don't understand," said Rinka. "What do you mean 'allowed' to?"

"Descendants from dragons can change form for generations, but the rules of the monarchy prevent anyone further from the throne than the twelfth in line for succession from doing so. It's an attempt to prevent civil war, although as you might remember from your history lessons, it hasn't been entirely successful."

Rinka did vaguely remember learning something along those lines in school, now that he mentioned it. Not that she ever imagined she'd be close enough to the monarchy to need to retain the knowledge of their rules.

"Here comes Ceri, showing off as usual," said Idris.

The white dragon dove sharply and then did a somersault before rolling down to land. The crowd cheered even louder, with a number of high-pitched screams from the younger ladies present.

Idris rolled his eyes.

The last dragon to land was the king. He circled overhead, closing on a large wooden figure in the shape of a man at the northern end of the lawn.

"What's that?" asked Rinka.

"I'm not sure," said Idris.

"It's called a wicker man. A local tradition to ward off foul spirits and protect the crops for the upcoming harvest," said a man who had walked up beside them while their attention was distracted. "How do you do, your highness?"

Though Rinka had never seen him before, she recognized him at once: this must be Lord Ainsley, Keir's father. Their resemblance was uncanny—the same brown eyes, the same strong jaw.

Rinka had heard a lot about this man from Alison in her letters, and none of it was good.

"We are well, Merelor. Did I see you arrive by motor carriage?" asked Idris.

"Yes, your highness. Would you like to see it later? I could take you for a drive."

"Perhaps another time. I have already promised this evening to Lady Rinka." Idris looked at her meaningfully, and she had to turn away to conceal her blush.

"How do you do, my lady? I've heard that you're staying with us as well. So great of you to come, and from as far as Paistos."

Rinka had forgotten to ask Idris for any information about Paistos.

But she was also in a playful mood, and she remembered Idris's advice: speak confidently and few would dare to question you. Especially in the company of the crown prince.

"It was quite a journey," she said, "but I'm grateful to stay in such a lovely and quaint estate."

Lord Ainsley's eyebrow twitched at the word "quaint." "Are the estates somewhat grander in Paistos?" he asked, attempting to conceal his doubt.

"Oh yes. My family's villa is constructed out of the entire mountainside. Still, the smaller homes here in Wilderise have a certain charm."

Lord Ainsley's smile remained pleasant, but Rinka could see the hint of a smirk pulling at his left cheek. "Mountainside? I believed Paistos to be on the sea."

She had truly pushed a button then to have earned such a contentious response, but she pressed on. "The mountains meet the sea in Paistos, yes. Much like the eastern coast of Wilderise."

"Of course," said Lord Ainsley. "Forgive me; I was never much for geography. If you'll both excuse me, I'm needed to greet the royal family. Or—the remaining members of the royal family. Forgive me, your highness."

"Buffoon," said Idris once he was out of earshot. "A nice dig you got in there, though. Done with all the passive aggressive animosity of a real courtier."

"Thank you, your highness," said Rinka with a smirking half-curtsy.

"Don't forget what happens when you call me that," growled Idris, sending a pleasant shiver down her spine.

The crowd stilled as the king made his final approach. He passed low overhead, cutting a straight line to the wicker man.

Then he roared, fire leaping from his open mouth to the wooden figure, bursting it into flame.

The crowd went wild.

"He does have a flair for the theatric," said Idris.

Rinka would not admit it to him at this moment, but she did find it pretty entertaining.

With the king finally landed, the royals shifted back into their regular forms with a series of loud cracks that bounced from the walls of the manor like thunder. They were each wearing fine robes in the exact same shades as their scales, Rinka realized.

"The only bit of magic my father has patience for," said Idris. "As much as he hates it, he could never stand for the royal family changing form in the nude."

"A pity," said Rinka. "I'd like to see that."

"You'd like to see my father naked?"

"I—shoot. That one got away from me a bit there."

"Don't worry," said Idris. "I understood your meaning."

"Excuse me, your highness. The king has requested your presence," said a woman in uniform.

"Come, my lady, it's time to meet the family," said Idris, offering his arm.

"I'm sorry, sir, but the king only requested that you come. Not the young lady." The woman in uniform nervously looked at Rinka, hoping this wouldn't be a problem.

"Well, won't he be delighted then when he gets the both of us?"

"Rule-breaker," muttered Rinka as she allowed him to lead her past the courtiers to the field where the royal family was gathered.

No one was rude enough to tell her to leave once she was there already, and so Idris introduced her to his closest relatives, who all greeted him with a surprising amount of kindness and delight at seeing him again after so long.

All except for the king and Princess Ceri, at least.

Princess Ceridwen looked very little like her brother. She was pale where he was tan, short where he was tall, her hair silver where his was black, and her eyes blue where his were brown. And yet the eyes were the same exact shape, an almond shape that must have belonged to their mother because they looked nothing like the king's.

King Derkomai shared Idris's imposing figure and his daughter's coloring, but little else with either of them. Still, he was a handsome man for his age, his full head of silver hair windswept underneath a silver crown studded with deep red jewels to match his royal robes.

His pale blue eyes sparkled with mischief or perhaps cruelty; it was difficult for Rinka to say.

"Prince Idris," he said. "How good of you to join us."

The words were sweet, but the tone was acidic. Rinka gulped, trying to remain calm.

"And you've brought a pet," said Princess Ceri, looking at Rinka.

Idris went stiff while the king chuckled malevolently.

"Play nicely, children. People are watching."

"Sister," said Idris. "You're looking as miserable as ever."

"Better miserable than pathetic," she bit back.

"Enough!" said the king. He lowered his voice. "I will not turn this occasion into yet another spectacle. Idris, I don't know what you're here to achieve, but I'd suggest you do it without another word to your sister."

He turned to Ceri, his voice far gentler. "Ceri, my sweet. Remember what we've talked about."

"Yes, Father," she said, pouting her bottom lip.

Idris held up his hands in surrender and backed away.

"Very good," said the king. He left without another word to them, heading to an elevated stand overlooking the crowd.

"I didn't get your name," Ceri said to Rinka once he was out of earshot. "Was it Boots? Fluffy? Miss Kitty?"

"Stop it," hissed Idris.

"What?" asked Ceri, her face full of mocking innocence. "Surely she's not courting you, on account of—"

"I said stop!" said Idris loudly enough that his father turned to shoot him a lethal glare. He continued, keeping his voice to a whisper. "You are twenty years old. Stop acting like a child."

She sighed. "You never were any fun."

The two of them exchanged barbs throughout their father's welcome speech, and they hadn't stopped by the time dinner arrived either. Rinka had been dressed in the first of the evening gowns Lydiach had made her: a pale mauve silk number with a chiffon overlay embroidered with delicate gold filigree.

"You must tell me the name of your seamstress," said Ceri to Rinka after a particularly cruel exchange with Idris. "That gown is magnificent."

Rinka suspected she was being mocked, but it was not the only compliment she received that night. She was seated across from Princess Chloe, Idris's aunt, and not only had she been complimentary of Rinka's attire, but she also made for delightful company in general, even more so with each glass of Wilderisen whisky.

"And then there was the time he got stuck in a dining chair," said Princess Chloe. "He must have been five or six, and he loved to sit backwards in chairs. You know, sitting with his skinny little legs wrapped around the back, kicking and making faces through the gaps, just being a little boy. His mother, Queen Yuling—this was before she was forced to return home—told him not to a hundred times, but he always did it as soon as she left the room. Well, she had a new set of chairs brought into the music room from her home, and they had a little slot in the back where his legs would fit. He slid both in there one day and couldn't get back out! It was the funniest thing. The carpenter was on his way by the time he got control of his magic and freed himself."

Rinka laughed, but she didn't quite understand the story. "Couldn't one of you have freed him?" They all seemed to have mastery over the same magic Idris used, at least in keeping themselves clothed in flight.

"Ah, the king prefers we don't use magic unless absolutely necessary. He's a believer in modern technology. I would have done it anyway, but Idris wasn't in distress. He was laughing just as hard as the rest of us."

In return for her fine tales, Rinka shared with her the story of their escape from the pirates, which earned her the attention and admiration of most of her end of the table. By the time she was able to speak to Idris again as they watched an elf courtier play the pianoforte late that evening, she had won over much of his family.

"You seem to be quite at home," he said to her, pulling her to the back of the room for as private as a conversation as they were allowed under the circumstances. "Aunt Chloe has already asked if she can invite you to stay with her in her town home this autumn."

"They're different than I expected," said Rinka. "More…"

"Ordinary?" Idris offered.

Rinka nodded, hoping it wasn't rude to say.

Idris smiled. "There isn't as much of a need to put on a show when it's mostly family around. Of course, all the usual rules still apply, especially since there are other courtiers present, but some of us care more about that than others."

"I see," said Rinka.

"For example," said Idris. "I absolutely should not be thinking the things I'm thinking seeing you in that gown."

His voice was barely a whisper. Rinka looked around to see if anyone had noticed, but they were all quite focused on the performance.

"And what are you thinking?" she asked him.

"I'm thinking," he said, leaning closer, "of just how easy it would be to tear this lovely thin fabric from your shoulder, just here." He traced his fingertips over the chiffon of her right sleeve without turning to look, his eyes fixed on the pianist.

"Not a chance!" whispered Rinka out of the corner of her mouth. "I've never had a gown this nice before, and I would sooner tear a painting in half than this work of art."

She glanced sideways to look at him before she continued, and the heat in his eyes threatened to ignite her. "If you wished to remove it, you'd need to undo the hooks just back here—" She glanced around the room and then took his hand, placing it on her back.

"I see," he whispered, running his fingers over the gown's closures. "So many hooks. An exercise in patience, I suppose."

"Some things are worth the wait," said Rinka.

"But waiting is hard," he said.

Out of the corner of her eye, Rinka could see him shifting his weight a little, the minute movement of his hips as he adjusted himself.

She shivered.

The applause began then for the end of the elf's performance. Idris withdrew his hand to clap, leaving Rinka to feel the echo of his touch.

"You aren't the only one who won't be sleeping tonight," said Idris quietly, his words drowned out by the applause. And then, louder, for everyone else to hear: "Good night, Lady Rinka. I hope you have the sweetest dreams."

Chapter Twenty-Two

THE DAM

Alison

Early the next morning, Keir brought Charlotte to see the garden he and Alison had made into a memorial for her inside of Alison's hedge maze.

The summer flowers were putting on their absolute best show: great blue globes of massive hydrangeas filling the shady corners; sunny white daisies with yellow centers and sweeping stems of bright pink cosmos near the bench; pale pink roses that scaled the garden walls, twining dramatically with deep purple clematis; the elegant tea rose Alison thought Keir had pruned to death in the spring standing front and center, blooming wildly with massive flowers of a delicate peach shade; and tall spires of catmint and lavender filling the ground underneath it all, absolutely covered in bees.

They brought Charlotte to the rock they had painted with her old name. Keir knelt to remove it, but she stopped him.

"Leave it," she said. "That part of my life is over. Let it stay buried here in this beautiful place."

They left her there with a book she had brought to read. Alison watched her exhale as they left, watched the tension drain from her shoulders, felt the peace of the garden working its magic and bringing her the closure she deserved.

❧❦❧

After a pleasantly uneventful ride into Fossholm, Alison and Keir made their way around the Midsummer Festival, taking in all the sights and sounds of celebration.

There were buffet tables full of summer delights: fire-grilled meats and platters of mouthwateringly ripe fruits, bowls of fragrant punch, and even a station serving treats chilled in an enormous ice box. It wasn't quite as spectacular as the feast in the fairy forest, but Alison enjoyed a cone of ice cream as they walked past groups of musicians playing lively tunes; lawn games of badminton, cricket, and croquet; competitions to lift heavy stones and throw logs a great distance; and children with painted faces, laughing and running around a great bonfire where the wicker man had burned the night before.

The courtiers walked among the common folk, and although the royal family had their own separate tent to gather in, Alison spotted Prince Idris and Rinka walking near the river.

"Why don't you introduce me to the prince?" Alison asked Keir.

He looked at her, confused, but slowly understood her meaning. "Of course," he said. "Let's meet his lovely companion as well."

Rinka looked so pretty in her cream-colored day dress, her red hair tucked under a wide-brimmed hat to keep the sun off her face.

There were others around, and so they made their false introductions before Alison asked Lady Rinka if she'd like to take a turn with her about the river.

Arm in arm, the ladies walked until they were a distance from the other festival-goers.

"Well?" asked Alison. "Tell me everything."

Rinka caught her up at length about her time in the manor: her grand chambers and her new beautiful clothes which arrived by the day, the fancy dinners and evenings of entertainment, and her harrowing introduction to the royal family and the better encounters that followed.

"And Idris?" asked Alison. "Is he treating you well?"

"Very well," said Rinka. "He's…"

Alison noticed the blush on Rinka's grey cheek as she turned to look at him.

"It's just for the summer," said Rinka, sounding as though she was trying to convince herself as much as Alison. "But I'm having a wonderful time."

"I'm so glad to hear it," said Alison.

Keir and Idris approached them once more. "It's time for the demonstration," said Keir. "Is everything ready?"

"I hope so," said Alison. She hoped the korrigans would come through.

A crowd had gathered on the opposite side of the drive from the main celebration. There was a narrow stream there that met the river south of town, and a dam had been constructed across it from concrete, widening the stream behind it into a pond.

"The future of Herot's Hollow, if we're unsuccessful," said Gwenla as she walked over to join them.

The dam allowed a small amount of water through an opening at the top, which sent it streaming into the low creek bed beyond like a fountain. There was also a blocked opening at the bottom in front of a round pillar which was currently stationary.

On the other side, they had set up a table with a music-player on top of it. It was the kind that ran on 'lectrics in Arcas Dyrne, with a great box beneath it for amplifying the sound. A long cord ran to a box near the top of the pillar.

The king approached, flanked by Lord Ainsley and a pair of dwarves. Keir gripped Alison's hand when he saw his father.

"I should have spoken with him before you found Charlotte," he said. "I'm not sure I can do it now without resorting to violence."

"There's no rush," said Alison. "I imagine he's so preoccupied with cozying up to the king, he won't even notice you here."

She was right—Lord Ainsley did not appear to spot his son in the crowd.

"Your majesty," he began with a bow. "Ladies and gentlemen. Thank you all for gathering here today to witness a most extraordinary sight. I bring you the future of Wilderise—plentiful 'lectric power for all, generated for free from our own natural resources. Andsaz, if you please."

"Andsaz? Of Andsaz Industries?" asked Alison. "That's my former employer." Alison had known her employer was involved in construction works among their many other ventures, but it had not occurred to her that they might be involved in the Wilderise modernization scheme.

"He must have driven that other one off. Or the vine did, I suppose," said Gwenla. This was indeed a different dwarf than the one Lord Ainsley had brought to town a few months prior.

Andsaz went over to the demonstration dam and moved a lever on the side. The water ceased flowing from the top and began to flow at the bottom instead. As the water reached the pillar, it began to turn. Then there was a whirring of gears followed by a crackle of sound from the music-player.

The slow, distorted sound of a brass band playing a march began. The tune shifted in and out of pitch before finally settling into the recognizable tune of Loegria's national anthem.

"Bravo!" shouted the king. The crowd echoed the cheer.

Alison looked at Gwenla nervously. "Any minute now…"

As the song continued, it began to speed up. Andsaz fumbled with the lever and the gears before running over to the music-player, trying to understand what could be going wrong.

"Just a little bit too lively there," he yelled to the crowd over the music, which was climbing higher and higher in pitch. "Just bear with me a moment…"

Alison saw what was happening. The water coming through the base of the dam was rushing far too fast. The pillar was spinning wildly, looking like a top about to go flying off a table.

"That's it!" said Gwenla. "Look—"

Andsaz shouted as the music-player made a loud booming sound, smoke rising from the box below. Then there was a series of loud cracks, almost like the sound of the royal family shifting form, but the king had not changed. He was backing away from the dam, his livid eyes on Lord Ainsley, who leapt over the creek bed to help Andsaz in a panic.

Moments after his jump, water began to shoot through the cracks which were now visible in the dam wall. "It won't hold," yelled Idris. "Run!"

The crowd ran in a panic, stumbling up the bank as the dam burst behind them. Alison turned back to look as a surprising amount of water—an unnatural amount—rushed forth in its collapse, tipping over the music-player and sweeping Lord Ainsley and Andsaz off their feet.

And then just as quickly, it was over. The water receded, leaving Lord Ainsley and Andsaz drenched but unharmed on the ground among the chunks of broken concrete and shattered 'lectrics from the music-player.

"They came through!" said Gwenla and then caught herself before anyone heard her speaking of the korrigans, who had undoubtedly been responsible for the sudden surge in water level. "The duke and the industrialist," she clarified. "Everyone is alright."

Everyone did seem alright, if a bit shaken, except for the king. "Merelor!" he shouted at Lord Ainsley, shaking water off the bottom of his cape. "What kind of fool do you take me for? You said it was guaranteed. No way to fail."

"Your majesty, I've never seen anything like it. Andsaz operates several of the greatest dams in Loegria—"

"Save it," said the king. "We're going with the coal mine and power plant. I won't waste any more time on this."

"Of course, s-sir," stuttered Lord Ainsley as he rose, dripping, to his feet. "I'll send for the great mining families at once."

"See that you do," said the king. "I want to break ground by the end of summer."

"Coal mine?" asked Gwenla, incredulous. "What have we done?"

❦

They gathered afterwards in the inn at Fossholm—Alison, Keir, Gwenla, Idris, and Rinka—taking a private room at the back to avoid being overheard.

"I was right the first time," said Gwenla. "Back when we first heard of the plan to build the dam. I said we should just let it go—knew that's what Lady Willana would have done—and then I went and got caught up in yet another foolhardy scheme. And now instead of an extra lake, the entire countryside will be coated with soot."

The innkeeper brought over a bottle of whisky, which Keir poured into glasses and passed around. Alison hadn't yet developed a taste for the stuff, but she took hers anyway.

She needed it at the moment.

"We just need to convince the king that this area should be preserved," said Rinka. "Idris, your aunts and uncles are reasonable people. Do any of them have the king's ear?"

"Not really," said Idris. "Not once he's put his mind to something. Well, Ceri might, but good luck convincing her."

"I read a book once on land conservation efforts in the New World," said Keir. "The native humans there led a campaign against goblin strip-mining with the help of a man from Wilderise. They published a series of articles about the wild beauty of the lands there, gaining support among the elvish settlers and eventually establishing outstanding areas of beauty as parks to be kept free of development."

"Lady Sibba suggested something along those lines using my poetry book," recalled Alison. "Perhaps we could add an essay or two about the value of conserving land for future generations to the pamphlet."

"Will it be ready soon?" asked Rinka. "If we can get it out in a couple of weeks, I can try to figure out who we need to convince."

Gwenla sighed. "I suppose it can't do any harm. At worst, maybe it will help you make a name for yourself, Alison."

"I'll head back and finish up my drafts as quick as I can," said Alison. "Weyland won't take long to add them to his illustrations. Keir, do you want to write the essays? Since you're the most familiar with the subject?"

"I'll ask Lady Sibba to help," said Keir. "Two voices are better than one."

"The only way I can see this working is if we get Ceri onboard," said Idris. "I'll see what I can do to mend the fences with her, but Rinka, you may have more luck."

Rinka looked uncertain of that, but she didn't protest.

"Here we go again," said Gwenla. "Let's hope this time we don't convince him to bring in a bulldozer and push the entire Hill Country into the sea."

Chapter Twenty-Three

A SUMMER'S BALL

Rinka

The evening brought with it the first ball of summer. After her dance lessons in the afternoon (which were unfortunately given to her and Idris separately), Ms. Murray dressed Rinka in yet another splendid gown, this one in soft gold with thousands of tiny beads and sequins sewn into a floral design. Rinka marveled at the intricacy of the embroidery. It seemed impossible that something like this could be created so quickly, but then she recalled that Lydiach was a fairy, and their magic was quite formidable.

She tried to remember all of the things she'd learned that would be needed to succeed this evening. Names, dance steps, proper introductions, personal histories, people to seek and out and those to avoid. This evening was an audition, her tryout for the part of a lady of the court. If they rejected her, or worse, if she drew Princess Ceri's ire, she'd be of no help to their plans to convince the nobility that Herot's Hollow was worth saving.

She was running the names of the Loegrian duchesses through her mind once more when she saw him at the top of the stairs.

Idris.

He'd looked splendid the night before in his dinner jacket, but in his immaculately tailored tuxedo, he was breathtaking.

It was difficult to imagine that this was the same man Rinka had met on the train in rags. The same man who had said such delightfully naughty things to her just hours earlier. He was the picture of class and grace in white tie, the long coat accentuating his impressive height, the lines of the jacket highlighting his trim, muscular figure. She forgot not only the names she was trying to remember as she looked at him.

She forgot her own name.

He hadn't seen her yet, and she relished the chance to watch him without his knowledge. It was like being let in on his secret, private world for just a moment, watching him adjust his cufflinks and run a hand through his slicked-back hair.

Then he spotted her. His lips parted and his eyes followed the lines of embroidery on her gown down her body, drinking her in.

It was so open, such a brazen display of his desire and appreciation, that it raised goosebumps on her arms.

"You look ravishing," he said when he met her at the bottom of the stairs. "Are you sure you want to go to this ball? We could always spend the evening under the stars."

Gods, it was tempting. But she had a purpose here. The stars would have to wait.

"And waste all of those dance lessons? I, for one, would like to see how you move," said Rinka. It was true. She was deeply looking forward to watching him move around the dance floor, to the light, teasing touches they would be allowed to share there.

It wouldn't be enough—not by a long shot—but at this point, she wasn't sure if she could get enough of him.

"Very well, then," he said. "You know, I usually hate these things, but I'll admit I've been looking forward to it all day."

"And why is that?" asked Rinka.

Idris looked at her as if she were being quite obtuse. "Because of you, of course."

"Because of the opportunity to play our little game?"

Idris shook his head. "No. I mean, yes, of course that. But truthfully, I'm just looking forward to seeing you in the crowd. Watching the way you interact with people—I'm not sure you even notice it, but you light up every room you're in. Your joy—it's infectious. I feel guilty for keeping you to myself."

Rinka didn't know what to say. "I—thank you."

They arrived at the queue into the ballroom. There, they were separated, seeing as they were unmarried, and each introduced to the party alone.

"Idris, Prince of Loegria and Wilderise."

Idris entered the room to quite a few looks from the crowd gathered there, and more than a few looks from the eligible young ladies. Rinka wondered if any of them would be the one he'd marry, and she found herself surprised at the pain the thought gave her.

"Lady Rinka of Paistos."

Rinka descended the grand staircase to the ballroom, and she felt every eye in the room turn to her. It was truly a magnificent gown to have earned such attention, she thought.

Before she was even off the staircase, an elf gentleman with long, blonde hair had approached her. "Might I ask you for a dance this evening, my lady? I'm Roderas, Duke of Westmark."

Westmark. Rinka tried to recall what she'd been told about him—was he the one who enjoyed fox hunting? Or perhaps it was falconry.

"It would be my pleasure, your grace," she said with a curtsy.

"Pencil me in for the second waltz. I'm afraid I'm hopeless with the quadrille."

It took Rinka mere minutes to fill her card. She left two dances open: the first and the last. Idris hadn't asked her to, but surely he would once she found him again.

And where had he gone anyway? The room was full to the brim with courtiers, and so many of them wanted to talk to her. This was exactly how she was hoping it would go, but she found that everything was just a bit less fun without him around, as if the room had lost some of its color.

"There you are," said Idris finally, coming up behind her during a conversation with the Countess of Mossbury and placing his hand on her back. "I hope you've saved a dance for me."

"Two, actually," said Rinka, and he beamed at her.

"Let's see which ones." He took the card from her and steered her away from the countess. "The first waltz—very good. Lots of contact in that one. And the last one—a polka. No, that's no good. Sorry, Mr. Alfred Herrington. No tango for you this evening." He scratched off poor Mr. Herrington's name and replaced it with his own. "Trust me on this."

"How rude of you," said Rinka. "What if I happened to like Mr. Herrington?"

She couldn't really remember exactly who he was at the moment, but the point remained.

"Do you?" he asked.

"I might have if I'd gotten the chance to dance with him," said Rinka. "Wasn't that part of the point of our whole exercise? To give me the chance to meet someone?"

She regretted it as soon as she'd said it. Not just because they could have been overheard, but also because she had been happy to forget about that detail. In truth, she hadn't found any of the gentlemen she'd met so far appealing, but she also had found herself unable to give them much of a fair chance.

He looked for a moment as if she'd slapped him. "Yes, I suppose that is true," he said when he'd recovered.

"Idris—"

"No, no, you're quite right. Have your tango with Mr. Herrington, then. See how much I care."

It stung to hear him speak that way. "I didn't mean it," said Rinka. "It was just a jest gone too far."

"Rinka, I'm not bothered. You are free to dance with whomever you wish."

He could say it all he liked, but his voice betrayed him.

He was jealous.

"Very well, I will," said Rinka. He was the one who had suggested the entire arrangement. She didn't see how he had the right to then complain about it once he realized that it might go exactly as he'd said it would.

The orchestra began to play then, and those who had found a partner made their way to the center of the room while others moved to the sides to give way for the dance.

"Shall we?" said Idris tersely.

"Let's," responded Rinka through gritted teeth.

They walked quickly together and took their place in a great circle of couples who were facing each other. On cue, they bowed and curtsied to their partners. Idris's bow was stiff and formal. Rinka curtsied mockingly low and deep.

If he was going to behave like a petulant child, she would do the same.

It was time then for him to take her in his arms. He took her hand and placed the other on her back and then pulled him to her, tight.

"A little close, don't you think, your highness?" she muttered as she rested her free arm on his shoulder, leaning back so that her throat was exposed to him.

"I don't care," he said. "Let them look."

There was no humor in him as they began to turn about the room. She could feel his barely restrained rage just beneath the surface as they moved, the tension in his arms, the stiffness of his legs.

It was ridiculous. She'd done absolutely nothing wrong. She was here at the ball to make friends, to identify the courtiers who might be sympathetic to their cause. He'd even said he was looking forward to seeing her do so. And when most of the night was spent dancing, how else was she meant to achieve that?

He released her then to perform the first underarm turn, and once she was back in his arms, he spoke to her in a voice so low it was almost a growl.

"I don't want to share you," he said.

On his breath, she thought she caught a whiff of smoke.

Rinka lost her step. She should be angry—she was angry. He had no right to say such a thing. No right at all.

And yet…she could not deny the fire it lit within her.

To feel wanted. To feel his desire for her laid bare.

No, she could not deny how it made her feel, but she would not give him the satisfaction of knowing how it had affected her. Not yet.

"I believe it's customary for an unattached lady to dance with many suitors," said Rinka. "There would hardly be a point to the dance card if that wasn't the case."

"It's different with us," he said.

"And why is that? Because you're the prince?"

"No." He gripped her hand tight, dipping her back low so that his mouth was near her throat. "Because I can't have you, and they can."

Rinka shuddered, her mind filling with images of what it would mean for him to "have" her.

There was truth to what he said, in theory. She could marry one of the men on her dance card. Even if they knew who she really was, knew she was a commoner, it wasn't unheard of. There was every possibility that someone would fall in love with her and not even care about her lie or her station or the ruse with the prince or any of it.

But marriage on the table or not, she knew they could not have her. Not really.

"No, they can't," she admitted, her heart in her throat. He turned her again in time with the music, and when she returned to face him, she was dizzy.

"You already have me," she whispered, her voice breathless.

He moaned and dipped his head dangerously close to hers, gripping her even tighter to him.

Maybe it wasn't forever, but for now, she was his.

"Meet me at midnight," he said, his lips pressed close to her ear. "By the stables."

She nodded, scarcely daring to breathe for fear that the movement might make her implode.

❦

The ball was still going at midnight, although with all of the dances from the dance card completed, the crowd had thinned somewhat as guests began to take their leave.

Rinka had given the tango to Idris after all, apologizing to Mr. Herrington for double booking and promising him the final polka. She begrudgingly admitted Idris had been right about the dance: it was far too intimate to have been shared with anyone else, at least in her present state of mind.

He had slipped away during the final dance, Rinka spotting him exiting onto the balcony as she pretended to laugh at Mr. Herrington's jokes. Mr. Herrington was actually quite funny, but Rinka's mind was elsewhere entirely.

She finally managed to make her own escape after one last conversation with Princess Chloe, who had spotted her dancing with Idris and wanted to share with her what a lovely pair they made. Rinka was flattered, and she felt an ache in knowing that it was all just temporary, that there would be no stay with Idris's aunt in her town home come autumn.

A refreshingly cool breeze blew on the balcony of the manor. There were others out here, some enjoying quiet conversation, others walking arm in arm in the moonlit gardens, waiting for a moment to steal away from watchful eyes.

The air was heavy with fragrance as Rinka made her way to the stables: the sweet scent of honeysuckle; the bright scent of freshly cut grass; the soft, sensual smell of jasmine; and the varied aromas of a dozen different roses, some fruity and light, others dense and ancient with hints of myrrh. It was an intoxicating bouquet, and when combined with the soothing, pulsing rhythm of the crickets and cicadas, it made Rinka feel as if she'd slipped into a dream.

She was pulled out of it by the sound of someone crying on the other side of a hedge.

Rinka paused, uncertain of what to do. There were no other voices around, no signs of movement. The sobs were quiet, with no obvious signs of distress. It was possible that whoever was crying had come out here to be alone with their sorrow and their thoughts, and that Rinka's intrusion would not be welcome.

And then there was the fact that Idris was waiting for her, and that she both desperately wanted to meet with him and didn't want to disappoint him by being late.

Rinka sighed. She couldn't leave whoever it was alone without checking to see if she could help. It just wasn't in her nature.

"Sorry, Idris," she muttered under her breath as she went around the hedge.

There, seated on a low bench on her own, was Princess Ceri.

The princess coughed, choking down a sob and standing upright as Rinka approached.

"I'm fine," she said. And then: "Oh, it's you."

"Your highness," said Rinka, curtsying to the princess. "Do you need any assistance?"

"No," said Ceri. "I don't want to talk to you."

Rinka didn't really want to talk to her either. Princess Ceridwen had been nothing but rude to her since their first meeting. She was just about to turn to leave when the princess let out another sob.

Ceri tried her best to conceal it. "Go away," she said. "I'm fine."

"You're very clearly not fine," said Rinka. "You don't have to talk to me, but perhaps I can just sit here with you for a little while. So you won't be on your own."

The princess did not say anything. She did not move, but she also did not protest when Rinka took a seat on the bench.

Rinka waited in silence, hoping that Idris would forgive her for the delay.

Ceri sobbed once, and then again, and then finally on the third sob, she sat down next to Rinka, holding her head in her hands.

"Nice weather we're having," said Rinka.

Ceri laughed and sniffled through her tears. "It's a perfect night." She wiped her nose on her handkerchief and turned to Rinka. "That's another lovely gown you're wearing."

Rinka could hear no mockery in her voice. Perhaps this was the princess's version of small talk.

"Yours is lovely too, your highness." Ceri's gown of dark green silk blended with the hedges in the dim light, nearly making her vanish from some angles.

Rinka waited again. In the distance, church bells chimed midnight.

"Is my brother nearby?" asked Ceri.

Not near enough, thought Rinka, but what she said was, "No. I came out for a walk on my own to cool down."

"I know you're not who you say you are," said Ceri.

Rinka blinked, looking straight ahead and trying to keep as straight of a face as she could. "What do you mean?"

Ceri placed her gloved hand on Rinka's forearm. "Don't worry," she said. "I'm not going to expose you. But I know you're not from Paistos. And I know you're not nobility."

Rinka's heart pounded in her ears. Idris had warned her about Ceri, about her games and schemes. And Rinka had seen her playful cruelty firsthand. What if this was some kind of trap? Some way of blackmailing her into doing something she didn't want to do?

Rinka looked at the princess. Her pretty blue eyes were puffy from the tears, and she looked so small sitting there, so young. She may have been a princess, and perhaps the things Idris said about her were true, but Rinka found it hard to feel anything but sympathy for her in that moment.

"You're right," she said. "I'm not."

Ceri nodded as though she appreciated Rinka's honesty. "Idris has a habit of falling for the wrong person," she said.

Rinka's heart skipped a beat on the word "falling."

The princess continued. "It's a trait we share, it turns out."

"Is that why you're out here?" Rinka ventured to guess.

To her surprise, the princess responded. "Yes," she said, her voice trembling as she began to cry once more. "He's engaged."

Ceri collapsed into tears. Rinka lifted a hand and gently rested it on Ceri's shoulder, moving slowly, cautiously, as if she was trying to catch a rabbit.

Ceri leaned into Rinka, nearly toppling her over, and sobbed violently on Rinka's shoulder. "He said he loved me," she choked out. "He still loves me. But he can't marry me. He doesn't want it, any of it. Not the title, not the crown. Not the life in the castle."

Rinka patted the princess's back in shock.

"How could he love me?" Ceri continued. "That's all that I am. That's all that I have. I'm not like Idris. He's wanted something else for as long as I've known him. But I don't. This is the life I want. So how could he love me? How could he love me if he could leave me for someone else?"

Rinka could see that Ceri was hoping for a response, some kind of wise answer from someone older that would give her comfort.

"To be honest, your highness, I know little of love. But I think it's possible to love someone very much and not be right for them. That sometimes love isn't enough, even though it feels like it should be. Even though it feels like the only thing that matters. And I know that sometimes, the right thing to do is to walk away from someone to let them have a chance of being happy. Maybe he left you because he loved you so much, he didn't want to make you miserable."

Ceri cried quietly for a while, but eventually, her tears slowed. "I'm not sure I believe that's true, not for him at least, but I hope you're right," she said. "It's a pretty thought. You have a kind heart, Lady Rinka. I can see why my brother cares for you."

Rinka sighed as the princess released her from her embrace.

"May I ask what happened between you? You speak fondly of him, and yet I've seen you do nothing but argue since you arrived."

Ceri wiped her face with her handkerchief. "My brother and I...He's much older than me, you know? Nearly twelve years older. By the time I was born, our mother was spending most of her time in her homeland. And our father, well, you've met our father. But Idris…he was there for me. I idolized him. Even as Father turned against him, even as he did his best to keep us apart. Idris didn't care. He'd come and interrupt my lessons to take me outside to fly kites from the castle walls. He'd bring me books and dolls and toys from far-off places, writing to traders and merchants to find me something I'd never seen before. He taught me to draw, taught me to skim stones, taught me how to find blackberries in the woods to eat at the end of summer.

"And then one day, he left for university, and he didn't come back. I thought he'd forgotten me."

"That must have been hard," said Rinka kindly, "thinking you'd been abandoned."

"Father took me under his wing then, and I hated Idris for years. I was cruel to him every chance I got. By the time I'd heard more of what happened between them, he hated me too."

"He doesn't hate you," said Rinka. "I think he just believes that you're on your father's side."

Ceri smirked. "Idris never learned how to manage Father. There's an art to it, in getting him to believe that your idea is his own. And it requires a certain willingness to play the part he wants you to play. He believes I'm a spoiled brat, and so I am. Idris never wanted to play along. Although, given everything that happened with them, I'm not sure it would have made a difference."

She took Rinka's hand and looked at her with a great deal of sincerity. "Lady Rinka, you've been kind to me, and so I'm going to tell you something that I think you need to know. Idris is going to be furious with me, and he's going to accuse me of using this to get back at him or to manipulate you or something, but if I were you, I'd want to know, and I'm pretty sure he hasn't told you."

Rinka's mind raced. What in the world was going on? Was this a part of the princess's trickery? She had just admitted to playing a part, so Rinka knew she could act if the occasion required it.

Rinka was in over her head.

Ceri continued. "Do you know about the Curse of the Air?"

"Oh," said Rinka, relaxing once more. "Yes, he did tell me that. He can't fly."

"That's the part everyone knows," said Ceri. "But it isn't just the Curse of the Air. It's the Curse of the Air and the Heir."

"I don't understand," said Rinka, unable to hear the difference.

"The *heir*," said Ceri again. "The heir to the throne. Idris will have no heir. It was the second part of the curse, the part my father went to great lengths to conceal."

"What?" asked Rinka. Her head was spinning. What did it mean to have no heir?

"He'll never have children," said Ceri. "I'm sorry. I thought you ought to know."

Rinka was at a loss. She had no idea how to respond, and she was certain that she wore her lack of certainty on her face.

If this was indeed a manipulation, Ceri must have known that it had worked.

But Ceri, to her credit, did not show a hint of joy or triumph or mockery on her face. Instead, she just looked sad.

"I—thank you, your highness," said Rinka finally after a long pause. "For telling me."

"I'm glad that you're here this summer," said Ceri. "I hope that doesn't ruin it for you. And I hope you believe me that I took no joy in telling you. You were going to find out eventually."

Rinka nodded.

"Would you like to walk with me back to the manor? It sounds as though the ball is winding down now," said Ceri.

"No, I think I'll stay here for a little while," said Rinka. "I need a moment to think."

"I understand," said Ceri. "Thank you again, Lady Rinka."

The princess left Rinka with her thoughts.

The Curse of the Heir.

The first thing Rinka felt was sympathy for Idris. What a terrible, terrible thing to curse a child with, and for something he didn't even do. Rinka could not imagine losing so much so young, especially not when, as a member of the royal family, he was expected to marry and have children.

Rinka understood then why his father wanted him to abdicate the throne, why he wanted to himself. And she realized what must have come between him and his former fiancée, the part of the story he'd kept from the mermaids.

It was only then that she thought of herself.

If Idris didn't plan to take the throne, there was no real reason he couldn't court her. She hadn't considered it before; she had just assumed that either he didn't want to court her truly or he wasn't certain about abdicating, and therefore her commoner status was a detriment.

But perhaps the real reason he chose not to court her had been that he could not have children.

It would have been unkind for him to keep such a thing from her if they were actually courting, that was true.

But they weren't actually courting. He didn't owe her this piece of information, especially not when it was so damaging to him and to his family.

So why did it still hurt her to hear it?

He was expecting her now, was probably wondering where she was and why she was so late.

But she couldn't face him, not yet. She wanted to be sure of what she was going to say before doing so. She was afraid that at this late hour, she'd say something indelicate and damage their relationship permanently.

And so she returned to the manor house alone.

◦§◦§◦

At breakfast the next morning, Rinka could see the exhaustion and disappointment in him. She watched him pick at his food, barely touching it and refusing to meet her eye.

When they finally were able to leave once the king had finished his meal, she approached him.

"I need to speak with you," she said quietly.

"You didn't come. I waited for hours. Were you unable to get away?"

"Come, let's take a turn about the garden," she said loudly enough for the others to hear.

"It looks like rain today," said Princess Chloe. "Better bring a brolly, just in case."

The footman that had originally greeted them brought them a pair of umbrellas. Idris refused his.

"Thank you," said Rinka to the footman before remembering she wasn't supposed to thank him.

She shook her head. All of these stupid rules.

The sky was overcast with dark grey clouds on the horizon. A warm breeze burst through, whipping up the skirt of Rinka's white day dress and nearly taking the closed umbrella from her hands.

"Did you change your mind?" asked Idris. "Was it something I did?"

"No," said Rinka, leading him to the same spot where she'd found Ceri. It was a secluded area; she wanted to be sure no one would overhear them.

"Idris, I was coming to meet you last night when I found Ceri right here. She was alone and crying. I spoke with her for a while."

"Ceri? Out here crying alone? What happened to her?"

Rinka considered how much to share with Idris. She felt certain that Ceri had shared her story in confidence, not wanting her brother to know. "Just looking for a bit of womanly advice, I think. She's fine, or she will be. But Idris."

She took a deep breath to steady her voice. "She told me about the Curse of the Air and the Heir."

Idris smiled sardonically and shook his head. "Of course she did. Of course she would."

"It wasn't like that," said Rinka. "At least, I'm fairly sure it wasn't. She wasn't trying to hurt you. I think she was just trying to help me. Since we're courting, at least as far as anyone knows. She felt like I had a right to know."

"Unbelievable," said Idris. "I knew she wanted to be queen, but I never thought that she would pull something like this to hurt me. To hurt you. I had no idea how far she would go."

"Idris," said Rinka softly, trying to calm him down. He was nearly shouting. "Perhaps I'm naïve. Perhaps you're right that she did this to hurt you, to drive us apart. But…it wouldn't. Not even if we were truly courting, which we're not. But even if we were, I wouldn't care."

Idris froze in place, unspeaking.

Rinka kept going. "The only part that upset me when she told me is that you felt you couldn't tell me. But even that didn't upset me for long. We've only just met, after all. And you never promised me anything more than a bit of fun for the summer. I understand why you didn't want me to know."

Idris sat down beside her, but still he said nothing, so Rinka kept talking. "One day, you'll find someone you do want to be with. And I hope you'll tell her early. Because there are some people that will care, but there are many who will not. There are people who won't care about your crown or your heirs or anything else. There are people that will love you for you. I hope you know that."

Idris sighed. "My father forbade me to tell my fiancée the truth," he said after a long silence. "He refused to believe in the curse himself despite seeing what the other half of it had done to me, and he paid off or imprisoned anyone who wouldn't agree to keep their silence. The rest of the story I told the mermaids was true—I did truly love her, and I did realize that she didn't care for me at all. When my father refused to let me break the engagement, I told her the truth."

"And she ended the engagement?"

"Yes," said Idris. "Although I'm not sure if it was because of the children or because she realized that my future as monarch was in jeopardy. By that point, I didn't want to find out. He paid her and her family handsomely for their silence. Then at some point, he realized he could pin his hopes for his legacy on Ceri instead."

"But if you can't have a child, why do you need to abdicate? Wouldn't she become queen once you're gone?"

"I told you I work at the University, the King's College near Arcas Dyrne. My area of study is curses—well, dark magic more generally, but I specialize in the study of curses and their effects. I believe it's likely that the wording of the curse makes it so that if I take the throne at all, I will have no successor. Not just a lack of a child heir, but my sister will be prevented from taking the throne for some reason. There are many ways that could play out, none of them nice."

"Perhaps you should take the throne and abolish the monarchy," said Rinka, trying to lighten the mood.

"I've thought about it," said Idris seriously. "At first, as an answer if something were to happen unexpectedly to my father, a way to protect Ceri and the rest of the family. It would meet the terms of the curse. And who knows? If I were to abdicate or abolish the monarchy, I may be able to have children after all."

"And perhaps you could give a voice to the people as well," said Rinka. Being amongst the nobility had given her a newfound awareness of just how little of a voice the common folk had.

"Are you telling me you doubt the ability of those pompous buffoons you saw preening and prancing around last night to represent the will of the people?" asked Idris with a laugh. "Preposterous."

He took her hands in his. "Rinka, I'm sorry I didn't tell you. I wanted to. But it's been my darkest secret for so long—my own colleagues don't even know it's my own curse that I'm researching, or if they do, they think it's so I can fly once more. I hope it hasn't put a damper on things."

"Not at all," said Rinka. "I hope you find the answer you're looking for one day, whatever that may be."

He sighed and reached for her, stroking her cheek. "Was that truly the only reason you didn't come last night? I was afraid that I'd been too forward, that I'd scared you off by taking things too far too fast. I know we're having fun, but I don't want you to feel pressured to do something you don't want to do. I was angry at myself for putting you in that position. I'm sorry I was cold to you this morning."

"Idris," she said. "I wanted to meet you so badly last night that I seriously considered leaving your crying sister on her own to do so. After she told me everything, I decided I needed a moment to think through what I wanted to say. That's all."

There was a clap of thunder in the distance, and the first drops of rain began to fall.

"Ominous," joked Idris.

"Although I don't mind if we take things slowly," admitted Rinka. "Not because I don't want to…well, you know. Not because I don't want *you*. But I very much enjoy the teasing. It's the best part."

"Rinka, I can promise you this: the teasing will not be the best part." He stood and pulled her up by her hands. "Come now," he said. "Before we get soaked."

The rain began to fall harder as they walked through the hedges back to the manor. Rinka opened the umbrella, but the wind kept blowing it backwards. She finally abandoned it entirely when it got stuck on a branch.

"Ah!" she screamed as the bottom fell out. She was drenched in mere moments, her white dress clinging to her, revealing everything underneath.

"Gods help me, what am I meant to do when you look like that?" asked Idris, and he pulled her behind a hedge out of view of the manor and kissed her.

It was absolutely pouring, and Rinka did not give a damn.

The kiss was a confession. It was a secret itself, shared between them, their eyes closed to it. It was the taste of the rain mixed with the taste of each other. It was the pull of his hand on her skirt, the lift of her leg to wrap around his hip. It was the clinging of fabric, the pressure of their bodies, the white-hot fire that burned within them that kept out the chill.

There was a flash of light through Rinka's closed eyes and the clap of thunder close by. Too close.

"Godsdammit," said Idris, pulling away entirely too soon. "I want you to know that I'm stopping this because I can't live with myself if you get struck by lightning on account of my passions and for no other reason."

He took her hand once more, and they ran for it.

Rinka laughed unabashedly as they pounded up the steps to the manor, everything that held her back washed away in the rain.

Chapter Twenty-Four

THE PAMPHLET

Alison

"Let's hear it," said Willow, her pointed ears twitching forward to listen.

Alison read out the lines that had been troubling her to the cat:

O'er heathered hills, with trees so high,
They reach like smokestacks to the sky.

"I like the alliteration, but that simile is tortured. Try again."

Harsh, but fair. The cat was an excellent critic; Alison had to give her that.

She was less helpful when it came to organizing Alison's papers. Willow's relentless need to see the inkwells pushed from Alison's desk onto the cottage floor resulted in disaster on more than one occasion during Alison's time drafting and editing her poetry for the pamphlet.

It did afford Alison the first success she had managed in working her magic on her own: apparently the prospect of a gigantic black ink stain on her sitting room rug was enough motivation to finally wrangle the power within her for some good purpose.

Alison had been at work on finalizing her poems and editing the essays for nearly three weeks, and she was ready to do just about anything else. It was difficult watching her friends come and go, heading into town and down to the manor to enjoy the summer festivities without her.

They had been kind enough to help her take care of herself as she worked: Gwenla bringing tea and helping her tend to her garden, Keir bringing dinners of spicy vegetable curries and a smoky salmon dish that he'd cooked with help from Charlotte, and even Rinka bringing the latest gossip from Fossholm on a visit to pick up some things from her trunk and satchel.

She had taken an afternoon off for Rinka's visit, enjoying a replacement strawberry welcome cake and showing her around Herot's Hollow at last.

"Oh, the houses are so charming!" Rinka had said when she'd seen them. "So much personality, so much history compared to Fossholm. I can see why you want to save it."

Alison brought Rinka to the inn where she met most of the townsfolk, becoming fast friends with Strelka and Charlotte especially, Charlotte apparently having become something of a legend there already on account of her ability to drink like a fish.

Mr. Smalls, the bard, had led them all in a rowdy song, with Keir leading them in a dance that ended up with more than one person on top of the tables, much to the consternation of the innkeep, Mr. Rainey.

Alison smiled at the memory.

"You're getting distracted," said Willow the taskmaster. "Get back to work."

Alison gave the cat a fake salute and lifted her pen to paper once more.

⁂

Keir helped Alison with the box of freshly printed pamphlets, carrying them for her up to the manor house where the preparations for the regatta were underway.

Gwenla had come along, of course, and Lady Sibba had as well. They were bickering as usual over the best way to get the pamphlets into the right hands.

"If you just hand them out, people will think they're rubbish and drop them to the ground," said Lady Sibba. "If we charge just a copper or two for them, they'll think they're worth something."

"Who could drop something so pretty on the ground?" asked Gwenla.

The pamphlets had turned out beautifully, that much was true. They unfolded into more than a dozen panels like a map, some dedicated to the essays Keir and Laddy Sibba had written, the rest covered in Alison's poems and Weyland's illustrations. "Preserve Herot's Hollow: A Place of Outstanding Natural Beauty," the pamphlet implored.

Alison hoped it would be enough.

The answer to their distribution problem presented itself as they arrived at a booth on the lawn where guests were being greeted ahead of the regatta.

"Ah," said Rinka, who had been waiting nearby. "Those must be the pamphlets. These go out with the programmes," she told a human who was handing out the programme of the day's events.

"Yes, my lady, of course," said the human. Keir sat the box next to him, and he took a stack of them and began handing them out with the regatta's schedule.

Rinka took a stack from the box. "Come, Ms. Lennox. We must introduce everyone to the poet responsible."

Rinka brought Alison around to a dozen courtiers—how had she possibly learned so many of their names in such a short time? Alison wondered—telling them all of her recent visit to the charming town of Herot's Hollow and handing them a pamphlet to enjoy while they waited for the races to begin.

Alison marveled at her friend. It was hard to imagine that this was the same orc who came home every night covered in blood a few months earlier. Her grace, her beauty, her good manners—Alison felt that this life was made for her. She knew that Rinka could be happy with her in Herot's Hollow, knew that Rinka could be happy pretty much anywhere—she was just blessed with the kind of easy good humor that eluded most. But Alison hoped that Rinka and Idris would find some way to continue once the summer had finished. It would be a shame to dull her sparkle.

They had made it back to Gwenla when Princess Ceri approached them. The princess wore a dress and hat that nearly matched Rinka's, her dress in white, while Rinka's was sage green.

"What do you think?" she asked Rinka, holding up the skirt of the dress as they curtsied to her. "I had them make me one to match yours."

Rinka looked surprised but flattered. "It suits you, your highness."

"What's that you have there?" asked Ceri, taking a pamphlet from Rinka's hands.

"It's a pamphlet about Herot's Hollow, the next town over," said Rinka as casually as she could manage, as if the entire plan didn't depend on the outcome of this conversation. "I visited recently. This is the poet, Ms. Alison Lennox. She's courting the Marquess of Caernock."

That was Keir's proper title—Alison wouldn't have been able to come up with that if asked. She marveled at Rinka once more.

"Well done," said Ceri to Alison. "He's very handsome. Are you coming to the ball this evening?"

Alison hesitated. "I'm afraid not, your highness. I've been hard at work on the pamphlet, and I haven't had time to secure the proper attire."

"The tailors here are superb; I'm sure they can make you something—wait, isn't one of them from Herot's Hollow? I thought that's what my lady's maid told me," asked Ceri.

"Yes, that's right," said Rinka. "Lydiach has been making most of my gowns, and she's from Herot's Hollow."

Ceri opened the pamphlet then, skipping the essays and flipping to the poems and illustrations.

Alison looked at Rinka and Gwenla tensely as the princess read. Rinka had told her that Ceri was a bit of a wild card, that she wasn't sure what the princess's motives were or if she could be trusted. It was a risk, trying to get her on their side.

"Oh, I like this one," said Ceri, holding up the pamphlet to the poem titled "The Spriggan."

Away! we go to the woods, away—
'Fore sun's last kiss has gone from day,
To seek and find Pan's champion,
To mend the circle once again.

Through wildcat hole and fairy hollow,
The elder sage, the spriggan, follows,
O'er heathered hills, through valleys fair,
The spring's awakening in the air.

He'll grow his arms of branches high,
To lift the stones to Sulis' sky,
And when the circle is remade,
He'll meet the stag and quit the glade.

Away! we go to the woods, away—
To welcome back the Queen of May,
Through dappled light and tree trunk's sway,
Away! we go to the woods, away.

"How did you come up with it?" asked Ceri.

"It really happened," said Alison. "Herot's Hollow is a magical place."

"Don't let my father hear you say that," Ceri warned. She leaned in closer. "But between us, I would like to meet him. The spriggan, I mean. He sounds fun."

"Of course, your highness," said Alison. She looked at Rinka. It seemed to be going well, at least.

"Why does it say 'Preserve Herot's Hollow'?" asked Ceri as she closed the pamphlet once more. "What's going to happen to it?"

"Well, it was going to be flooded to make way for a dam," said Gwenla. "And now there's talk of leveling it to mine coal from our hills for a power plant to be built here in Fossholm."

"And you are?" asked Ceri.

"Gwenla, your highness. I'm a friend of Ms. Lennox. We're hoping that if enough people learn about how wonderful Herot's Hollow is, the king might be convinced to preserve it."

Ceri laughed. "That won't convince my father at all," she said. "But I know what might. Come with me."

They followed the princess as she marched them to the royal tent where her father and Prince Idris were waiting, along with the rest of the royal family, for the first set of rowers to reach the finish line.

Alison, Rinka, and Gwenla looked at each other nervously. What could the princess possibly have in mind?

"Father, I'd like you to meet Gwenla. She's a dwarven industrialist from here in Wilderise, and she has a plan to bring 'lectrics here without ruining the beauty of the place."

Gwenla's grey eyes looked as though they might pop out of her face.

"Not this again," said King Derkomai. "I'm trying to watch the race."

"But Father," said Ceri, her voice a bit whiny, "Gwenla's idea is just marvelous. It's something brand new, and it's going to save so much coin. It barely needs any workers at all."

"No workers, you say?" said the king. He was on his feet now, watching the first boat come down the final stretch. "Come on!" he yelled.

Idris moved around behind his father to join Rinka, mouthing to her: *what's going on?*

"Very few," said Ceri. "Would you let her demonstrate it? Before the end of the summer, of course. I know you want to see Wilderise modernized soon. It's such a clever idea. It's going to change the face of 'lectrics here *and* in Loegria. A new wave."

"A new wave," repeated the king absently. "Come on! Row! ROW!" he shouted at his boat, which had just lost the lead. "Row, dammit! Yes! That's it!"

The king's preferred boat fought back, coming up from behind and narrowly squeaking ahead of their competitor right at the finish.

"YES!" yelled the king, crumpling his programme in his hands and pumping his fist. He turned then to Ceri to clap her on the shoulder, elated. "And what is it, exactly, this new idea?"

Ceri looked at the group. Alison looked at Gwenla, who looked at Rinka, who looked at Idris.

It was Gwenla who dared to come forward. "Why, it's the power of the sun, your majesty. The power of the sun, harnessed and yours to command."

"Two weeks," said the king. "You have two weeks before we're heading back to the castle. Or I'm building the coal mine. Understood?"

"Yes, your majesty. I'll prepare the demonstration at once," said Gwenla, curtsying to him as they took their leave.

Alison looked at the others, flabbergasted and utterly helpless.

"Well," said Ceri, following them from the tent. "Aren't you glad I was here to help?"

Chapter Twenty-Five

THE THIRD QUESTION

Rinka

"Thank you, your highness," said Rinka when no one else responded. "Your help was most…helpful."

Ceri smiled brightly. Rinka still didn't know whether to trust her—was this an intentional ploy to humiliate them, or was her suggestion to the king a genuine attempt to help the situation?

"Just what do you think you're playing at?" hissed Idris, coming up alongside Rinka to face his sister. "Another one of your schemes? Another plot?"

"Idris, don't—"

"Really? I've gone out of my way to help your friends, and this is the thanks I get?" Ceri was incensed. Rinka caught the smell of smoke on her breath.

Rinka gestured to Alison and the others to continue on. It was better if they weren't a part of this.

"Can we just stop this, Ceri? I don't know what I've done to you, but I just want this to end. I know what you told Rinka—" He looked around to check who was watching, and seeing that their argument had drawn the attention of quite a few onlookers, he stopped himself.

"I told her because I knew you wouldn't. Because you're a coward, and you only care about protecting yourself," Ceri snarled under her breath.

"Stop it, both of you," said Rinka. "This is ridiculous. You both care about each other—"

They turned to her and glared, the expression on their faces exactly the same.

Rinka couldn't help but laugh. "You're exactly alike," she said.

Idris said, "I'm nothing like her," at the exact same time Ceri said, "We're nothing alike."

"See?" said Rinka. "Pretty close."

Idris sighed heavily. "I don't want to do this anymore. I don't know what I have to say to convince you that I'm not out to get you, that I don't want to take anything from you, that I've never tried to hurt you. I don't care if you believe me or not; I just want you to leave me alone. Whatever game you're playing, leave me out of it. Leave my friends out of it. Leave Rinka out of it."

Ceri's eyes were full of tears. "It's not a game!"

People were turning to look at the princess getting upset.

"Come on," said Rinka, "let's go somewhere private."

Rinka led them back to the drawing room of the manor, which was empty with everyone out at the regatta. She took a seat on a sofa and gestured for them to join her.

Ceri did so. Idris remained standing.

"I've lost everything this summer, and you didn't even notice," said Ceri, her reddening eyes focused on her brother. "Isaac is engaged. Deepa, Elise, Jerta—they've all stopped talking to me. Do you even know who they are? Where have you been, Idris? Why did you stop coming home?"

"It had nothing to do with you," said Idris. "And the last time I saw you, you told me you hoped someone would break my other wing, so I didn't think I needed to ask your permission to stop coming to visit."

Rinka looked between them, shocked.

"I was hurt, Idris. You left me. You left me alone with Father." Ceri started to cry. "I just wanted you to come back. You were supposed to go to university and come back, and you didn't."

Idris stood with his arms crossed, refusing to comfort Ceri. Rinka looked at him, nodding her head towards the princess.

"I didn't mean the things I said," said Ceri through her tears. "I never forgot what you did for me. I'm sorry, okay? I'm sorry."

Rinka glared at Idris. If he didn't do something soon…

Idris sighed. He pulled the handkerchief from his pocket and held it out to Ceri. "'Dris," she said, her voice very small. "I miss you."

That did it. That was the thing that melted the ice wall Idris had built around the place Ceri occupied in his heart. Rinka could see it on his face, could see his expression soften as he continued holding the handkerchief.

"Come here, you," he said. He leaned down to hug her, and she wrapped her arms around his waist. "It's alright," he said. "I'm sorry too."

He took a seat down next to her. "Tell me about what happened with Isaac."

Rinka rubbed Idris's shoulder, proud of him. "I'm going to go see if I can catch up with everyone else. I imagine they're hard at work on a plan."

"But you'll be back in time for the ball?" asked Ceri.

"Of course," said Rinka. "Wouldn't miss it."

❦

Rinka found the others at the inn in Fossholm in a state of abject panic.

"It's just not possible," said Gwenla. "Rinka, thank the Gods you're here. Can you talk to the princess? Perhaps if we can find an actual dwarven industrialist, we could do this. But not in two weeks."

"I could try," said Rinka. "But I don't think she'll be able to buy us more time."

"That's what I said," said Lady Sibba. "We were talking about it before you got here. Keir and I read the same article in a journal a few years back—what Gwenla made up on the spot is actually possible. We could harness the power of the sun to run the 'lectrics here."

"I should have been a scholar," joked Gwenla. "I just thought it sounded impressive."

"It will take some time to research though, and even if we could meet with the scholar that proposed it, it's unlikely she would be able to help us make a working prototype. And even if she could do that, there's no way to have it in time."

"Which I why I said we need to get more time," said Gwenla.

"And you just heard it from Rinka that we don't have it," said Lady Sibba.

"If we just had a few more months, I could reach out to some of my extended family. There are a couple of industrialists in my mother's line that could help with the manufacturing—"

"Wait," said Alison. "What we need in two weeks is a working prototype of something that can harness the power of the sun to power, say, a 'lectric candle, right?"

"Right," said Lady Sibba. "What's your point?"

"We don't need a working prototype. We just need a prototype that *looks like* it's working."

There was a pause as they considered it. "You're saying we try to trick the king? But how?" asked Gwenla.

"Magic," said Alison. "We build something that looks like it would work—have Weyland make something that looks like what the scholar came up with in that article—and then we use magic, my magic, to make it seem like it's working. That will buy us more time to figure out how to actually make it."

"But the king hates magic," said Rinka. "I know he can recognize Idris's magic—he told us as much. Maybe he won't recognize yours, but it's a risk."

"Could you talk to Idris? And maybe Ceri? See if they have any ideas for how to conceal that we're using magic?" asked Alison.

"I can ask," said Rinka.

"How are they, by the way?" asked Gwenla. "That looked tense back there."

"They're better," said Rinka. "I'm sure they'll help us if they can."

"Lady Sibba, you don't happen to have a copy of that journal at the schoolhouse, do you?" asked Keir.

"No, I wouldn't. I throw out journals every couple of years. I can ask Duncan."

"I'll check the manor," said Keir. "I haven't been back to my library there in some time, but we typically hold on to our journals."

"Keir, are you sure?" asked Alison. They had been avoiding Lord Ainsley most of the summer.

"It's time I got it over with," said Keir. "Would you like to go to a ball with me?"

Alison smiled, blushing. "I would. But what will I wear?"

"I'm sure Ceri wouldn't mind you borrowing one of her gowns," said Rinka. "You're about the same size."

Gwenla downed the rest of her pint of ale in one long gulp. "Well, it's far from a sure thing, but it's better than the coal mine. Welcome to the family, Rinka. We're glad to have you with us. I'd say we do more than just harebrained scheming and plotting, but then I'd be lying."

Rinka laughed. "Harebrained scheming for a good cause," she said. "That's something I can get behind."

"Cheers to that," said Gwenla, who then realized her glass was empty. She picked up Alison's half-drunk glass. "Cheers!"

"Cheers!"

⚜

Ceri had invited Alison and Rinka into her chambers to dress for the ball together, which wasn't ordinary, exactly, but their family wasn't known for their respect for the rules.

"You simply must wear this one," said Ceri, handing a long piece of blue satin ribbon to her lady's maid to tie in Alison's hair. "It'll match your eyes."

The dress she had given Alison to wear was blue as well, a slinky column of sapphire blue silk with delicate sleeves.

Ms. Murray brought the three evening gowns Rinka had not yet worn to allow the other girls to help her decide.

"That one," said Ceri immediately, pointing to a red dress as her lady's maid helped her into a sleek black gown of her own. "It's Idris's colors. He'll love you in it."

The red dress was stunning, Rinka had to admit. And it was true that the beads and sequins that did somewhat resemble his scales.

"Red on red?" said Rinka, pointing to her hair. "Are you sure?"

"I'm certain," said Ceri.

Rinka glanced at Alison, who nodded.

They headed into the ballroom together once they were finally ready, a little late due to Ceri insisting on changing their hair accessories several times before settling on the right ones.

"We need to hurry," said Ceri. "Most of the dances have already been promised."

Rinka helped Ceri and Alison fill their dance cards as she filled most of her own. She was especially looking forward to dancing with Keir, whom she'd heard was an accomplished dancer and one of the most coveted partners tonight, although he hadn't been seen yet.

"Where are they?" asked Alison, speaking of their respective men. Idris was also nowhere to be found.

Alison finally spotted Keir as the first dance was just about to start. His collar was bent out of shape, and he was shaking his hand.

As he came closer, Rinka could see a bandage on his knuckles.

"What's happened? Are you alright?" asked Alison.

"Fine," said Keir. "Better than fine. My father and I have reached an understanding."

"Oh Gods, Keir, you didn't," said Alison.

"Didn't knock that smirk right off his face? I did, and he deserved it. I doubt we'll see Lord Ainsley around tonight. He's looking a bit worse for wear. Come, my darling. I'm feeling very much like dancing at this moment."

Alison shot Rinka a bewildered look as Keir took her to the dance floor.

Rinka shrugged. From everything she'd seen and heard of Lord Ainsley, Keir was right about him deserving it.

She was just beginning to regret saving a dance for Idris when he finally arrived. He was as handsome as ever in his tuxedo, and Rinka had to stop herself from jumping into his arms at the sight of him.

It's just for the summer, she reminded herself. At least her mother's voice wasn't here to judge her. It had been quite some time since she'd heard it—perhaps her outlandish actions had silenced it for good.

"You're late," she said with a flirty pout. "I did save the first dance for you, though."

"Rinka, may I speak with you?"

She was caught off guard by his serious tone. His face was serious too, and more than a little sad. It was almost haunted.

"Of course," said Rinka, her mind racing. She had just seen him a few hours ago. What could have possibly happened in their time apart?

They went into the garden once more, returning to the same secluded spot from a few weeks prior. "What's wrong?" asked Rinka. She rubbed the bare skin of her arms above her gloves nervously.

"You look unbelievable," he said, keeping her at a distance, as if he didn't dare move any closer. "Impossible. I can't take my eyes off of you." His voice was strained, breathless.

"I don't understand," said Rinka. She was terribly worried. Something was definitely very wrong here, but she could not fathom what it was.

"I almost didn't come here tonight," said Idris. "I wasn't sure I could handle it, not after today."

"Today? What happened today?"

Idris adjusted his cufflinks, staring at them, unwilling to look at her as he spoke. "It was the way that you were with Ceri. The way that you listened to her, believed her, comforted her even when I wouldn't. The way you took care of us both. You stayed with us and made sure we worked it out."

"You're not making sense," said Rinka. "Did I overstep? Did you want privacy?"

"No," said Idris. He sighed, turning away from her to look up at the manor. There was a nervous energy about him, something pent up inside that threatened to burst to the surface the longer they stood here. His shallow breaths raised and lowered his chest in a way that made Rinka worry he might faint. "I'm going mad. I'm sorry. I don't know how to say this."

Rinka felt her pulse flutter. Did he want to end their arrangement early? Did something change?

Or could it be that there was something that had always been true that had been left unsaid? Something that could no longer be denied?

"I know what I said a few weeks ago about what this could be. A bit of fun, a bit of a game. Something light and easy. But it's not that for me, not anymore. Maybe it never was."

"Idris," she said, closing the distance between them and taking his hand. "I want to ask my third question."

He startled, but he didn't pull away. "What?"

"My third question," she said. "The third question you promised you'd answer truthfully. I'm ready to ask it."

He swallowed, meeting her eye for half a moment. "Alright," he said. "Ask away."

She looked at him, and she could see the torture and the hunger and the longing, the last secret they shared begging to be revealed.

She dared herself to ask it.

"Is this real?"

He looked at her then, one eyebrow cocked in surprise. He was still for a long moment, his eyes studying her face, her neck, her shoulders. And then he reached out with his free hand and touched her arm on the sleeve. He stroked the delicate fabric, smiling slightly, perhaps remembering what he'd said about a similar dress their first night in the manor. Remembering the dream of it, the vision that haunted him night by night.

He moved then to graze the sequins on her waist, understanding their meaning. They were his, the smooth red beads so much like his scales, and she was his. Really, truly his. Not just for the summer. She had lied when she said it, had known it was a lie.

It wasn't enough. The summer wasn't enough.

Then he pulled her closer to him. He stroked her cheek delicately, tracing the line to her jaw and then once more to her lips. It wasn't just a pattern of movement; it was a ritual. A ceremony in three parts. An offering in prayer at the altar of her body.

Rinka's heart pounded, the pulse hammering in her ears. Her vision was in a tunnel, transfixed.

There was only him.

He leaned forward and touched his forehead to hers, their eyes so close they could not focus.

"Gods, I hope so," he whispered, and then he kissed her.

If the kiss in the rain had been a confession, this one was a revelation. The end of the mystery, the end of the games and the riddles and the secrets in the dark. This kiss was the truth laid bare.

And it was a demand for the closeness of skin on skin, the baring of everything, body and soul.

She followed him silently as he led her by the hand. As they walked through the moonlit gardens, there was a sudden boom in the distance and an explosion in the sky—fireworks.

They didn't notice.

There was only this.

Idris took her to the place near the stables. He pulled her to him hungrily, desperately. He kissed her lips, her jaw, her neck. She gasped as he pushed the fabric from her shoulder, revealing the flesh there, smooth and grey and oh-so-soft, and he kissed it too. The dream of it made real.

Then he hesitated, remembering what she said about the other dress. He reached for the hooks on the back.

"No," said Rinka, tugging on his hands. "I can't wait. I want you right now."

"Fuck," said Idris. He moaned, low and deep. "I need you." And then he slipped the red gown from her shoulders, but it didn't tear. It stretched, his magic expanding it so that it fell from her to the ground in one fell swoop.

He was on her then, Rinka pulling him to her, begging him not to stop, not to hold back. There would be time for all of that later, time for anything and everything, but for now, this was all she needed.

His lips on hers, their bodies entwined.

It wasn't enough, would never be enough. But for now, at least, she was satisfied.

Chapter Twenty-Six

THE PROTOTYPE

Alison

Two weeks flew by in a blur of research, planning, and testing. Parts were ordered from Loegria—a 'lectric generator similar to the one Andsaz had attached to the pillar spinning in front of the dam, a number of small metal parts whose functionality Alison wasn't sure of, and a great 'lectric candelabra, which they hung from a movable scaffolding to demonstrate the new technology.

There had been setbacks. Alison didn't fully understand all of the issues they'd encountered with concentrating the sunlight and connecting the various components, but she had seen the piles of scrap metal and discarded parts, and more importantly, witnessed Weyland's frustrations and concerns with the entire plan.

"It won't work," he said as she joined the group in the workshop behind his forge. Gwenla, Lady Sibba, and Keir were all there already, Keir having come from a house visit to check on Minra and her young twins.

"It doesn't need to work," reminded Alison. "Looking at it now, I'm fairly convinced that it's possible."

The apparatus looked impressive enough. There was a great dish of hammered metal, as big around as Weyland was tall, mounted on a platform which could be rotated to face in the direction of the sun. In the center was a column which held a vessel containing water, heated by the concentrated light in the way that pointing a magnifying glass in the wrong direction on a sunny day could start a fire. It connected through the back of the dish to a series of boxes containing some sort of fan and the 'lectric generator, and then it connected to the candelabra through a short wire.

So far, the candelabra had failed to light up. The issue, as Weyland explained it, involved containing the steam to generate enough pressure to rotate the fan. "I need it to work," said Weyland.

It wasn't an issue of his ego. It was the risk to them—to Alison in particular—if the king were to find out the demonstration was false. Weyland knew better than anyone what failure could mean for them, and Alison understood his concerns.

Still, what choice did they have? If they gave up and admitted that they couldn't create their solar machine in time, there was no guarantee that the king wouldn't punish Gwenla, the face of the operation, in the same exact way he'd punished Weyland.

Alison sat with the others drinking tea as Strelka, Weyland's apprentice, came over with a newly crafted central vessel, the final attempt they would make before bringing the prototype to Weldan House, working or not.

"Any progress?" asked Gwenla. She was referring to Alison's attempts to light the candelabra herself.

"I can heat the water well enough, but if Weyland can't contain the steam, it still doesn't matter," said Alison.

"Can you light it directly? You know, channel the energy of lightning itself or something."

"I don't think even Idris can do that," said Alison. Idris and Rinka had stopped by to check on their progress earlier in the week. Alison was happy to see them looking especially cozy, and she was even happier when she heard the news from Rinka that they were truly courting now.

But Idris hadn't been able to help in the way of the magic situation. His powers were only as useful as Alison's were, although his control over them was far superior, even with Keir helping Alison direct hers. He could rotate the fan in a consistent manner that eluded Alison, but there was still the problem of his father being able to detect his interference.

They waited as Strelka and Weyland heated various pieces of metal and wire, detaching the existing assembly and attaching the new one.

Finally, it was time for the final trial.

"Turn it a bit more, a bit more, there," said Weyland as they rotated the dish to face the sun. The day was lightly cloudy, and it took a couple minutes for the sky to clear enough to heat the water in the vessel.

Weyland paced around between the front and the back of the dish, checking for leaks.

But they didn't come.

"Wait," he said, "I think that may be—"

The 'lectric candelabra flashed on.

"You've done it!" shouted Gwenla.

Everyone gathered around the assembly, Weyland gently pushing them away from the exposed components, which were quite hot.

As they watched, a huge cloud passed overhead, and the boiling slowed. The candelabra flickered and went out.

"Let's just hope it's a sunny day," said Gwenla. "Do you think Idris can control the weather?"

Chapter Twenty-Seven

LIGHT AND POWER

Rinka

The demonstration took place at the last festival of summer. The day was hot and humid, the cooler weather of fall still weeks away, but with the royal family leaving, it felt like an ending.

Rinka and Idris still hadn't discussed what would happen next. He wasn't due back at the University for a few more weeks, and Rinka was looking forward to spending time with him away from the watchful eyes of the nobility. She hoped that by the time he was due to return to Loegria, they'd have a better idea of what to do about the distance.

The festival was much the same as the one at the beginning of summer, with a great feast, a bonfire, and a number of activities and competitions taking place around the manor grounds. There were also a number of celebrations for the first harvest, a process Rinka had been removed from in her previous city life: a ceremonial reaping of the first grain from a field behind the manor; the baking of bread in a clay oven, which was then thrown onto the bonfire as an offering to the Gods; and the crafting of dolls from hay and garlands from dried herbs to ward off evil spirits and protect the remainder of the harvest yet to come.

"Of course, the dolls do little for true agricultural curses," said Idris, walking arm in arm with Rinka. "In most cases, you'd be better off hunting down the originator of the curse and burying them in the field instead."

"Would that work?" asked Rinka.

"No," said Idris, "but it would be deeply satisfying."

At midday, they joined a crowd gathered for the 'lectric demonstration. Idris joined the king and Princess Ceri, but Rinka slipped away to join Alison, who was standing off to the side, trying her best to appear natural.

"Are you ready?" asked Rinka. She had heard from Alison earlier in the day that there was a chance if the weather held that her powers wouldn't be needed at all, and she hoped that would be the case.

"I'm ready as I can be," said Alison. Her face was pale, and Rinka could see that despite her words, she was frightened of what might happen.

Keir came up to join them then, gently rubbing Alison's shoulder before taking her hand. "We've got this," he said, but when he smiled at Rinka, his brows were furrowed.

Gwenla stood next to the king, and on his signal, she moved forward to address the crowd. "Lords and ladies and gentlemen," she began. "Er. Lords and ladies, and ladies and gentlemen," she tried again. There was scattered laughter from the crowd. "Oh, forget it," said Gwenla. "All of you lot listen up. I'm Gwenla, originally of the Rodaz Mountain industrialists, and I'm here to demonstrate a most miraculous new technology: the power of the sun harnessed to run 'lectrics. It's the wave of the future, a new hope for Wilderise and Loegria, and you get to see it here first."

There were a few claps, mostly from the villagers from Herot's Hollow come to support Gwenla.

"Get on with it," said the king.

"Right away, your majesty," said Gwenla. She looked nervously at the sky, and Rinka understood her concern.

An enormous group of clouds was rapidly approaching. The wind picked up, sending a few of the ladies' hats into the air, including Gwenla's.

"Oh," she cried, reaching for it. "Just a moment, sir," she said, chasing it down. "Perhaps it would be best to wait—"

The wind picked up again, and this time it lifted the great maroon sheet they'd draped over the dish.

Light hit the dish then as Gwenla scrambled with the sheet, her eyes on the clouds that would be over the sun in moments.

"What are you doing?" asked the king. "Is it ready to work or not?"

"Just another quick adjustment—" started Gwenla, but it was too late. There was a sound of boiling water and the flowing of steam, and the 'lectric candelabra began to glow, its light illuminating the black sheet they'd placed behind it to better demonstrate the effect.

"Oh," said Princess Chloe from the crowd. "It's working!"

It was working, at least at that moment.

"Behold!" shouted Gwenla, finally getting her hat back on. "The power of the sun!"

"Not bad," said the king. "Tell me about the construction. How many of these will be needed to power the manor?"

"Your majesty, I have a paper with the figures right here," said Gwenla, thrusting a chart Alison had number-crunched based on the original research towards the king, hoping to take his attention away from the prototype before the clouds passed overhead.

"Just give me the gist of it," said the king.

"Of course, your majesty," said Gwenla, squinting at the paper without her spectacles. "One apparatus can generate the power of approximately eight horses—no, sorry, three—over the course of a normal day, which should be enough to fully power several ordinary homes, although the manor is much larger—"

"What's happening?" asked the king. "Why isn't it working?"

The clouds had arrived, casting a cool shadow on the manor grounds. The prototype continued to work for a moment as the water continued to boil, but it was slowing down, causing the candelabra to flicker.

"Ah, just a little issue with the water," said Gwenla. "The apparatus will continue working even in the sun's absence because of the inherent storage mechanism. Let me just make an adjustment." She ran around to the back, shooting a glance at Alison as she went.

Alison tensed and began to concentrate on the water. Keir's eyes focused on the king, sweat dripping from his brow.

"Wait!" whispered Rinka. "Let me try."

"What?" asked Alison.

"Idris channeled magic with me, and I was able to do something to help him."

"I didn't think orcs could do magic," said Keir.

"I bet the king doesn't think so either," said Rinka. "Perhaps he won't recognize it."

"Alright," said Alison. "But hurry. We've got to get it working again."

Rinka took Alison's hand and felt the surge of power within her. It felt different than Idris's power had, and Rinka panicked for a moment that this wouldn't work.

"Are you alright?" asked Alison, feeling her fear through the connection.

"Give me just a moment," said Rinka.

She remembered what Idris had said—magic was a negotiation. She did not try to take Alison's power from her. She simply asked it if she could borrow it for a moment.

It traveled between them slowly, begrudgingly.

Gwenla banged a wrench against the prototype uselessly. "Almost there!" she shouted.

"I can feel it," Rinka said to Alison.

She felt Idris's eyes on her as she focused on the water vessel. She smiled at him, trying to affect a casual air that said she wasn't doing anything suspicious. Just enjoying the show.

The water had slowed to a simmer in the vessel. With Alison's power, she could sense it, could feel it across the lawn.

"Just a little warmer," she murmured. She asked it nicely. *Wouldn't you like to be just a tiny bit warmer? Isn't the heat nice?*

It did not respond.

"It's not working," said Alison. "I'm just going to have to—"

Rinka felt something else then. More power joining Alison's—Keir's. And then further still—Idris's, who had clearly worked out what they were up to. His power was weaker over the distance but still present, and the familiarity of it felt like a warm hug.

"Come on," begged Rinka of the water vessel. "Just a couple of little bubbles."

Nothing, nothing…

And then, there it was.

One little bubble rising up the window of the vessel. And then a couple more.

"That's it!" cried Gwenla. "Give it just a moment to boil again."

The bubbles continued, one by one, until the vessel was boiling wildly. The steam whistled through the pipes, sending the fan whirring and the generator turning until at last the candelabra was lit once more.

"Very good," said the king. If he noticed anything amiss, he gave no sign. "Now, how many did you say the manor would need?"

"I'd guess twenty or so for the manor alone," said Gwenla. "We'll need to run water to them, of course, your majesty, just like any other steam engine—"

"That's well underway," said the king. "Lord Ainsley assures me the manor will have its plumbing up to snuff as soon as the guests are gone. How long to get fifty up and running?"

"Fifty?" asked Gwenla.

"For the entire Hill Country," said the king.

"Well," said Gwenla, looking at Alison for help before realizing they were still preoccupied maintaining the power, "if we start them straight away, I'd suspect we can have them within a year." Gwenla raised her grey eyebrows in question to Lady Sibba when the king turned his back. Lady Sibba shrugged.

"You have three months," said the king. "Come, Ceri. Let's see this pedal-cycle you've been raving about."

The king led Ceri away, and the crowd began to disperse. Rinka, Alison, and Idris were finally able to let go of the magic as the sun returned overhead.

Alison turned to Rinka, her face exhausted from the effort. "Three months?"

Epilogue

"Three months?" said Gwenla, joining them once the last of the nobles with questions had gone. "It doesn't work for three minutes consistently. What are we going to do?"

"Come up with another wild scheme, I suspect," said Idris as he joined them too. "Well done, my dear," he said to Rinka, kissing her hand. "You're quite an extraordinary woman."

She followed the group back to the inn, the town saved for the time being, at least.

Three months wasn't long, but it was time enough for another plot. Time enough for another harebrained adventure with her friends.

About the Author

Amy Yorke is an author of light and cozy fantasy and lover of all things magical and romantic. She is half English, half American, and she offers her sincere apology to readers of both languages for her idiosyncrasies in word choice. In her spare time, she enjoys gardening, playing video and tabletop games, and chasing after her cats.

Join her mailing list to receive news, updates, and promotions, including free advanced reader copies prior to new releases: https://www.amyyorke.com.

Read on for a preview of *The Ancient and the Amber*,
Book Three of the Wilderise Tales

Chapter One

WELCOME TO WINWOLD

Ceri

It was the autumn of Princess Ceridwen's reinvention.

The summer had been a disaster. Her father had dragged the entire court out to the middle of nowhere, and what was worse, she'd lost just about everyone she cared about.

The breakup with Isaac had set the whole thing off, but as she had realized in the weeks since, it had been a long time coming.

Ceri hadn't known how her ladies-in-waiting really felt about her until she watched them abandon her one by one. It was the loss of Jerta, her closest confidante other than her brother since childhood, that had hurt the worst. Their final argument out on the terrace of Weldan House had struck Ceri to the core, and not just because of the cruelty of Jerta's words.

No, like all of the best insults, Jerta's words had hurt because there was, within them, an undeniable kernel of truth.

Ceri had dismissed it at the time, but Jerta was right about her.

She was selfish. She was spoiled. She was manipulative and, at times, cruel, and she was a terrible friend.

It hadn't always been that way.

Ceri hadn't had the easiest upbringing in the castle. Her mother was in and out for most of her childhood, unable to bring her children with her due to the iron will of her husband: Ceri's father, King Derkomai. Prince Idris, her only brother, had left her alone there when he went to university. She'd been raised by a series of nannies, governesses, and tutors, but none of them could keep her from her father's influence once he set his sights on her as his potential heir.

Ceri learned quickly how to adapt to her father's mercurial moods. She let him spoil her when he wanted to, she stayed out of his way when he didn't want her around, and she learned to talk to him in such a way that he allowed her to do what she wanted at least some of the time.

She was just pretending to be the person he wanted her to be, but perhaps if you pretend to be someone else for long enough, you can't help but become someone else in the end.

Ceri didn't notice herself slowly turning the skills she'd learned to survive her father onto her friends, but once it was pointed out to her, she knew it was true.

It was done now.

She was starting fresh at Winwold College. Her father hadn't understood her sudden change in attitude towards attending university. She'd fought him on it the previous year when she had finally been old enough to enter, but, if she was being honest, she hadn't wanted to go not due to a general lack of interest but because Isaac wasn't going to be there.

She would be making no further decisions based upon the location of a man, no matter how handsome he was.

King Derkomai had been even more baffled when Ceri had told him she didn't wish to attend King's College, his alma mater and the nearest university to the castle.

No, she would be going to Winwold. Its primary advantage, other than being as far as from the castle as one could get while still being in Loegria? Idris would be working there this autumn as a guest lecturer, while the friends he'd met over the summer worked with a professor about that sun-powered 'lectric machine she'd helped them "invent" a few weeks earlier.

Fine, so she supposed that was one final decision she made based on the location of man, but that man was her brother, and she had missed him terribly.

Ceri's carriage conveyed her from the town of Norgate along a narrow, wooded path into the mountains. Winwold College's campus was mainly in the town below, but the first-year students, colloquially known as "freshers," were all sent to High House, a former manor which overlooked Norgate. High House was visible in the distance from the town, but it vanished from view the moment the carriage reached the tree line.

Indeed, in this dense forest, there was little to see at all. Ceri had never experienced a wood this deep and dark. The sun was so thoroughly and perfectly blocked from view that it had managed to fool an owl, which hooted softly in the distance even though it was still hours until nightfall.

At last the carriage reached an ancient bridge. Ceri leaned out the window, grateful to feel the sunlight on her pale skin and silver hair for a moment before being plunged back into the darkness of the forest.

Gods, it took so long to travel this way. Ceri had insisted on the carriage: arriving by air in her dragon form wasn't exactly conducive to her goal of blending in. Finally, after what felt like hours, the carriage took a steep turn up a hill, emerging from the woods.

The road rose sharply to cross another bridge which led to the gatehouse, its filigreed iron emblazoned with the school motto: *SIC ITUR AD ASTRA*. Behind the gates stood High House.

It wasn't exactly a manor house, but it also wasn't exactly a castle. Ceri could see the similarities with a real castle, the King's castle, Corycus, where she spent most of her childhood, mostly in the lower levels of stone. But there were additions in stone and wood and plaster, spires and towers and turrets which served no apparent function. They had been added during the manor conversion for aesthetic purposes alone, Ceri figured. She knew exactly what her father would say about them: "Waste of bloody coin."

It was hard to deny the picturesque charm of it though, standing as it did on its own with the mountains rising behind it and the yellowing trees of the dense forest nestled up against it.

The gates opened at the royal carriage's approach, and a man burst out a door from the gatehouse. He was wearing academic formal attire just like Ceri: knee-length robe, white shirt with black tie, and a black mortarboard hat, although his robe was crimson while hers was black to indicate his higher degree.

The carriage stopped before him. "Your royal highness," he said, bowing so low to the carriage Ceri thought he might kiss the dirt.

"Rise, sir," said Ceri. "Are you the dean of students?"

"Dean Whittaker, at your service," he said.

Dean Whittaker was a half-elf of roughly middle age. His hair had gone grey, and his belly had gone round, but his nose and jaw were still fine and sharp. Winwold College had had just one other dean in its four-hundred-year history, Dean Whittaker's mother, a full-blooded elf who had run the college for most of that time.

"May I show you to the royal suite? I'd be happy to take you on a tour of the grounds once you're settled in."

"That won't be necessary," said Ceri.

"The tour?"

"No, the suite." Although she'd agreed to arrive a day earlier than any of the other students, she had not agreed to the royal suite. "While at Winwold, I'd like to be treated just as any other student. You understand, don't you?"

Godsdammit. There was that manipulation again. It wasn't enough just to make her wishes known. Ceri had added that little innocent question at the end: *you understand, don't you?* Those were the words she used, but she knew what the question conveyed: *you know who I am, don't you? Will you dare to defy me?*

"Of course, of course. Ms. Asher, see to it that Ceri's things are brought to a room. Yes, one of the ordinary rooms."

"Right away, sir," said a human who stood in the doorway. She hurried up the road to the main building as if she were being chased.

"If you wouldn't mind, we can start with the tour to give Ms. Asher time to make the new arrangements," said Dean Whittaker.

Ceri nodded, and the Dean gave instructions to the carriage driver, who dropped them off at a pair of grand double doors that marked the entrance into High House.

The Dean led Ceri through a series of rooms that were both familiar and peculiar to her. The great entry hall was lined with statues, busts, suits of armor, and so many paintings and tapestries that it gave the room a claustrophobic feel, as if the amount of space required far less than whoever had decorated it could allow. There was more variety here than in her father's castle and various estates, but the contents were largely the same.

The scale of the accommodations was familiar as well, though the later construction meant there were more hallways than were present in the royal castle and palaces. The style had once been to connect rooms directly, but here at High House, there were long wood-paneled corridors, the weak 'lectric lanterns too few to illuminate the entire lengths such that they appeared to fade into shadows, giving the illusion that they went on forever.

There was something eerie about this place, but Ceri couldn't quite put her finger on it.

"And around this corner is the library. If I recall from your letter, you're considering a course of study in Comparative Literature?"

This was a surprise to Ceri, who hadn't exactly written the letter requesting her admittance far outside of the ordinary admissions window. Truthfully, she didn't know what she wanted to study.

"It's one option I've considered," she said. "I understand that Winwold doesn't require choosing a concentration until the second year of study? I'm hoping to keep my options open."

"Very wise, your highness," said Dean Whittaker. "Of course, Professor Sandak runs an excellent program in the Literature department, but there are no bad courses of study here. Now, let's see if Ms. Redclaw is here—"

From beyond the closed library doors, there came a terrible crash.

And then a scream.

All the color drained from Dean Whittaker's face.

"Oh," he squeaked. He coughed and cleared his throat. "I'm sure it's nothing, but I better go see if Ms. Redclaw needs—"

Dean Whittaker reached for the door just as it swung open with such force that it clattered against the wall, shaking some of the hallway paintings.

"How many times have I told you?" yelled a woman's voice from within.

"But Ms. Redclaw—" began a man. Ceri tried to look inside the door, but Dean Whittaker blocked her view.

"Excuse me, Ms. Redclaw, are you quite all—"

"There's been an incident," said the woman, who must have been Ms. Redclaw, to the Dean. "The library is closed."

"Ms. Redclaw—"

"*Closed.*"

Glancing around the Dean, Ceri caught glimpse of a small, grey-haired woman in a wheeled chair. She didn't seem particularly intimidating, but Dean Whittaker backed away immediately, pulling the door closed behind him.

He took a moment to readjust his tie. "I'm sorry about that. Ms. Redclaw is very particular about her library. We'll have to come by at another time."

Ceri agreed, but the truth was, she was intrigued by the commotion. There were few things that were more tempting to her than closed doors. A lifetime of wandering the halls of the castle had taught her that most interesting things happened in the private places where people thought they couldn't be overheard.

Ceri allowed the Dean to drag her along through the rest of the halls. He showed her the various departments with their offices and classrooms, noting with special pride the fine rooms which had been given to Prince Idris during his stay, no doubt at the expense of some tenured old fellow who would resent him for it greatly. (The prince himself was out for the day to greet his arriving companions.) He brought her into the grand dining hall, which was apparently a former cathedral to the Gods of Loegria, though the iconography and stained-glass windows had been replaced with depictions of scholars and significant moments in history, including the conquering by Ceri's own ancestors.

Finally, the Dean led her through a pair of doors into a cloistered courtyard.

"Destroyed in the Great Fire, but the east wing remains intact. It's handy for avoiding the cold when walking to the dormitories during winter, but on a fine day such as this, it's nice to walk outside, don't you think, your highness?"

It was a fine and sunny day here in the courtyard, the oppression of the halls forgotten in the open air. Ceri could imagine groups of students lounging out here on the grass, reading books and discussing important things. She hoped she'd find a way to be among them.

"I said go away!" Someone was yelling in the far corner of the courtyard near the lone stand of trees.

Dean Whittaker once again put himself between Ceri and the commotion. "On second thought, it might be best to show you the way you'll walk in winter," he said, attempting to steer her back into a doorway.

"Go on! Get! I said GET!"

The distant figure seemed to be arguing with a crow.

"Who is that?" asked Ceri.

Dean Whittaker looked pained. "Groundskeeper Tomasar is…passionate about his work. Nothing to worry about."

Particular and passionate. The staff at the college were much more daring than Ceri had expected. The staff and servants of the castle operated under the strictest code of conduct. Her father would have fired anyone who behaved as the librarian and the groundskeeper had done, but Dean Whittaker seemed almost afraid of his staff. Almost as soon as she had thought it, he delivered a warning. "Just don't mess with the old yew there, whatever you do."

"The yew?" At the base of the group of trees, a small cast iron fence had been erected with a sign that said *KEEP OUT*.

"That's the Norminster Yew," said the Dean, gesturing to the trees. "It's all one very old tree; the middle part has rotted away. Tomasar is quite attached to it."

Tomasar, an elderly dwarf in overalls with a scarred face and a long, grey beard, waved the rake he was using to frighten away the crows to Dean Whittaker and Ceri. The Dean waved back weakly as he led Ceri past the trees, through the breezeway beyond, and into the dormitories.

There, the human from earlier was waiting. "Your highness, your rooms are ready." They followed her up a flight of stairs to a nondescript door with a set of small brass numbers: 213.

The room was small—no, tiny. Ceri's dressing room at the castle was larger. Somehow, they'd managed to cram two single beds, two wardrobes, and two writing desks with chairs into the narrow space. Ceri passed the furniture and her trunks, which filled almost the entirety of the open floor, and headed to the window.

Through the heavy leaded glass, Ceri had a fine view of the courtyard, including Groundskeeper Tomasar's continued fight with the crows.

"It's perfect," she said.

"I'll leave you to get settled in," said the Dean. "Dinner begins at six; there aren't many here on campus yet, so we'll all be eating at the head table. Generally, it's rare for students to be invited to the head table, but of course, you are always welcome to do so."

"That won't be necessary," said Ceri. "Thank you for the tour."

The Dean fidgeted with his tie, looking around the small room as if he wanted to say more about Ceri's choice of accommodations, but he didn't dare to do so. He bowed a little less low than he had the first time and took his leave.

Ceri pushed her trunks to the side of the room that had a little less space. Truly an unselfish choice—she hoped her new roommate would appreciate how generous and accommodating she was.

Her new roommate. Ceri had never shared a room with anyone before. She had dreamt as a child of having a sister; not that she didn't love her brother, but Idris was nearly an adult in Ceri's first memories, and she'd always longed to have someone her own age to play with. She'd had a number of friends, but they had been required to keep their distance on account of her station, and they frequently were sent away along with their parents at the king's whims, no matter how much Ceri cried and begged for them to stay.

But now, she would share her space with someone else. Someone who would know her on a level that none but the servants did.

It was thrilling. And also terrifying.

Ceri began to unpack some of her things, brand new clothes in scholarly styles: straight skirts in dark wool that reached to the knees, finely starched shirts, warmed knitted jumpers, and ties in the college colors of crimson and black. There were new undergarments here too, lacy Gallic designs that could be put on without the help of a servant. (Her aunt Chloe had helped her procure those without the king's knowledge.)

The wardrobe was filled with the contents of just the first trunk, with four more to go just like it.

That was a problem for another time. Ceri looked out the window to see the Dean reentering the dining hall on the other side of the courtyard.

Perfect.

She slammed shut the wardrobe, leapt over the trunks, then forced herself to slow down to pull the dormitory door closed quietly behind her, looking up and down the corridor. No one was there to stop her.

She headed back to the library.

Outside its double doors, she could hear nothing within. There were no voices, no crashes or bangs or any sounds of movement whatsoever.

Perhaps she had missed it.

She gently turned the right-side door's brass knob, a creaking sound escaping from the hinges as she pulled it open.

The room was dark beyond, pitch black even compared to the poorly lit hallway she'd come from. She felt around, trying to orient herself but reaching into nothing but open air.

She considered stepping back out into the hallway and returning with a candlestick, but the door snapped shut behind her, engulfing her in darkness.

Something drew her further in.

She took another tentative step forward, her hands reaching into the darkness and the silence. The air in here was unnaturally hot, a stifling, oppressive heat that made it hard to draw air into her lungs.

Her hands found a bookshelf, old worn wood bowing under the weight of countless volumes. Her fingers grazed their exposed spines, feeling the variety of textures: stiff modern cloth with cool patches of neatly inked lettering, smooth leather with deep grooves where the titles and authors had been burned in by ancient hands, fraying linen with thick threads which caught under her nails and seemed to pull at her, almost in invitation.

A droplet of sweat formed on her forehead as she moved along the shelf and further into the library, entranced.

She reached the end of the shelf, keeping one hand on it as she stretched to find the next one. Then there was a crash off into the distance to her right, and the sound of thundering footsteps rapidly approaching.

She backed away, letting go of the shelf in her haste and reaching behind her for the door she'd just come through.

It wasn't there.

She felt something moving to her left. Something, or someone. She panicked, twisting backwards away from the noise to her right and the movement to her left, desperate to find the door, to find her way back into the hallway and back to her room where she should have just stayed and minded her business, far away from whatever was moving here in the dark.

And then it collided with her, sending her to the ground as something else moved in.